BREAKING the CYCLE

MEGAN LOWE

Breaking the Cycle © 2016 by Megan Lowe

Breaking the Cycle is a work of fiction. All names, characters, events and places found therein are either from the author's imagination or used fictitiously. Any similarity to persons alive or dead, actual events, locations, or organizations is entirely coincidental and not intended by the author.

For information, contact the publisher, Hot Tree Publishing. www.hottreepublishing.com

Editing: Hot Tree Editing
Formatting: RMGraphX
Cover Designer: Claire Smith
ISBN: 978-1-925448-16-0

10 9 8 7 6 5 4 3 2 1

DEDICATION

*To the people who come into our lives, enter our hearts
and never leave; for the family we choose, and those we don't.
I love you all.*

GLOSSARY

Breaking the Cycle is written in Australian English and has a colourful collection of colloquialisms and slang. Enjoy discovering some new and wonderful terms.

Saos: A delicious savoury cracker biscuit. Great with cheese or Vegemite.

Profiteroles: Mouth-watery dessert. A profiterole, is a filled French pâte à choux pastry ball with a typically sweet and moist filling of whipped cream, custard, pastry cream, or ice cream

Op Shop: Short for opportunity store. Aussie version of a charity shop or thrift store.

Firies: A firefighter

360: *AFL 360* is an Australian football talk show.

Boot: Nope. This is no shoe. A boot is the US equivalent of a car trunk.

Roo: Nick Riewoldt, an Australian rules footballer.

Arvo: Short for afternoon.

Speccy: Also known as 'specky' and 'speckie.' To look and spectate.

Mark: A skill in football where a player catches a kicked ball that has travelled more than fifteen metres without anyone else touching it or the ball hitting the ground.

BREAKING
the CYCLE

CHAPTER ONE

BRIA

I've been on the go all day and am starving. Having been to Wheels a few times, especially when I'm too lazy to cook after my shift at the supermarket across the road, I'm no stranger to popping in to grab a burger. They are to die for after all. Okay, so maybe I've been here more than a few times. A few times a week possibly. The girls at uni rave about the hot men who hang out here, but whenever I come in, they're always all over the more scantily-clad girls, who call themselves students, but I doubt they've ever seen the inside of a lecture theatre. Not that I'm jealous. Trust me, given the opportunity, no one chooses the girl in the Coles supermarket uniform over a girl wearing a few scraps of fabric.

Besides, manwhore isn't my type. I see them come into work to buy condoms. Of course, they never stop and talk to me.

Instead, they just give me a smile and continue on their way with the swagger so many of them seem to have.

Walking in, Wheels looks like any other diner, albeit a bit larger, with a bar to the right and a huge dining area with an open window into the kitchen to the left. I've managed to miss the dinner rush, so there's no one else here. This isn't unusual since it's a Wednesday night and this isn't a big town. Booker is a glorified uni town, three hours east of Melbourne and an hour and a half from the coast. It's quaint and quiet and the perfect setting for someone to focus on their studies.

I take a seat in one of the booths along the front wall and before long, I'm greeted by two of the cutest men I think I've ever seen.

"Hello, my name is Christian. Welcome to Wheels. I'll be your server tonight," the smaller of the two greets.

At three feet, he can barely see over the table but I can see enough of his face to glimpse dimples, one on either side of his face, deep brown eyes, and a messy mop of dark brown hair.

I smile at his professionalism. "Thank you, Christian."

He smiles back at me. "What would you like dis evening?"

Steepling my fingers and resting my chin on my hands, I ask with mock seriousness, "I'm not sure. What would you recommend?"

He scrambles up on the seat beside me with excitement in his eyes and begins pointing at the menu. Behind him, the other half of the cute duo chuckles quietly. At what I guess is at least six feet two and solidly built, he runs his hand through his head of longish brown hair, the movement exposing

2

glimpses of ink on his arms that have been covered by a black-and-white long-sleeved baseball tee, stretched over an impressive chest.

"So is dat what you want?" Christian's voice interrupts my reverie.

"I'm-I'm sorry?" I stutter, and the god behind Christian chuckles again and I blush. He looks up at me and his green eyes make me gasp.

"Uncle Reed!" Christian whines.

"What's up, buddy?" the god, Reed, says.

"You said da next pretty girl was mine!"

"What?" I ask as Reed chuckles again and holds up his hands.

"I wasn't doing anything."

"You were! You were doing dat eye thing again!"

"Eye thing, huh?" I ask Christian.

"Yeah, he gives all da pretty girls dis look and dey go all mushy."

"They do, do they?" I glare at Reed, who holds his hands up again.

"Yes." Christian huffs and crosses his arms over his chest.

"Well here,"—I take one of Christian's hands, point his finger, and poke it into my chest—"does that feel mushy to you?"

His eyes go wide at his finger being near my modest C-cups and he shakes his head earnestly.

"See? So not *every* girl goes mushy."

"I also never copped a feel within two minutes of meeting a girl, but hey," Reed mumbles.

3

"But he did do da eye thing," Christian accuses.

"Maybe, but it didn't work. I only have eyes for the man sitting next to me." I nudge his shoulder gently.

"Really?" he asks in awe.

"Absolutely," I reply solemnly. "So tell me, handsome, are you single?"

"All right, all right, that's enough of corrupting my nephew for one night," Reed says as he picks Christian up and sets him down facing in the direction of the kitchen. "Go see your dad, buddy."

"Okay. Bye, girlfriend," Christian shouts to me as he toddles off.

"Damn kid. He was supposed to be my wingman. Instead, he snags the girl himself."

"And who says I would've gone for you anyway?" I ask, crossing my arms and leaning back against the booth.

"Don't be like that, angel. You and me, we're going to be great."

"We are, are we?"

"A romance for the ages."

"Does that mean you're going to woo me, Reed?" I mock purr.

"Whatever you want, angel."

"In that case, I'll take a bacon cheeseburger with onion rings and a caramel shake, thanks."

He clutches his chest as if I've shot him. "That's cold, baby."

"And so is you standing here, flirting with me without even asking for my name."

"I don't need a name, baby. To me you'll always be my angel."

"Oh God," I scoff. "Please tell me that line doesn't actually work?"

"I dunno." He shrugs. "I've never tried it before, so let me know. Your food will be ready soon." He winks before sauntering off towards the kitchen.

I have to admit, I hide a bit of a smile as he walks away.

Christian has only just come bounding out of the kitchen again with a bundle of cutlery in his hand when the back door bursts open. He freezes amid the shouts coming from the kitchen. I react immediately and am almost to him when a pot comes flying out of the window to the kitchen. I rush the last few metres, scoop him up, and rush back to my booth on the opposite side of the diner. He's shaking in my arms.

"Hey, shh, it's okay," I coo, rocking from side to side.

Through the window, I can see Reed and three guys going at it. One looks similar to him and I assume he's Christian's dad. The fists are flying fast and heavy, with the occasional kitchen utensil flying through the air. I move Christian under the table with me.

"I don't like dose guys," he says. "Dey're mean."

"You know them?"

"Dey're our rivals."

"Rivals?" I'm so confused by the rush of activity and the strangeness of his answer.

"My daddy, Uncle Reed, and my other uncles ride bikes, all sorts of bikes, and dey're da best. Dose guys don't like dem."

5

"Your dad and uncles ride bikes?"

"Yep. Dey're really good too. When I grow up, I want to ride bikes just like dem. My pop and my pa rided bikes too."

"Jesus, how many men are in this family?" I mutter under my breath.

"We're all men," Christian says proudly.

"Yeah? What about your mum?"

"She died, just like my ma and my nan. Dey're all in heaven."

"Oh, buddy, I'm so sorry." Instinctively, I squeeze him tighter in my lap.

"It's okay. My dad and uncles and pa and pop look after me."

"How many uncles do you have?" If they're anything like Reed or the glimpses of Christian's dad, that's one hell of a gene pool. While I've seen plenty of guys around this place before, I have no idea who's related to whom.

"Dis many." He holds up four fingers. "Uncle Reed, Uncle Liam, Uncle Mav, and Uncle Jax."

Above us, the window shatters.

My heart stutters, my hands shaking as I hide Christian's view from the craziness going on around me. I've never seen or known anything like this to happen before. We cower down even more and listen as more windows are busted. With each break, Christian whimpers and buries himself into my neck.

A few minutes later, I hear the back door slam and a frantic voice. "Christian! Chris! Where are you, buddy?"

"He's under the middle booth with me," I call, unable to keep the tremor from my voice.

There's glass all over the place, so I don't want to try and slide out from underneath the table with Christian clinging to me.

A grown-up version of Christian sticks his head under the table, his lip split and a cut over his eye not able to mask his concern for his son. I recognise him as a regular.

"Chris," he breathes, reaching for the boy.

"Daddy!" Christian squeals and scrambles into his arms.

"Careful of the glass, buddy," I say, helping him get to his god-like father.

"Thank you," the hunky god says, looking at me somewhat curiously.

"No worries. I couldn't leave my boyfriend at the mercy of those thugs." I smile and offer Christian a wink, trying to cut through the heavy tension. It also helps to dissolve my own pounding fear.

"Boyfriend?"

"Yeah, Chris snagged the angel," Reed's voice says.

I make my way out from underneath the table and am immediately set upon by Reed as I straighten. His hands come up to cup my cheeks, his eyes boring into mine, concern written all over his face. Electricity zaps through my body on contact and a sense of calm and peace washes over me.

"You okay, angel?" he asks.

"I'm fine, but you're not." My voice shakes once more, but this time because of the feel of his skin against mine. He has blood dripping from his nose and a bruise on his jaw.

"So, angel, or daughter-in-law to be," the god says, "you have a name?"

I smile, and not breaking eye contact with Reed I introduce myself. "Bria Marie Adams."

Reed smiles and presses a soft kiss to my cheek. More electricity zaps through me.

"Angel," he whispers as we break apart.

"Nice to meet you, Bria *Marie* Adams." His voice is light and jokey as he mimics the use of my middle name when he introduces himself. "I'm Parker Nathaniel Ryan. You've met my son, Christian Nolan Ryan, and that's my brother Reed Cooper Ryan," Parker introduces.

"Nice to meet you, Ryans," I say as Reed releases my face but slings an arm around my waist. I surprise myself by leaning into him. With my adrenaline finally calming, I need the support of his comforting touch.

"Seriously, Bria, I can't thank you enough for looking out for Chris."

"It was no problem. Like I said, I couldn't leave my boyfriend at the mercy of those thugs." I tap Chris's nose.

"Yeah, about that—" Parker begins before Chris interrupts.

"You're bleeding, Daddy."

"Huh?"

"You're bleeding." Christian lightly touches his lip.

"Here, give me Chris and you two can get cleaned up," I offer.

"Chris?" Parker asks.

"Come on, boyfriend," I say, extending my arms to Chris. "Let's let Daddy and Uncle Reed get cleaned up." Without a backwards glance, Christian leaps from Parker's arms to mine.

"Go on, get cleaned up. We'll be right out here," I say.

Reed smiles before turning and heading to the restroom. Parker lingers before reluctantly following his brother. I understand his reluctance, especially after all that's just transpired, but Chris seeing his dad's bloody lip can't be a good thing.

"My uncle likes you," Christian says as I walk us over to the bar area, since it seems to be the most free of glass.

I chuckle. "I'm sure your uncle likes a lot of girls."

"Yeah, but you're different. I can tell."

"Oh, you can tell, can you?"

"Yep," he replies confidently.

I jump, clutching my chest when two older men burst into the diner. From the looks of them, they're obviously related to Parker, Reed, and Christian.

One of the men rushes to the kitchen before moving on to the restrooms while the other stops to survey the damage. Finally, his gaze comes to me and Chris, who has hidden his face in my neck at the sudden arrival.

"Sorry, miss, as you can see we're closed. We're in a bit of a state at the moment. I'm afraid you and your son will have to go elsewhere," he says. He's of similar height to Reed, six one or six two, but with grey running through his black hair and age written all over his face and in his green eyes.

"Actually, I believe this is your grandson."

"Chris?" he asks. The little boy's face is still buried in my neck. I rock side to side and pat his back gently, nodding at the older Ryan.

"Great-grandson. I'm Jay, by the way."

9

"Bria. I'm looking after him while Parker and Reed clean themselves up."

"Oh." He rubs his face. With concern evident in his heavy sigh, his gaze flicks on me and then Chris.

"Is there a problem, apart from the obvious?" He seems reluctant to leave Chris with me. Okay sure, I'm a stranger, but considering the situation and that I'm only trying to help, I would have hoped that would be enough to ease any of their concern.

"To Chris you might be."

My brows dip in confusion. "What? I'd never—"

"It's nothing against you personally. The fact Chris has taken to you like he has speaks volumes. Usually he's a bit uneasy around women. Stems from issues with his mother."

"He told me she died."

Jay nods and looks at Christian, who's now fast asleep, clinging to my neck tightly. It seems the anxiety of the last few minutes took its toll pretty quickly.

Jay takes a seat across from me. "To say Emma was a mess would be putting it lightly. The girl was a disaster and if not for the fact she gave birth to my great-grandson there, I'd say a waste of perfectly good air, but it's rude to speak ill of the dead."

Initially, I have no idea how to respond. The information seems way too personal to be shared with a stranger. Yeah, I've been in the diner a fair bit, and maybe they recognise my face, but that's it. I'm tempted to nod, hand over Chris and run for the hills, but I'm pretty sure my wobbly legs won't allow that to happen.

"So, erm, what did she do?" It seems my curiosity wins.

"I take it you've met Parker? Chris's dad?"

"Briefly."

"Well, Parker and Emma never dated. From what I hear none of my grandsons do. It was a one-night thing."

My brows shoot up at this bizarre information. I'm too damn intrigued for my own good so I nod for Jay to continue.

"You see, we Ryans have a problem with women: we can get 'em, but keeping 'em is another story, a kind of curse you could say. My wife, Marla, died after having Nate, the boys' dad. We'd only been married a year at her passing. Our relationship was eighteen months all told."

Despite the years since this happened, sadness lurks in his eyes. "I'm so sorry, Jay." I reach over to pat his hand, wanting to offer comfort.

"Nate did better with his Liz. They were together almost ten years before cancer took her, but Park... well, let's say he had the worst luck of all. Unfortunately, it didn't just affect him, it got to this little one too. To this day, I don't know how she got her talons in my grandson, but she sashayed in and he was hooked. Dropped everything and everyone. He was only twenty-two and his career was about to take off. We warned him not to get too caught up but it didn't matter. He was already gone. Emma was the lowest kind of person. She had seen Parker's star was on the rise and wanted on board the gravy train.

"It was clear she was only with him so he would pay for everything, and that included what she put up her nose."

I can't hold back my gasp. Jay seems unfazed as he

continues while I look around the diner, wondering if Parker's going to re-enter any minute and demand Jay shut up. Hell, there's no chance I'd want all of my stories shared with strangers. But like a deer caught in head lights, I can walk away. I need to hear this story.

"She claims the condom broke, but we have our own suspicions. She did right by Chris, at least while he was in her belly, but the moment he was out, she went back to snorting all of Park's money. When Chris was almost one, Park had to go away to compete. Emma wanted them to travel with him, but Chris had a bit of a cold so Park told them to stay at home. Emma was livid. She tucked Chris into bed and invited all her druggie friends around for a party. Chris woke the next morning and as he usually did, went into her room to wake her up, only she didn't wake up. He stayed with her until the next morning when Park came home. She'd OD'd. It wasn't a surprise to any of us. I just wish Chris wasn't the one to find her."

Tears well in my eyes. No child should have to deal with that. "The poor darling," I say, and hug him tighter.

"So you see, him getting close to you is a big deal." He leans back, his gaze roaming over my face. "Yep, you'll do."

With wide-eyes, I sit back and try to work out what he means. It seems Jay's just told me I've become a part of this family of men and their world. I have not a clue what that is going to entail. If it's anything like tonight, it will be a bumpy ride.

CHAPTER TWO

REED

Looking at my reflection in the mirror, I'll admit those fuckers got in a good shot or two. The bruise on my jaw and the blood dripping from my nose are proof of that, but I'm betting they'll be pissing blood for days, along with some nicely broken ribs.

"Holy shit, those fucks," Park fumes as he comes back into the bathroom, first aid kit in hand. His lip is split and there's a nasty gash over his eye that'll need to be sewn up.

"I know."

"And Chris…. I don't know who that girl is, but if you don't marry her, I will."

I smile at the thought of Bria being mine. I've seen her in here before and think she works at the supermarket over the road. I seem to remember her in those god-awful tan-and-white shirts they wear. Even those couldn't hide her beauty. She's the most stunning girl I've ever seen. About five six, midlength blonde hair, and a killer body with curves for days and a nice rack. I'd love to have that body wrapped around me, her squirming underneath me as I rock her world. I chuckle as I remember Chris's scolding. He always says I'm doing an eye thing, but what he doesn't know, what he *can't* know, is I've never been so affected by a woman's gaze as I am by my angel's.

It's then that Pop bursts through the door.

"You boys all right?" he asks, surveying us.

We both nod.

"Where's Chris?" he asks, noticing that the little guy isn't with us.

"He's with Bria," Park answers.

"Who the fuck's Bria?"

"The girl outside with Chris," Park explains.

"Chris is with a *girl*?"

"A woman, *Reed's* woman," Park says.

"That so?" Pop raises an eyebrow at me.

I shrug, not willing to argue it. I was already stricken, but seeing how she looked after Chris and handled the fucked-up situation, there's nothing more I want but to get to know her better.

"Must be some woman for Chris to take a shine."

"Judging by R's reaction, I'd say she's a game changer." Pop raises an eyebrow again, and again I shrug. Let it never be said we're not an expressive family.

"Come on, let's get you two cleaned up."

Two stitches later, we exit the bathroom to see Pa sitting with Bria, Chris asleep in her arms.

"Good Lord in heaven, would you look at that?" Pop swears when he sees them.

"Told ya, game changer," Park says as he walks past.

"I know it's a risk," Pop says to me, "but if you let that one go, you're an idiot."

"Trust me, already miles ahead of ya," I answer as I pat him on the back and head towards my girl. She doesn't know it yet, but she is.

"Holy shit, Chris never goes to sleep without a fuss," I voice as I approach Bria and kiss her on the top of her head. "You got the magic touch, baby." She jumps at the contact. I'm being overly familiar with her, acting like I've known her forever, but her pull is strong.

"She's definitely worked her magic on young Chris here," Pa agrees.

"He's not the only one." Park grins and nods in my direction. Pa raises an eyebrow and I shrug. He nods, approving my choice.

"Parker, do you have anywhere I can put him down? I can't imagine this is a very comfy place to sleep," Bria asks.

"I don't know. You look like the best kind of pillow," I say and she shoots me a look, her one brow raised. I flash her my best smile and she gasps. I've got her!

"We live in the house at the back. Come on, I'll show you," Park says.

"I'll watch him," Pa volunteers. "Leave you young 'uns to the hard work."

"Actually," Bria pipes up, "I can stay with him if you want. This place is a mess, and the faster you can get it cleaned up, the faster you can get back up and running."

"Angel," I breathe, and wrap her in my arms, or as best as I can with a sleeping Chris, "you don't have to do this, you know."

She freezes at the contact, her eyes raising to mine. Upon contact, she releases a breath and her shoulders relax.

Clearing her throat, she looks away towards Parker. "I know, but this little guy needs me and Jay is needed here. It makes sense I stay with him."

"Really, Bria, it's not necessary," Park says.

"Guys, come on. I don't know everything but I do know Chris being this close to a woman is a big thing. Just go with it, yeah?" It really is. Not one of us can deny it.

We all look to Park, who nods.

"You really don't have to do this." I lower my voice when I speak, looking into her eyes. She shifts Chris slightly and even in his sleep, he clings to her tighter.

"I don't mind, but it seems your nephew does." I smile at her and get a shy one in return.

"Come on, I'll show you." With a hand on the small of her back, I guide her to my childhood home. Park, Pop, and Pa all kiss Chris on the forehead as we leave.

CHAPTER THREE

BRIA

Reed guides me to the house behind the diner. It's old. Some would go so far as to call it ramshackle, but I wouldn't. The colonial-style home has a wide veranda and a screen door that has rips in it, but I like it immediately. It's a little worn down but it's tough, much like I imagine the family that inhabits it is.

"You grew up here?" I ask Reed as we cross the gravel driveway.

"Yep. Until I moved out a few years back, this was the only home I knew."

"I like it. It's rough but it has character."

"Like me?"

I shake my head and laugh. "Oh, you're smooth, Ryan, real smooth."

He chuckles and opens the door for me. I step into what appears to be the living room, filled to the brim with trophies.

"Are you guys secretly trophy hoarders?" I ask.

"Nah, my pop just likes to display all the trophies my brothers and I have won." He shrugs.

"Do you think you have enough?" There's barely a spare surface.

"There's always room for more. Come on, Chris's room is down here." He leads me down a corridor, stopping at the first door.

"This used to be mine," he says, raising his eyebrows.

"And how many thousands of women have seen the inside of this room?" I ask as I walk past him, the words spilling out. I have no idea where my confidence or my questions are coming from, especially since I don't know the guy. A blush heats my cheeks and I'm relieved he's behind me so he can't see.

"A few"—he shrugs—"but none as stunning as you." He kisses me on the cheek as I'm rolling my eyes before he goes to the small bed and pulls back the covers.

It's the second time his lips have touched my skin and each time, my breath has caught in my throat. There's such ease and casualness between us. I've never known anything like it before.

Takin a deep breath to get my hormones under control, I sit on the bed while Reed kneels down and takes off Chris's shoes and socks.

"This really is incredible," he says, standing up again.

"What is?"

18

"Chris being this comfortable with you. Not that I blame him. I'd give my right arm to be wrapped around you like that. But for him,"—he lifts his arm, exposing a tight expanse of abs and hint of that male V, and rubs the back of his neck— "it's nothing short of miraculous."

Heat once more travels across my skin at his compliment. Shifting Chris onto the bed, I pat his back as he settles again. It's a welcome distraction from the heated looks Reed keeps sending my way.

"Your pa told me about Chris's mum and your brother. Sounds like the little guy's had a rough start."

"He has. Emma was, well, she was a fucking nutcase to put it mildly, but Chris was more than worth the trouble."

"I can tell he's well-loved."

"The centre of our universe," Reed says as he runs his hand over the little boy's head.

I risk a glance at him, wishing I hadn't. He's so gorgeous and distracting that I can't think straight with him so close. "Well, I think he's down for the night if you want to get back to the diner." Distance will be good. It means I can start acting like me and not this crazy woman who happily leans into a stranger's touch. But, boy, the simplest of his touches are divine.

"Are you sure you want to stay here? You don't have to."

"I know, but I seem to have developed a soft spot for this little guy."

Reed cups my face. "You're amazing, Bria."

I smile shyly. "Go on, you're not using me as an excuse to get out of cleaning up."

"Damn, baby, way to shut a man down."

"I think you can handle it."

"For you, I'd handle a fuckload more." With a quick kiss, this one edging closer to my mouth he's gone.

About an hour later, after some Saos and vegemite—a girl's got to eat and my burger was never cooked—I've gotten myself settled on Chris's small bed with him cuddled into my side when another dark, brown-haired head pokes into the room.

He starts and then comes to stand in the doorway. There's no denying he's a Ryan, but shorter than Reed and Parker, probably more my height, and a little less built but still solid.

"Over the years, I've become used to finding beautiful women in bed with my brothers, but never in my wildest dreams did I expect to find one in bed with my three-year-old nephew."

"And you didn't partake in these shenanigans?" I ask with a smile.

"Honey, I'm the straightest gay man you'll ever meet."

I raise an eyebrow and am met with a nod. "I dunno." I tilt my head. "I've dated a few who could give you a run for your money."

The new Ryan raises his eyebrow and I shrug.

"Your family doesn't approve?" I ask.

"My brothers appreciated me leaving all the women for them. I am the prettiest, after all."

I laugh.

He comes further into the room and offers me his hand. "Liam."

"Bria."

"So, explain to me how you're here?"

"I was in the diner when all the shit went down. I grabbed Chris until it was over."

"And he went willingly?"

"He's my boyfriend." I shrug.

"Boyfriend?"

"He got jealous of Reed."

"Right. Well, if you're okay here?" he asks, still puzzled at my presence.

"We're fine. Go help your family."

With a quick kiss on Chris's forehead, Liam leaves to join the rest of his good-looking family.

CHAPTER FOUR

REED

We're an hour into the clean-up, with all the glass swept up, when Liam waltzes in.

"I don't know who hooked that girl in there but whoever did, if you don't marry her, you're queerer than I am," he says, picking up a sheet of plywood to cover the window.

"That would be our nephew, but I'm trying to unhook his claws," I reply.

"I gotta tell you, man, that girl with Chris, dismissing the fact that *she's* with Chris for a minute, she's something else."

"I'm already with you, man."

"She's R's game changer," Park chimes in as he fits more wood into the window.

"Game changer, huh?"

I shrug, my standard reply when I'm struggling to put into words exactly who Bria is to me.

"You could do a hell of a lot worse and probably not much better."

"I don't think I can do any better. There *is* no one better."

Liam raises an eyebrow. "Yeah, Bria's a game changer, all right."

It takes another couple of hours for us to board the windows and clean up the kitchen, but by two we're finally finished.

Liam heads back to our place while I go to check on Bria and Chris.

In her sleep, she's curled around him and he is tucked tightly to her side.

I sweep her hair off her face. "Angel," I say with a quick kiss to her cheek. She stirs a little then curls tighter around Chris.

"Come on, wake up for me, pretty girl," I whisper in her ear, nuzzling her neck.

This gets her pretty brown eyes to blink slowly.

"Reed?" she asks sleepily.

"Hey. I thought you might be more comfortable in a bigger bed."

"You've finished cleaning up?"

"Just got done. Come on." I hold out my hand to her.

"What about Chris?"

"He'll be fine. Park, my pop, and Pa are here."

"He'll be fine, Bria," Park says behind me. "But thanks for all this. I'm pleased you were here for him."

23

"It was no problem," Bria says, getting up and tucking Chris in. "He's an amazing kid. You've done a great job with him, Parker."

"Look at my girl, sucking up to the bro-in-law already."

Bria just glares at me and I chuckle. "Come on, let Chris get his beauty sleep." I take her by the hand and pull her through the house and outside.

"Where are you taking me?" she asks with a hint of annoyance.

"To my place."

"I don't live far. I can—"

"No. Come on. It's been a long night." The last thing I want is her disappearing on me. After the drama of earlier, I want nothing more than to spend time with her.

She glances at me, seeming to deliberate something. "Your place? Where is that exactly?"

"Here," I say, unlatching the gate that divides my family home from mine. "Liam and I share."

"So when you moved out, you moved *behind* your house?" Her brows lift and a small smile plays on her lips.

"It's a separate property, so technically I did move out, but I wanted to be close and this was available so here I am," I say as we walk up the back steps and into the kitchen.

"At least it's clean." She grins, looking around at the slightly dated décor. The house isn't as old as our family home, and Liam and I have made some improvements over the years.

"For a couple of bachelors, Liam and I do okay. Come on, my room's through here." I tug her into my room. I pulled the age card—I'm twenty-four to his twenty-two—and snagged the master suite, and at the moment, I'm glad I bothered to make my king-sized mahogany bed this morning. I pull back the covers and gesture for Bria to get in.

"I can just take the couch."

I shake my head and nod towards my bed.

Rolling her eyes, she adds, "You just expect me to climb in bed with you, a complete stranger?"

That's exactly what I'm asking her. Saying it aloud, it's sound crazy even to my own ears, but the thought of her not spending the night or lying close to her sends panic through my chest. "I've seen you around," I admit. "You work at Coles, right?"

She nods.

"So," I continue, "we're not technically strangers. Hell, you've already met my whole family."

She bites her bottom lip.

"Please."

She hesitates before saying, "You know this doesn't mean anything, right?"

"Whatever you say, angel," I reply as I take off my shirt and jeans.

I turn back to the bed and hear a soft gasp. I pull the sheets back and indicate for her to get in. With a small sigh, she kicks of her shoes and climbs onto the bed. I get in beside her and pull her towards with me, trapping her against my chest, my arm around her shoulders, holding her to me.

"Reed."

"Shh, angel, just sleep. It's late."

After a few minutes, I can still feel her mind going a mile a minute.

"How did you manage to bewitch six members of the Ryan clan in one night?" I ask. Not only has Chris taken to her like a house on fire, but her in my bed fully clothed is another miracle in itself. I won't lie and say I'm not dying to see what's hidden beneath the clothes, but I don't want to fuck this up by pushing her even more. Park was right when he called Bria my game changer, because she is. Already, from her care and kindness, she's making me want to be different. That she's so damn beautiful helps too. She's not a one-night stand, like so many—*too* many—girls before her. No, this girl, this *woman* has already cemented her way into my life, my heart, and my family and I like it, I *welcome* it.

"It's a talent," she finally answers.

"It's something."

"And to think all I wanted was a burger," she says and I chuckle.

I kiss the top of her head. "Goodnight, angel."

"Goodnight, Reed."

CHAPTER FIVE

BRIA

I wake up wrapped around Reed, my head resting on his defined chest, my arm around his waist.

I take a moment to study his face, the thick black lashes framing his beautiful eyes, before moving on to his chest and arms, covered in intricate black-and-grey ink.

He shifts in his sleep and I feel his rather large erection poke me in the side.

I'm imagining all the things I'd like to do with it and him when he runs his hand down my back, breaking me from my naughty thoughts.

"Morning," he says in a sleep-laced voice.

"Good morning to you, too." I smile at him and he

stretches his back, pushing his dick against me again, and I blush.

He catches sight of my cheeks reddening and gives me a cocky smirk.

I arch an eyebrow at him.

"Sorry, but when a man wakes up with an angel in his arms, there's only so much he can do."

"You are so smooth, Reed Ryan."

"Not smooth, baby, truthful. You're an angel. Not just in looks, though you're a fucking knockout, but what you did for my family last night…. I know we keep harping on it, but Chris doesn't trust women, at all, but with you, it was like bam!"

I smile. "He's a great kid."

"The best."

"His family, especially his uncle, aren't bad either."

"Aw, thanks, baby."

"I meant Liam."

"You know Liam is gay, right?"

"I do. He mentioned you all were thankful he left all the girls for you because he's the prettiest."

He chuckles. "Yeah, that's my little brother for ya, always looking out for me."

"Well, it's not like you couldn't use the help," I joke and am rewarded with a full-on laugh.

"Damn, angel."

"Well, someone's got to keep you grounded." I shrug.

"But if I'm grounded I'll never get to fly with you," he says, getting serious.

"Reed," I breathe.

"Bria." He cups my cheek, "Seriously, you're amazing and unlike any girl I've ever known." I stare into his green eyes searching for deceit, but find none.

Everything is moving so fast, rationally I know this, but I don't have that little voice in my head, or even my heart telling me to slow down.

We stare at each other for a moment before he leans into me and kisses me.

The kiss is soft and gentle, but enough for my heart rate to spike at the contact. He gently leans on me, pushing me to my back before situating himself in between my legs and grinding into me. On contact, I moan in his mouth, my hands clutching at his chest. It doesn't matter that we only exchanged words a few hours ago. It doesn't matter that I know so little about him. How can any of that matter when everything about this moment, this contact feels so perfectly right?

Need moves me into action and I lift my hips to meet him. His lips travel to my neck and I tilt my head to accommodate him while his hand slips under my shirt. He pinches and kneads at my breast, sending ripples of pleasure straight to my groin, drenching my panties.

"Reed," I pant.

"I know, angel," he says before returning his lips to mine, the hand on my breast navigating south.

When he reaches the button on my jeans, he pauses, waiting for me to object. When I don't, he unbuttons them, pulls the zip down, and rubs his hand over the front of my panties. I arch up against him, running my nails down his back when he slides his hand inside, running his fingers up and down my slit, feeling my wetness.

"Damn, baby, you're drenched."

"I know," I gasp. "What are you going to do about it?" In any other situation, I would have laughed or been horrified at my boldness, but with fierce desire pushing me on, I mean every word.

He growls, capturing my lips once again while he slips a finger inside me. I moan as he glides easily in and out.

"Oh God." I gasp as he adds a second finger, the heel of his palm rubbing my clit. I start grinding myself against him and feel my insides tightening.

"That's it, baby," Reed coaxes. My breathing is loud and shallow. There's a light sheen of sweat covering my body, and my nails are probably leaving marks down his back. The thought makes me clench around his fingers. I like the idea.

"Reed," I breathe again.

"Come on, baby, come for me," he whispers in my ear before sucking behind it, sending me over the edge into orgasmic bliss.

He continues sliding in and out of me as I slowly become aware of my surroundings, running my hand through my hair.

"Good?" Reed asks above me, a smug look on his face.

"My toes are tingling."

"Good," he says, giving me a quick kiss. "Thank you for letting me see that. You were amazing."

A small smile tugs at my lips. I've never been thanked for allowing a guy to get me off before. It's all a little surreal. "What about you?" I ask, suddenly aware of what has to be a rather painful erection digging into my stomach.

"Don't worry about me. I'm a big boy. I can look after myself."

"I can tell." I lift my hips to his and am rewarded with a groan.

"Seriously, Reed, do you need me to—"

"That was about you, angel. I'll live."

I bite my lip in indecision.

He unsnags my lip from my teeth. "Seriously, angel, I'll be fine. That was something I wanted to do for you. Watching you come apart was so much more than I imagined." He leans down and gives me another kiss.

I grab the back of his neck, holding him to me while my tongue explores his mouth, his wrestling with mine. While he's distracted, I reach down and slide my hand beneath his black boxer briefs. He's too much of a temptation. He jerks when my hand comes into contact with his hard cock, and he tries to pull away from the kiss but I hold him to me, running my hand up and down his length.

"Bria," he growls against my mouth.

"Shh, relax," I say, squeezing him a little harder. I continue moving my hand up and down, and his hips begin to thrust in rhythm with me.

"Baby, I'm close," he pants, and a few pumps later, he comes all over my hand and his stomach.

I bring my hand to my mouth, and look at the fluid. My eyes flash to his and he's staring at me with such an intensity, that my tongue snakes out and licks his salty cum off my skin. He groans and covers his face with his hands. I love what I'm doing to him.

Exhaling a deep breath, he stares up at me with wonder in his eyes.

"Who are you? And what on earth did I do to deserve that?"

I grin. "Just giving as good as I got. And now I've got to go, and you need to have a shower," I say, getting out of the bed and grabbing my shoes. If I honestly didn't have anywhere else to be, I'd be so tempted to stay in bed all day.

"Can I see you tonight?" he asks, leaping out after me.

"We'll see," I say over my shoulder as I walk to the door. It takes everything in me not to skip on my way out.

~

Heading into Wheels that night, I try convincing myself I'm only here to check on Christian, but really, I know I want to see him, be near him again. I definitely had *not* been thinking all day about the toe-curling orgasm he gave me this morning. I stop at the door and press my thighs together to help ease the ache.

I step inside and notice the windows once again have glass in them. It only takes a minute before Chris is rushing through the diner and attaching himself to my legs.

"Hey, buddy," I say, ruffling his hair as who has to be another Ryan comes up to us. It's a face I recognise from my previous visits, but apart from that, I have no clue who he is.

He's probably between Liam and Reed's heights, five nine, five ten maybe, more similar in build to Liam, and probably a few years younger.

"Who've you got here, Chris?" Young Ryan asks.

"Bria, she's my girlfriend," he replies.

"Your girlfriend, huh? And just how do you know my nephew?" he asks me.

"Which brother are you?" I ask.

"Jax, the youngest."

"Bria," I introduce myself and extend my hand. He shakes it.

"So you know Chris how?" he asks again.

"I was here last night." I pick Chris up.

Awareness crosses his face. "Ah, you're *that* girl."

"Yep," Chris answers. "She's Uncle Reed's girl. He's in love with her."

My heart flutters at an incredible pace and I try to brush aside the child's words.

"You're R's girl?" he asks as a warm arm slides around my waist and a kiss is pressed to my temple.

"Yep," Reed says once his body is close to mine. "Bria's my girl." He moves behind me, pressing my back to his front and giving me a squeeze.

"Your girl?" I ask, raising an eyebrow.

"Yep, my girl," Reed confirms.

"Isn't it a bit early for that?" As soon as the words escape, the image of his fingers inside my panties, his mouth on mine, heats my system. I know my words make no sense.

"You're the one who came back."

"Maybe I came back for Chris." I give him a squeeze as he rests on my hip, his tiny fingers playing with my hair.

"Chris?" Reed asks, and taps his nose. "The kid's a flake, total commitment issues."

I'm still too flustered by the memory of this morning and how this conversation is playing out. I find my voice, feeling the urge to push him. "Maybe I'm not in it for the long-term."

"Don't kid yourself, angel. You're a long-term forever girl."

"How do you know?" I ask, momentarily taken aback.

"Because a girl like you deserves the world, which is why you're here right now and not in my bed."

"Pulling out the big guns, big bro," Jax says with what sounds like awe in his voice.

"For my angel, anything, *everything*," Reed says, kissing my cheek. A huge smile crosses Jax's face.

"Park was right," he says as yet another Ryan walks up to us.

This one has the same dark hair as all the other Ryans, and if not for a few years' age difference and grey-blue eyes, he could be Liam's twin. He also has roughly the same build as him too.

"Because seven Ryans aren't enough," I mutter under my breath.

"R, Park needs you in the kitchen," he says, then spots Chris in my arms. "What the fuck?"

"This is Bria. Chris's girlfriend and R's game changer," Jax says, smirking.

"Huh?"

"Bria was the girl here last night," Reed explains.

"Oh, right. Well, attachments aside, Park needs you in the kitchen."

Reed gives me a squeeze and another kiss on the temple and moves off to the kitchen. The young Ryan shoots me a quizzical look before moving off towards the bar.

Jax sees my frown. "Don't worry about Mav. He's the mysterious one."

"So if he's the mysterious one, which one are you?" I ask as I move to the booth I sat at last night, sliding along the seat, and bringing Chris with me. Jax slides in opposite me.

"I'm the cheeky one." He shoots me a dazzling smile.

"And Liam's the pretty one, which leaves what for Parker and Reed?"

"Park's the serious one, was even before the champ here came along,"—he taps Chris's nose—"and Reed, he's the fun one." He wiggles his eyebrows at me.

"Of course he is." I sigh.

"Which one am I?" Chris asks.

"You're the handsome one," I reply and tickle him.

"Although I guess there are a couple of others that Reed could go by," Jax says, seemingly lost in thought.

"Like what?" I ask, my interest piqued.

"The troublesome one, maybe. The angry one, although not so much anymore. Nah, the fun one fits him best."

"Why is or was he troublesome and angry?"

"Well he isn't so much anymore, more when he was racing."

"Racing?"

"You mean you don't know what we do? Who we are?"

"Chris told me last night you guys ride bikes, but that was it." I shrug.

"My brother is calling you his girl and you haven't Googled him?"

I shake my head and shrug again.

"Damn girl, you gotta do your research. Us Ryans are

some important people," he says in all seriousness. "None more so than me." He bursts out laughing.

"Oh my God, you're terrible," I admonish but can't help laughing along with him.

"I know but I'm lovable as well, so that helps." I roll my eyes. "Nah, Chris was right, we do ride bikes."

"Push bikes?" I ask, trying to picture Reed in skintight Lycra. I have to admit, the picture isn't half-bad.

"Nah, well sorta, but mainly motorbikes. Park and Mav do, or did in Park's case, motocross. Mav and I do freestyle motocross as well as freestyle BMX, and Reed and Liam are our factory racers, or again, used to be, in Reed's case."

"Whoa," I say, realizing just how involved the Ryans are in, well, motorsport.

"Yep, we're da best," Chris pipes up.

"Is that right?" I ask him, bouncing him on my knee, and he nods wildly.

"So Parker gave up because of Christian, but why did Reed?"

"Reed and this guy, Hunter David, came up through the ranks together, and because he's a local as well, there was always fierce competition between the two," Jax begins. "It only got worse the higher the level of competition. Hunter is a great rider, stupidly talented, but he never wanted to work hard and took every shortcut he could. Reed didn't have as much talent but he worked hard and was persistent. He never gave up. Realistically, Hunter should've smoked him every time, but because he didn't want to do the hard work it evened them out.

"Anyway, it was towards the end of the season and at every race there were parties and all the favours that come with them, if you know what I mean."

I nod and Jax continues.

"Well, it had been a not-so-hidden secret that Hunter was indulging a little too much, but Reed never had enough proof to go to the race organisation. I mean, racing is a dangerous sport, guys have died doing it, so the last thing anyone needs is to be racing against a guy still living last night's high. Finally, Reed got proof of what Hunter was doing and took it to the race organisation. They banned Hunter for the rest of the season but he was allowed to compete the next."

"They made him go to rehab and counselling, right?" I ask.

Jax shakes his head. "Nope,"—he pops the P—"and so Hunter had six months to develop a fully formed habit and stew in his anger. By the time the next season rolled around, he was an addict hell-bent on revenge. He ended up making every race an opportunity to try to take Reed out. Reed told the race organisation this would happen, and everyone could blatantly see what Hunter was trying to do, but because there were never any crashes that could be labelled as more than racing incidents, their hands were tied."

My eyes widen in surprise. It's like hearing a soap opera for motorsports. "Was Reed hurt?"

"A few broken bones and he was sore more often than not, but nothing serious."

"I don't understand why the race organisation wouldn't do anything."

"Neither could anyone else. In the end, after a particularly nasty crash, Reed had enough. He went to the race organisation and said one day Hunter was going to kill him or someone else and he refused to put the other riders at risk. He said that if they wouldn't put a stop to Hunter and his vendetta then he would, and so he quit."

"It seems like such a shame." And it really does, especially if Reed is as good and as passionate as his brother says he is.

"It is. Reed's a great rider. The sponsors and the crowd loved him, but Hunter was getting more reckless. He didn't care who he took out on the way to getting Reed, and Reed refused to put the other riders at risk."

My chest constricts painfully at the thought of Reed being seriously injured. The emotion was raw and unfamiliar. "So what happened to Hunter?"

"He ended up losing sponsors because of his behaviour and had to drop down to the lower classes."

"So why didn't Reed go back?"

"His body had changed. He'd bulked up, which wouldn't have been an issue to lose, but he'd also grown, and crouching on those bikes is hard enough without having to worry about the gangly-arse legs he's got going on. Besides, Liam had been working his way up and making a name for himself and Reed didn't want to trample on any progress he was making."

"So Liam rides with Hunter?" I ask. I don't disguise the worry in my voice. These men who I barely know already matter to me.

"Nah, they managed to miss each other, but every now and again if a ride comes up for Hunter, they'll race each other."

"And how does that go?"

A smug smile crosses Jax's face. "Liam leaves him in his dust."

"Yeah!" Chris cheers from my lap and we laugh.

"Liam's like the love child of Reed and Hunter. He has Hunter's talent and Reed's work ethic, which makes him unbeatable. Hunter can't stand it. I mean, you saw what happened last night."

Shock at just how serious this is rips through me. "That was him?" I gasp.

"Him and his goons. It seems the more success Ryan Racing has, or every time something happens with his outfit, we get the blame."

"So what happened to cause this latest attack?"

"I heard Hunter missed out on a ride for the race on the weekend, so naturally it must be our fault. It has nothing to do with the fact he can barely walk in a straight line, let alone race a 1000cc bike at 300 km/h."

"He's not a nice guy," Chris says.

My eyes drop to Chris and I offer a small smile. "It doesn't sound like it." I give Chris a quick squeeze. "So who does this Hunter race for?"

"Devil Racing. No idea why they still sponsor him, but it's their loss."

My face pales because despite not knowing about the world this lot of good-looking men inhabit, I *do* know Devil Racing.

CHAPTER SIX

REED

I walk into the kitchen determined to make this a quick chat. I've got plans for my girl and me.

"What's up, man?" I ask Park. "Bria's here."

"She is?"

"Yeah, Chris is with her right now."

He peers through the window into the dining room. Shaking his head, he says, "For as long as I live, I will never know how she got to him."

Looking at her as she laughs at something Jax says, my heart swells in my chest. "I think I'm beginning to understand."

"Yeah?" Park cocks an eyebrow.

"There's something about her."

"There really is."

"She just fits. Tell me it doesn't feel like she's been a part of this family for years."

"No, you're totally right, man. She does fit, almost perfectly."

"No almost about it. So what did you want to talk to me about that's keeping me from my girl?"

"You got the parts for Liam's bike for the weekend?"

"Yes, Park, I have. They arrived today as I told you they would. I *have* done this before, you know. In fact, I used to do this for a living."

He sighs and stops flipping burgers for a second. "Yeah, I know, and we all know how much you gave up for the field and for the family. It's just—"

"It's just the pre-race jitters don't lessen even if you're no longer the one on the bike. I get it."

"You could've been great, you know."

I don't want to hear it. I know what I gave up. "Wasn't meant to be." I give a one-shoulder shrug. "You know that as well as I do."

"But at least I got Chris out of it."

"And I got my life. Seems like a fair enough trade."

"Especially when a girl like Bria comes along, am I right?" Parker chuckles.

"Damn straight. So can I go out there and get her now?"

Park laughs. "Yeah, sure, have fun." He offers his fist. I pound it out before exiting the kitchen.

Bria looks lost in thought when I get to the table where she sits with Chris on her lap, the lucky bastard. I slide in beside them and Bria snaps back to reality.

"So what does it take for a girl to get a burger around here?" she asks in her sweet voice.

"A whole lot because you and I are going out."

"We are?"

"Yep, on a date. Our first in fact," I say, grabbing Chris and swinging him over the table to stand beside the booth.

"And if I wanted to stay here?"

I slide closer to her, running my hand from her knee up to her thigh, my lips at her ear, and say, "Please, angel, I just want to be alone with you, get to know you better. I'm not above begging."

She turns her head and gives me a quick, chaste kiss on the lips. "Okay."

"Okay?" I ask, shocked she gave in so easily. I hope that means I'm getting through to her, but I just don't know her well enough to make that distinction, *yet*. But I'm determined it won't be long until I can.

"Yep, I've decided you need to woo me, so let's get to it." A brilliant smiles curves her lips as she playfully pushes me out of the booth.

As soon as she's out of the booth, I grab her hand and race towards the door.

"Bye, Reed, bye, sis, have fun!" Jax calls out as we burst outside.

"Did Jax just call me sis?" Bria asks as she tries to keep up with me. I don't answer; I'm in too much of a rush to begin our night.

CHAPTER SEVEN

BRIA

Reed pulls me through the diner in a rush and I admit, I'm as eager as he seems to be to start our date. It appears sometime during the chaos that was last night, this band of men have wormed their way into my heart, none more so than Christian and his eldest uncle.

Reed comes to a stop in front of a shiny, pearlescent-blue bike—a very fast one by the look of things.

"Have you ever ridden on one of these?" he asks, grabbing helmets, one off the handlebars and the other out of a lock box on the back.

I bite my lip and shake my head. The ones I used to tool around on when I was younger were nothing like this.

Reed tugs on my chin to release my lip. "Do you want to?

If you're uncomfortable, we can take my car."

I've always wanted to learn how to ride a motorbike, but have been scared shitless to actually do it. I mean, if something goes wrong, there's not a lot of protection between you and the road, but I'm not scared with Reed.

"No, the bike is fine. Just don't go too fast, okay?"

Reed steps up to me, both of his hands finding my hips and pulling me flush to him. "Angel, I promise I will never do anything you don't want me to do. Putting you at risk by speeding doesn't sit right with me, so if you want me to drive at 10 km/h that's what I'll do, okay?"

I smile nervously and chuckle a little. "I don't think going that slow will be necessary, just don't go speeding off."

"Sure thing." After a quick, chaste kiss, he puts the helmet on my head, adjusting the chinstrap before putting his own on.

He picks me up and puts me on the back of the bike, and hops on in front of me. He then reaches back and pulls me tight to his back. My arms are crossed securely across his very tight abs, my thighs hugging his narrow hips.

"If you want me to slow down, just tap my stomach, okay?"

I nod and Reed starts the bike, bringing it to life beneath us. He moves easily with the bike, leaning into the corners, taking me with him, the cool night rushing around us.

It's exhilarating, the sense of freedom coming from not being in the confines of a car. I feel like I'm almost part of the scenery I'm riding through. Beneath my helmet, I wear a massive smile.

We ride for about twenty minutes before he pulls over to

a rest stop off the side of our town's main road. Just because we're in the middle of nowhere really, it doesn't mean we're behind the times. Even all the way out here, we follow culinary trends. A rickety old food truck is sitting in the clearing, and the smell of herbs and spices permeates the air.

Reed helps me off the bike, running his hand through his hair, making him look even more irresistible than he already is. I bite my lip beneath my helmet before taking it off, my hair drifting around me in a blonde cloud.

I manage to just get it off my face before Reed crashes his lips to mine.

He sucks my bottom lip before his tongue begs entrance and I grant it. I moan into his mouth and Reed growls and pulls me tighter to him. His tongue explores my mouth, the minty taste of the gum he must have been chewing seeping into mine. His body feels amazing against mine with the tight abs I was hugging a few minutes ago and strong, muscular arms keeping my body next to his.

Finally, he breaks the kiss, leaving us both panting a little. "Damn, baby."

"What?" I ask, still trying to get my bearings.

"You have no idea how incredible you look, do you?"

"An incredible mess, you mean?" I say, running my hand through my mop of hair.

"Baby, you are so far from a mess it's not funny." He pulls me tighter to him. "You are so goddamn amazing, and you have no idea."

Heat crawls its way to my cheeks. "I'm just a uni student."

"Oh, angel, you are so much more than that already."

"What do you mean, already?" I ask as Reed takes hold of my hand and pulls me towards the truck.

"I mean that quickly, so quickly, almost instantly, you have brought a lightness to our family."

The quick and instant is right. I've been barely able take a breath and get myself together since last night and meeting him. But it's another word that catches my attention. "A lightness?"

"I can't explain it, but it's like we can smile again or something."

"Reed, I've known you and your family for"—I glance at my watch—"twenty-two hours now."

"I know, and that's the crazy thing. You've just slotted in like you've always been there. Anyway, let's get some food and we can talk about this over dinner."

"Reed!" a voice from inside the truck says.

"Hey, man, how the hell are ya?" Reed asks.

"I'm good."

"That's good. Hey, meet my girl, Bria," Reed says, pushing me forward.

"Bria, huh?" the voice says as I step forward, and I recognise Mike, the owner. "How you doing, girl? The usual?"

"I'm good, Mike, and the usual will be fine, thanks." I smile at Reed's wide eyes.

"You know Mike?" he asks.

"Been coming here about as long as you. I'm kind of amazed you two have never run into each other. You're both here enough, but I see you found each other anyway. I am a bit surprised a woman of your intelligence is with a bum like this one, though," Mike says, nodding towards Reed.

"Hey, man, not cool!" Reed says, pulling me back to him, my back to his front, and resting his chin on my shoulder. His grin doesn't match his offended tone.

Mike chuckles. "Hell, man, she's a smart girl. Figured she already knew that. So what are you eating?"

"Give me a rack of ribs with baked beans, fries, coleslaw, and a Coke."

"Gotcha. Go take a seat and I'll bring it out to you."

"So you know Mike, huh?" Reed asks as we take a seat at a nearby picnic table.

"I do." I shoot him a smile.

"So was he right?" Reed asks as he reaches across the table and twines his fingers with mine.

"About what?"

"That you know I'm a bum but you're here anyway."

"Of course I'm here. It's undeniable. I'm sitting right across from you." I poke out my tongue.

"You know what I mean."

"No, I don't think you're a bum; in fact, I think there's a lot more to you than meets the eye."

"Jax told you the story."

"Jax told me *a* story. I don't know if it's *the* story."

"What did he tell you?"

"That you used to race, you had trouble with a guy named Hunter. He was a danger to you, the other racers, and himself and the race organisation didn't do anything to stop him so you quit."

"Yeah, that's the story."

"That was a very selfless thing you did."

47

"Yeah well, he had to be stopped. Now he just comes after us in different ways."

"Before we get too into this, I've got to tell you that I may be unfamiliar to a lot, basically all, of the motor racing world, but I *have* heard of Devil Racing before."

"Okay," Reed says hesitantly. "A lot of people have."

"There's a little bit more to it than that."

CHAPTER EIGHT

REED

I'm not gonna lie, when she says there's more to it, I'm seriously starting to freak-out. Does she know Hunter? How well? Did they used to date? How come I never met her before? And more importantly, can I walk away from her knowing she's close to Hunter?

I take a deep breath and try to calm down. "I gotta tell you, I'm freaking out a little here."

"It's nothing bad," she rushes to reassure me, "but I grew up with one of the guys who rides for Devil."

I've now got the entire roster of that piece-of-shit outfit running through my head. "Who?"

"Roman Thomas. I haven't spoken to him in years though. He, um, he changed after signing with them."

I have to admit the name doesn't ring a bell, but Devil has so many guys going through the garage, all of them with hopes of becoming the next Mick Doohan but then shoved in development classes or used as test riders. The fact he, Bria's friend, changed after he signed with them, well, devil by name, devil by nature.

"Can't say I know of the guy but I appreciate you telling me of the connection."

"Rome's a great guy. Well, he was before he got involved with them, but when they first started talking to him, it was like he forgot who he was and what he stood for. He caused a lot of heartache."

"For you?" My heart starts pounding. I really don't like the idea of my girl being an ex to one of these guys.

"No, not to me, to my best friend, Grayson. Her and Rome, they were 'the' couple in our high school."

I exhale a deep breath. "You really had me going for a minute there, angel. I had all sorts of crazy thoughts running through my head."

Bria gets up and comes around my side of the table. I turn and draw her into my lap and she wraps her arms around my neck, my hands resting on her hips. On contact, I ease into her touch and affection. Effortless. Everything about Bria is so natural, as easy as breathing.

"I just didn't want something to happen and for it to come out that I know him and you be blindsided by it."

"Thank you, baby."

"It's just, I think we've got something here, you know?" I catch the slight shake in her voice, her nerves rising to the surface.

"Oh, I know." I bounce her a little in my lap, which turns out to be a very bad idea judging by the tightening in my groin. "But I do appreciate it." I draw her face to mine, our lips seeking each other out. I take the time to explore her mouth. My lips feel bruised from our earlier kiss but I don't give a fuck.

God, this girl. I'm almost certain I never want to let her go, and I've got a feeling it won't take long for that "almost" to disappear.

One of my hands moves to her arse while the other travels up to her chest to graze her breast. I lightly rub her nipple and feel it harden under my touch. She moans into my mouth and I pull her tighter to me, my cock pressing hard against my zipper now.

We're interrupted by someone clearing his throat.

"Sorry to interrupt you lovebirds, but I figured you wouldn't want to let this food get cold," Mike says, two giant plates in his hands.

I clear my throat as Bria hides against my neck. "Yeah, thanks, man."

He snickers as he puts the plates down. "Enjoy." He walks away.

I look to see what Bria ordered and laugh. It's the same as mine but she's ordered different sides.

"You're a fucking dream," I mutter before I crash my lips to hers again.

I finally manage to tear my lips away from hers. "Come on, let's eat before it gets cold."

Mike comes back to deliver our drinks, a Coke for me, a

milkshake for Bria, but not just any milkshake. There's syrup and cream running down the sides, four wafer sticks sticking out, plus... "Are those profiteroles on top?" I ask.

"They surely are," she says, taking a long sip.

"Is it as good as it looks?"

"Better." There's a twinkle in her eye.

"Want to give me a taste?"

"Nope." She wraps her lips around the straw again.

As soon as she releases it, I grab the back of her neck and bring her lips to mine, kissing the shit out of her.

"Mmmm, caramel," I say as I lick my lips, taking a wafer stick with me.

Grinning, she shakes her head.

"Come on, the food's getting cold," I say and gesture to our meals.

"Mac and cheese, sweet potato fries, and potato bake, huh?" I ask, swinging a fork over her plate.

"Food of the gods," she says and shovels in a mouthful. She closes her eyes and moans. My dick twitches. He still hasn't fully recovered from our make-out session before.

"Wanna share?" I gesture to my sides.

"Sure." She shrugs and snags one of my chips.

"So tell me about Bria Marie Adams."

"What do you want to know?"

"Anything, everything."

"I'm an only child. My parents, Aaron and Lacey, have been together for twenty-eight years. They live in Mooresville, about an hour and a half from here on the coast."

"So my family must be a total culture shock compared to yours."

"There are a *lot* of you," she concedes.

"What else?"

"I'm doing honours at Booker, a journalism/PR major."

"You live on campus?"

"Yep, with my best friend, Grayson. We managed to snag a suite. It's nice."

"You guys grew up together, right?"

"Yep, our parents are best friends and we're only a few months apart in age so naturally we were always together."

"That's cute. She a journalism major too?"

She shakes her head. "Geography and meteorology."

"Really?"

"Don't ask."

"Okay, so you're an only child, who's relatively local, and a journalism student who likes delicious food. What do you do in your spare time?"

"I read or listen to music, shop. You know, girl stuff."

"What do you like?"

"Besides good food and caramel milkshakes?"

"Yeah."

"Not much, really. I'm a simple girl, Reed." She takes another sip of her drink.

"I don't think there's anything simple about you," I say and tuck a strand of hair behind her ear, "except for how seamlessly you've become a part of our lives."

"So why bikes?" she asks, turning the focus onto me.

"Why not? My pop and pa rode them and that filtered down to us. There wasn't much of a female influence for most of us, so we didn't have a mum around to tell us or my pop and pa that motorcycles are dangerous and young boys shouldn't be on them."

"Would you have listened even if there were?"

I smile and shake my head. "Probably not. We're all stubborn and when we find something we love we hold on to it, for the most part…." I trail off, thinking about the women who have left our lives.

"Your pa, Jay, right?" she asks, and slides a hand over mine. I nod. "He told me about your mum and grandma."

"Obviously I never knew my grandma, and I was six when my mum died."

"Do you remember much about her?"

"Little bits. Park was eight and he remembers a little bit more, but still not a lot."

"I'm sorry." She squeezes my hand.

"It is what it is. We just have bad luck. Well, if the stories my pa and pop tell are true, extraordinarily *good* luck and then extraordinarily *bad* luck." Suddenly I see Bria in a whole new light. Not as a girl I'm insanely into, someone I have no doubt I could have a future with, but as someone who, if she continues her relationship with me, could very well become a victim of our family's shitty luck as well.

CHAPTER NINE

BRIA

We finish dinner chatting about general things. Towards the end, Mike comes out and joins us, giving Reed a hard time and trying to convince me to stop seeing him. We both laugh him off.

It's only when I start yawning do we realise how late it is.

"Come on." Reed stands and offers me his hand. "It's late and you've probably got class tomorrow."

"I do, but tonight is worth any tiredness. I had a great time."

"Me too." He kisses me before putting the helmet on my head.

He puts me on the bike then gets on himself, and I have to admit that being wrapped around him is a major advantage of this mode of transport. I slip my hands under his shirt and rub them over his tight abs, his muscles contracting from my touch. With a quick squeeze of my knee, Reed starts the engine and we're off into the night again.

This time I enjoy it more, knowing what to expect. I think if Reed and I go anywhere, I'm going to insist on taking his bike. The freedom and feel of flying combined with being wrapped around him? I doubt there are too many better feelings on the planet, except for maybe his kisses. Reed's kisses could probably cure cancer if, you know, kisses could do that sort of thing. Okay, so I'm getting caught up in all that is Reed Ryan, but anyone coming under the onslaught I have and I'd like to see them try and resist it. I bet everything in my bank account, which at the moment is sitting at $113.42, that they won't be able to. I'm only human, after all. Just a normal twenty-two-year-old girl who has caught the eye of a motorcycle god and is trying to keep her composure. It's not easy in the face of all his charm. Sure, I've dated in the past, but no one like Reed.

We get back to the diner and Reed spins to face me. His hair is a mess from his helmet and he quickly restyles it, the movement showing off his bulging biceps and giving him an irresistible "just been fucked" look. I get why he found the same thing with me irresistible. He takes mine off and smiles when we make eye contact.

"Can I see you tomorrow night?" he asks, bashfulness crossing his features.

"Three nights in a row? Are you sure you won't get sick of me? Plus, people will talk. The famous Reed Ryan, notorious womaniser, seen with the same girl three nights in a row."

"I'll never get sick of you, angel. We could be together for ten lifetimes and I still won't get enough."

"Reed…"

"Shh, angel." He presses a finger against my lips. "I know this has been fast, but there's something drawing me to you, something I've never experienced before. It's making me want to do things I've never done, like spending three amazing evenings with you. I know I have a reputation, we all do, my brothers and I, but my pa and pop always told us that when we find the girl we're meant to be with nothing will stop us."

My heart beat speeds up at his words. "And that's me?"

"It is."

"Oh." I don't know what else to say.

"I know it's soon and I'm probably freaking you out, but I don't want to leave you in any doubt as to what you are to me, Bria. I don't want there to be any doubt of what we've got, what we're building here."

I nod.

"Okay?"

"Okay," I reply and Reed exhales in a rush.

"I really like you, Bria."

"I really like you, too."

"Good." He smiles his brilliant smile. "So I'll see you tomorrow, now tonight?" he asks, looking at his watch.

"You don't want to wait until the weekend? It is Friday. We could hold off and do something Saturday."

"Liam has a race on the weekend. He's down there now

with Mav and Pop. Jax and I are going to go down Saturday morning."

"Oh." My shoulders slump. I'm not doing a great job of acting coy. It's one of my weaknesses. I'm an open book.

"Hey." He lifts my chin with a finger. "I'd love if you'd come with us."

"Really?" Excitement courses through me.

"Yeah, you can be Liam's umbrella girl."

"Umbrella girl? I won't have to wear anything skimpy, will I?"

He laughs. "As much as I'd love to see that, I don't want anyone else to, so no. Just one of our tees and jeans, or shorts if it's hot."

"I won't be in the way, will I?"

"Nah, we'll see if Pa and Chris want to come, that way Park can have the diner to himself."

"It won't be too much for him?"

"It'll be easier for him actually, especially if we take Chris with us; then he won't have to worry."

I nod, discovering even more about the inner working of Reed and his family. "So you all usually go?"

"Depends, but how about we talk about this over dinner tonight? It's late and I don't want you to fall asleep in class."

I laugh. "I won't, don't worry about me."

He takes a step closer to me and pulls my hips flush with his. "Baby, that's just not possible. You're mine to worry about now."

"So does that mean I can worry about you too?"

"There's nothing to worry about, and I don't want you to trouble yourself about little old me."

"That's not possible," I say, echoing his words, and reach up, grabbing the back of his neck and bringing his lips to mine.

We quickly get lost in the kiss and it's only when we're both gasping for air that we break apart.

"Damn, angel," Reed says, his forehead resting on mine.

"I should probably go," I say, but make no attempt to move.

"You could stay."

"Reed…."

"Okay, but will you stay tomorrow night? We won't do anything you don't want to do, but it'll mean we can leave straight from here."

I smile. "Fine, I'll stay tomorrow."

"Good." He smiles, kissing my nose before stepping back and releasing me. I grab his hand and walk him over to my trusty Honda Civic. It's almost twenty years old but has never failed me yet.

Reed opens the driver-side door for me, and after I get in, he bends down and fastens my seat belt.

"Can never be too safe."

"There's that worrying again."

"I promise you, angel, I'll always worry."

"Don't. I'll see you tonight, around six?"

"Sounds perfect, I'll see you then." With one more kiss, he gets up and closes my door.

I start my car and drive out of the diner's car park, Reed watching me before he's finally out of sight.

The journey doesn't take long, especially when I'm caught up in replaying our sweet kisses. Before I know it, I pull into my spot outside my dorm at just after one. I've just closed our suite door when I hear her voice. "You're coming in late."

I jump and try not to let my heart beat through my chest.

"Jesus Christ, you scared the life out of me."

"That'll teach you for thinking you could get anything past me. You didn't come home last night and you're coming in late tonight. So, who is he?" Grayson's eyes light up and she bounces on our op shop couch.

I cringe. Having been so involved with Rome, Grayson is well versed in the racing world and will likely know all about Reed and his gorgeous brothers.

I sigh and take a seat on the couch. The breakdown of her and Rome's relationship was rough, really rough, and I've barely got my nose out of a book long enough to notice the opposite sex, so this kind of gossip has been rare between us.

"His name is Reed. Reed Ryan."

"As in Ryan Racing, those Ryans?" she asks, the pitch and volume of her voice rising.

"Yep, that'll be them."

"Them? You mean you've met them?"

I nod. "Yep, all of them: Nate, Jay, Parker, Reed, Liam, Mav, Jax, and Christian."

"You met the father and grandfather?" she asks incredulously.

"Last night. I was at the diner and some shit went down and I got caught in the middle."

Her face falls. "Was Rome…? Did you see…?"

I place my hand over hers. "I didn't see anyone, least of all Rome."

She nods. "Okay."

"So I take it you know about the Ryans and Devil Racing."

"Everyone knows. From what I hear, Hunter is full-on pure hatred."

"Well, I don't know who was there last night, whether it was that Hunter guy himself or some other guys, but it *is* full-on. Have you been to Wheels?" I ask.

"Once, ages ago. Rome took me in the hopes of meeting one of the Ryans, but they weren't there. That was before…." She trails off.

"Hey." I grab her hand again. "It's okay."

"It shouldn't hurt this much, *still*!" Grayson says, wiping at her eyes.

"I know, honey, but not everyone works to a timetable."

"Ugh! Okay, enough of this. Tell me about the Ryans. Are they as hot as everyone says they are?"

"Hotter." I sigh.

"So Parker's the one with the kid, right?"

"Yep, Christian, he's such an adorable kid. I ended up looking after him last night when everything went down."

"The mother's dead, right?" A frown creases her brows as she waits for my answer

"From what I've been told she wasn't ever really a mother, but yeah, she's dead."

Nodding, she continues with her follow-up question, which in Grayson's world means jumping from one train of thought to the other with no logic, "Tell me about Reed. I've heard he's a major player." To her credit, she bites her lip as she says this.

"Well he may have been, but he says with me it's different."

"Do you believe him?"

I pause, thinking about the last twenty-four hours. Smiling, I answer, "I believe how he's been with me."

"And how's that?"

"Respectful and sweet and hot, and I think I'm in real danger of falling for him."

"He is really hot," she concedes, but I can tell she's worried.

"He is, but it's more than that, way more than just his incredible looks. I can't describe it, Gray, but there's something pulling us together. He says he feels it too."

"Have you slept with him?"

"No. Not entirely."

A loud laugh spills around the room, and she shakes her head. "What do you mean, not entirely?"

"We shared the same bed last night."

"And…."

"There *may* have been some touching," I say quickly, blushing.

"Bria Marie Adams!" Her hands fly to her mouth, but I know is covering a smirk.

"What? It's not like I'm a virgin."

"I know. It's just, my little girl is all grown up." She mock sniffs and wipes at her eye.

I shove her shoulder and she falls back on the couch laughing.

"I'm going to bed. I won't be here tonight."

"A sleepover! Already?"

"Shut up! Liam's racing this weekend and Reed has asked me to go. If I spend the night there with him, and he's promised to be a gentleman, we can leave straight from his house." Not that I'm quite sure I want him to behave, but I'm willing to let it play out and see what happens.

"Hmm, well, just be careful."

"I will, don't worry."

She sitting again, her smile gone. "It's just, I know guys like him, you know?"

"I know, but I think Reed is different. He's older than Rome, and by all accounts, his racing career is over."

"I just don't want to see you heartbroken."

I pull her to me. "I know and I love you for it, but Reed is different. Now, let's get some sleep."

"Okay," she says, but I can tell she's hesitant to believe me. I can only hope I'm as right about Reed as I think I am.

CHAPTER TEN

REED

I have to admit the idea of spending tonight with Bria, having another night with her in my arms, even if we don't do anything, has me psyched. I take a minute to reflect on how different that thought is. Usually I'm a one-and-done type. With all this shit with my family's so-called curse, I never wanted to bring a girl into the chaos, and to be honest, none has ever caught my eye to convince me otherwise.

Until Bria.

She's amazing. She's smart and funny and incredibly beautiful and so fucking hot it's a wonder I haven't exploded from how much I want her. I've been with my fair share of women but none I've wanted more than her. I feel like this dramatic shift in my usual MO should have me a little disorientated, but all I feel is excitement. Excitement about when I'm going to see her again and what we'll get up to, even if it's just making out. I genuinely just want to spend time with her. That's never happened before, and if I have my way, it'll never happen with anyone besides Bria ever again.

I walk into the diner's kitchen with a huge smile on my face.

"You'll be okay tonight without me, right?" I ask Park.

"Why? You got a hot date with sis tonight?" Jax asks as he hops up on one of the benches.

"Sis?" Parker asks.

"Yeah, Bria."

"You're calling her sis?"

"Dude, you're the one who called her R's game changer. I'm just making it official." He shrugs.

"Fair enough, but yeah, we'll be fine."

"Thanks."

"So what's the plan?" Jax asks.

"Dinner and then hang out. She's going to be staying with me tonight and then we'll drive to the race tomorrow."

"She's coming to the race?"

I shrug. "Yeah."

"Cool." Jax nods.

"Hey, have either of you heard of a guy called Roman Thomas? He rides for Devil," I ask as casually as I can. Bringing up Devil is never a good idea, but I want to know about Bria's friend.

"Roman?" Park asks.

"Yeah."

"I've heard of him, why?"

"He, Bria, and her best friend grew up together. I just wanted to know what sort of guy he is."

"He's been with Devil for a while, a lot longer than their usual lackeys, but I'm not sure why. I think he's had a few rides but that's it, mainly testing I think."

"What sort of rider is he?"

"He's good, too good to be wasting his time with Devil, but you know how they suck guys in."

"So you think he's just hung up on making it?"

"I guess so. I mean, it's not like I know the guy personally, but that's my best bet. Liam might know more."

"What about in general? Is he a good dude?"

"Are any of them good dudes if they ride for Devil?" Jax asks through a mouthful of chips.

"You never know. He grew up with Bria, so...."

"Oh, you are so whipped, man." Park chortles.

"Hey, man, you've seen her, she's beautiful—"

"She's downright smokin'," Jax interrupts, and I smack him on the back of his head.

"Get your own, fucker."

He laughs and stuffs another handful of chips in his mouth.

From the dining room, we hear Chris yell out, "Bria!"

"Speak of the devil," Park mutters as I race out to see her.

When I get to her, she has Chris in her arms and is giving him a hug. I bring her as close to me as I can with Chris hanging on to her, and take her face in my hands.

"Angel," I breathe and crush my lips to hers.

She giggles as we break apart. "Hey."

"I missed you," I say, still not releasing her cheeks, and feel them heat beneath my palms.

"Me too," Chris chimes in. "You're pretty and you give good hugs." We both chuckle.

"Well thanks, handsome," Bria says and gives him another squeeze.

"All right, buddy," I say, reaching for Chris, "you've had enough cuddles with my girl today. It's my turn."

Bria giggles again as I take Chris into the kitchen.

"Hey, sis," Jax says as he pokes his head through the window.

"Hey," she says and gives a little wave while I beam. I love that she's taken to my brothers and they've taken to her, but if they're anything like me, we never had a chance.

I drop Chris off in the kitchen.

"She here then?" Park asks.

"Yep, see ya." With a quick kiss to Chris's head, I dash out to my girl.

"Hi, sis, bye, sis," Park says, poking his head out through the window as well. I arch an eyebrow at him and he shoots me a shit-eating grin. I shrug and flip him the finger. If they want Bria to be a part of our family, then I'm not going to dissuade them, but it doesn't mean I've lost my edge.

"You ready?" I ask and take her hand, pulling her out of the diner.

"Where are we going?"

"I made dinner. I thought we could go back to my place."

"So the wooing's over, huh?" she asks with a wry smile.

I stop and pull her to my chest, holding her tight to me. "Oh, babe, I will *never* stop wooing you. If I do, I give you permission to do really bad things to me."

"Really bad things, huh?" She raises an eyebrow at me.

"Absolutely." I kiss her nose.

"Like what?"

I consider for a minute. "If I've been *really* bad, I suppose you could withhold blow jobs." I grin at her and throw her a wink

She snorts, shaking her head. "Blow jobs, huh?"

"Yeah, I think that's fair."

"Are you forgetting something?"

"No." I shake my head. "No, I don't think I am."

"Well, in that case, I don't think there's much reason for me to go inside that house with you."

"What! Why?"

"Because clearly your skills in bed are so poor I've forgotten we've even slept together." She dances out of my arms, laughing as she runs away from me.

I manage to catch up to her, pick her up, and swing her around. "You think you're funny, huh?" I ask.

"You brought it up," she says in between giggles.

Her hair creates a curtain around us, and she looks so beautiful in this moment I lose my breath. I put her down and brush her hair from her face. "Angel," I breathe, and crash my lips to hers. She responds instantly, pressing herself tightly against me, rubbing against me. My dick is about ready to burst out of my jeans. She moans and I swear it takes all of my self-control not to come.

We break apart and I run my hand through her hair. "Trust me, baby. When we have sex, you'll remember it." She moves her hand down and squeezes my erection. I throw my head back and groan. "Baby," I warn.

She smirks and squeezes me again, giving me an evil grin. "Judging by the bulge in your pants, I have no doubt you'll make it a night to remember." With a final squeeze, she dances through the gate and into my house for a night neither of us will forget.

CHAPTER ELEVEN

BRIA

I slip into Reed's house and stop short. The kitchen table has been set for two with flowers and candles in the middle.

"Holy shit," I whisper.

"Told you the wooing hasn't stopped," Reed says behind me, slipping his arms around me, bringing my back to his front.

"Reed," I whisper.

He doesn't respond except to brush my hair to the side and start licking and kissing my neck. I bring one hand up and run it through his hair; the other clutches his as he pulls me to him. I moan and shift my head to the side so he has better access.

"You keep up with those sexy-as-fuck noises, baby, and

this night will be over before it even begins." He pushes his erection into my back.

His hands start to travel north to my breasts.

"I thought you said if we don't stop the night will be over," I say, more than a little breathless.

His hands drop to his sides and he rests his forehead on my shoulder.

"You're too irresistible for your own good," he says.

"*My* own good?" I ask with a laugh.

He kisses my neck once before stepping around me. "Fine, *my* own good."

"So what's for dinner?"

"Beef bourguignon with fresh French bread, red wine, and mashed potato."

"And dessert?"

"Me, obviously." He winks as he opens a bottle of wine.

"Any other options?" I tease, though there's nothing more than I want than to ensure he is my dessert.

"You?" he asks and hands me a glass.

"Anything else?"

"Crème brûleé, but only if you eat all your veggies."

I laugh and clink my glass with his. "To nights to remember," I toast.

He arches an eyebrow. "To nights to remember."

"You cooked all this yourself?"

"Yep. Gotta impress my girl somehow."

"Your girl?" I'm so aware I keep throwing questions his way, but I feel as though I'm on a fairground ride. Everything is happening so fast, but I can't help but seize our connection and the happiness that it brings with it. But that doesn't mean I'm not crazy confused.

He takes a step back and a deep breath. "Yeah. Look, I know this has all happened really fast and we've spoken a little about what's happening here, but if you want to slow down or stop altogether then that's fine. Just say the word, okay?" He looks up with a forlorn expression on his face. "I've never done this before, and I really, *really* don't want to fuck it up, so if you're not ready for anything or everything, just let me know."

He looks adorable like this, unsure and sexy. I step closer to him and grab him by the shoulders. "Reed, just breathe, okay? All I was going to say was I really like being called your girl." I blush deeply.

"I really like calling you my girl." He cups my face in his hands.

"So I'm yours and you're mine?" I don't hide my grin.

"Absolutely." He kisses me.

Pulling away, my gaze roams his face. Honest eyes stare back at me. Whatever this is, my instinct nudges me to take a chance. Despite my fast beating heart, calm embraces me; I'm doing the right thing. "Let's eat," I say, and wait as he pulls out a chair for me before placing a plate in front of me.

Once he's seated, I take a bite and the beef melts in my mouth.

"Oh, my God! You cook like this and I might have to keep you around forever," I say through a mouthful of bread.

"Looks like I'm stuck with the cooking duties for life then." He smiles his panty-dropping smile and butterflies take flight in my stomach. For life? Oh boy.

We finish dinner before moving into the living room where Reed stretches out on the couch, pulling me on top of him, my back resting on his front, his legs either side of me. He twirls a length of my hair in his hands.

"So tell me more about you," I say, snuggling into his warm, broad, hard chest, his musky woodsy scent enveloping me.

"What do you want to know?"

"Everything."

"Okay, well I'm the second eldest of five boys, twenty-four and three-quarter years old."

"Twenty-four and three-quarters?" I ask, looking back at him over my shoulder.

"Yes. The three-quarters is very important," Reed says, and kisses my nose.

Smirking, I nod. "Okay, so keep going."

"I'm a retired motorbike racer who now works at his family's diner, garage, and racing team."

"You guys own a garage as well?"

I feel him nod. "It's just down the street."

"What else?"

"My favourite number is ninety-nine. My favourite colour is blue. I wear boxer briefs. My favourite food is ribs, with waffles and pizza close seconds. My favourite bands change but the core are Unwritten Law, Linkin Park, and the Foo Fighters, and my favourite movie is *The Sound of Music*."

"*The Sound of Music*?"

"Yeah man, it has singing, dancing, love, and Nazis. It's the ultimate movie."

"If you say so." I snuggle into him and an arm slips around my waist.

"What about you, Miss Adams?"

"What about me?"

"What are your favourites?"

"My favourite food is Chinese. My favourite flavour is caramel. I prefer white chocolate over dark or milk. My favourite colours are burgundy, gold, and magenta. I can never choose, and my favourite authors are Tijan, Kaylee Ryan, L.P. Maxa, and Cambria Hebert."

"Magenta?" Reed asks.

"It's a purpley-pink."

"Good to know. You ready for dessert?"

I nod and sit up so he can get up.

He comes back a few minutes later and gets back in his previous position. He wraps his arms around me, the crème brûlée in my lap. I reach for it and Reed smacks my hands away, instead digging in and feeding me himself.

I moan, tasting the bitterness of the toffee and the sweetness of the vanilla across my tongue.

Reed rests his head against the back of mine. "Baby, those moans…."

"I would say I'm sorry, but that's heaven."

His head comes around so he can look me in the eye. "Really?"

I nod. "Oh yeah."

He brings another spoonful to my mouth. I keep my eyes on him as my mouth closes around the metal, and see his pupils dilate and feel his cock twitch behind me.

"Mmm," I purr.

In a flash, Reed puts the spoon on the coffee table and crashes his lips to mine. Gasping for breath, we break apart and I get up.

"Wha…?" Reed begins before I sit back down, straddling his hips.

"Much better," I say, leaning in to kiss him.

He nips and sucks at my lips, my body rocking into his, my hips grinding against his, the friction feeling fantastic. He moves to kiss my neck, his hands sliding up my sides underneath my shirt. I stop rocking to tear my shirt off, revealing my black lace bra.

"Holy fuck," Reed breathes, "you really are an angel. A deliciously sexy angel, and you're all mine." My already drenched panties get wetter as Reed pulls me to him again, his hands kneading and pinching my nipples.

I run my hands down his chest, reaching between us to rub his impressive erection. He growls the minute my hand comes into contact with him and stands, my legs wrapping around his waist, our lips never parting as he walks us to his room. He kicks the door closed before putting me down gently on the bed. I stretch out, lying on the pillows, and Reed stretches out on top of me.

"You're so goddamn beautiful, Bria. What the hell are you doing to me?"

"You? Why me? You could have any girl you want."

"I want you."

"So do I." I bring my body flush with his, grab the hem of his shirt and pull it up. He gets the hint and pulls it off.

I run my hands over the ink on his arms, designs of smoke and flames, before reaching the waistband of his jeans and belt.

"Are you sure?" he asks.

"I'm yours and you're mine. Show me what it means, Reed."

"Baby," he whispers as we fumble with each other's jeans, eventually managing to get them off, followed by our underwear and my bra.

Reed's hands move up and down my sides before one slides between us and goes between my legs.

"So wet, baby," he says as his finger runs up and down my slit before slipping inside me. I arch against him, my legs falling open further to allow him room.

"God, baby, you feel so good." His lips run over my collarbone, my breasts brushing against his chest with every heaving breath I take.

Reed slides in another finger and curls them to hit my G spot; I cry out, my fingers digging into his back.

"Just there, huh?" He smirks above me.

I nod and bite my lip.

He stops his fingers and shoots me an evil grin. "I want to taste you, baby." I nod again. It seems my brain to speech link has gone kaput. His grin turns triumphant before he kisses his way down my body, spending plenty of time on my breasts before stopping between my legs.

He inhales deeply. "You smell divine, Bria." He bends his head and sucks up my arousal.

"Oh God!" I yell, my hands flying into his hair, holding him to me.

"So good," he says before circling my clit with his tongue. I'm on the brink when he slides a finger in and he hits my G spot again. I come so hard I see stars, my eyes rolling back in my head, my body arching off the bed.

"That's it, angel," Reed says as he rides out my orgasm with me. Eventually the waves subside.

"Welcome back." He smirks at me when I open my eyes again.

"Mmm." I move against him.

"God, Bria, you're like nothing else."

"You're not bad yourself," I say, cupping his cheek.

"I think I've fallen for you," he says quietly, almost bashfully.

"Good, because I've fallen for you." I have no desire to hold back the words. It all seems too late for that anyway.

"You have?"

"One hundred percent."

"God, Bria." He crashes his mouth to mine, my arousal still on his lips.

I lift my hips to invite him in. I'm desperate for him, for the contact. Slowly, he pushes inside me. I moan at the intensity of the rightness as well as the stretch.

"God, Reed."

"I know. You feel like a dream. You're fucking made for me."

He's finally all the way in and gives me a minute to adjust. It becomes too much. Too much stillness. Too much of being gentle.

"Reed, honey, I need you to move."

"Just a sec. If I move now, it's gonna be over. You feel too good."

"Reed," I whine. I *really* need him to move.

"I got you, baby." He begins to move in and out; simultaneously, we moan, and I arch into him.

He takes a nipple into his mouth and sucks it hard, kneading and pinching the other. I know my moans are getting louder, but there's nothing I can do to stop them. I reach around and grab Reed's arse, pushing him into me harder.

"That's it, baby," Reed pants.

"Oh God!"

"Come for me, Bria, I want to hear you, feel you."

"Reed!" I scream as I come hard around him.

He pumps into me a few more times before releasing into me, setting me off again. Reed collapses on top of me and rolls us so we're on our sides and he's not crushing me, his cock still deep inside me.

He brushes my hair away from my face and looks deep into my eyes. "You just ruined me."

"What?" I ask, my heart beating even more wildly.

"That was the best sex of my life and I'm ruined for everyone except you."

Oh, that's better. I giggle and bury my face into his neck. He wraps his arms around me and pulls me close.

"I think you ruined me as well in that case," I say.

He pulls back so he can look me in the eye. "Yeah?" I nod shyly. "So damn perfect," he whispers as he pulls out of me.

"Oh shit."

I sit up. "What?"

"No wonder it felt so good. We didn't use a condom. Fuck! I *never* forget. I'm so sorry, baby."

My eyes widen and I swallow. A tiny flutter of panic sits in my chest. While there's no chance of me getting pregnant, I now know enough about Reed to know he's been around a bit. "Umm…."

"Fuck, I'm so sorry, angel. Are you, you know, on anything?"

"Ah, yeah, I'm on the shot. I got it a few weeks ago."

"Okay, good," he says, and runs a hand through his hair.

"Um, are you, have you...?"

"Oh God, no, I've never done that before. I swear, Bria, I'm clean."

I blow out a breath. "That's good."

"I hate to ask."

"I'm clean."

He smiles and leans over to kiss me before going to the bathroom. I immediately miss the fullness of having him inside me.

"Open for me, baby," he says as he comes back in with a washcloth. I roll to my back and spread my legs so he can gently clean me up, something I've never had anyone do for me before.

"I'm so sorry for forgetting the condom, but you make me lose my mind."

"It did feel really good." I bite my lip.

"It felt fucking phenomenal, and I swear I've never gone bare before."

"It's okay. I trust you, Reed."

"Yeah?"

I nod.

He kisses me before throwing the washcloth back into the bathroom and hopping back in bed, pulling me to his chest. I run my finger over some of his tattoos as he runs his hand through my hair.

"So what's the deal with tomorrow?" I ask, breaking the silence.

"Well, the track's about two and a half hours away. Pa, Chris, and Jax will be coming with us, if that's okay?"

"It's fine. I love Chris and your pa, and Jax is awesome."

"Don't tell him that." Reed chuckles.

"I won't."

"Good." He gives me a squeeze. "We've got box passes for you, Pa, and Chris, the best seats in the house, although getting Pa to stay there will be a challenge."

"Where will he want to be?"

"In the pits."

"Where you'll be?"

"Yeah. I'm sorry I won't get to spend the race with you."

"That's fine. You've got to support Liam."

"You're not pissed I won't be with you?" he asks, surprised.

"No, you've got a job to do. Would I like to watch the race with you? Yeah, of course, but racing was here before I was. Plus, Liam deserves the best and that's you."

"No, angel, the best is you, but luckily for me, Liam is gay so I'll take care of you," he says, rolling me onto my back and situating himself between my legs.

"Oh, you will, will you?" I ask, lifting my hips to his and feeling his erection waiting for me.

"Angel, I will always take care of you." And he does, all night.

CHAPTER TWELVE

REED

I wake to my alarm blaring way too fucking early in the damn morning, but my hand cupped around one of Bria's tits makes it worth it. She's a solid C-cup, a nice handful for me. I give her a squeeze before shutting my alarm off. We've only had about an hour and a half of sleep but I couldn't help it. I just couldn't get my fill of her. I still haven't, judging by my rock-hard dick. I wasn't joking when I said I was falling for her and she'd ruined me for everyone else. For as long as I live, all I want is Bria, and that's what I'm gonna have right now.

I nuzzle her neck and gently roll her to her back. "It's time to wake up."

She swats at my face. "Just a little more sleep, honey, please?"

I fucking love that she calls me honey. I love that this incredible girl is mine and she's willing to overlook my history.

"I'm afraid not. We have to be on the road soon, and I need to have you before Chris comes running in here."

If I thought the amazing sex Bria and I had last night was a fluke, this morning wonderfully proves me wrong. It leads me to think sex with Bria is always going to be amazing and it's enough to not want it with anyone else.

She collapses on my chest and I hold her to me tight.

"With wake-up sex like that, feel free to wake me anytime," she pants.

I laugh and kiss her neck, inhaling her sweet, fruity scent. "Whatever you want, angel. If I remember correctly, I did promise to take care of you, so if this is what you need to get you going…."

She laughs and slaps my chest, climbing off me. "You're such a martyr, aren't you, Reed Ryan?" She winks at me over her shoulder as she walks that sexy arse of hers into the bathroom.

I get up and follow her immediately, like the whipped arse that I am. "Hey, a promise is a promise." I reach around her to start the shower.

Once it's warmed up, I pick her up, her legs wrapping around me, and walk us in. I sit us down on the bench, grab the back of her neck, and bring her lips to mine. I kiss the hell out of her while she reaches down and squeezes my still-hard cock.

"Can you go again, angel, or are you sore?"

83

"I'm a little sore but I'll deal. I want you, Reed."

"I don't want to hurt you."

"Only good hurt, honey. Don't worry."

"Baby…."

In the end, Bria takes matters into her own hands by sliding down on me again. If bed sex with Bria was amazing, shower sex is out of this world! She takes me so deep I almost lose my mind. This girl….

"Damn, Bria, I swear you're gonna be the end of me." I kiss her neck as I lift her off me so we can clean up.

"But you'll go happy, right?"

"I'll be fucking ecstatic, but I want more with you." I grab her and bring her body flush to mine. I can't stop touching her, and to be honest, I really don't want to. I'm so into this girl it's not even funny.

"Can I ask you something?" she asks as she lathers soap all over me.

"Anything." I run my hands up and down her sides.

"Do you miss racing?"

"I miss the competitiveness and the thrill of the race, but not all the bullshit that came along with it."

"Like what?"

"All the stuff that allowed Hunter to get such a foothold, and the pressure from the sponsors. It was insane. Now, I'm just happy to ride recreationally and leave all that shit to Liam. He's so goddamn talented I'm in awe of him, and so's the rest of the circus."

"So all the stuff that bothers you doesn't bother him?"

"It doesn't touch him. Liam's the star, the drawcard.

Whatever he wants or needs he gets."

"It must be nice."

"He's earned it and now he's reaping the rewards."

"And he's not in danger from Hunter?"

"You worried about my brother, angel?" I ask, bending so I can look in her eyes.

"Of course. He's your family, plus, all your brothers are lovable in their own right."

I'm so glad to hear her say that. My family and I are as close as we can possibly be, so any woman who comes into our lives is going to have to get along with them. Bria fits in like she was born to do it and that's good, because when the time's right, I'm making her one of us. Every time I think such a statement, I expect the panic to set in. There was a time the thought of settling and being with one person would make me rush out and find a new lay quick. But with Bria, there has been nothing but rightness and contentment. I'm happy to go along for the ride.

Just then we hear small fists banging on the door. "Uncle Reed, Aunty Bria, are you in dere?" Chris shouts.

I rest my head against Bria's shoulder. "I'll never know how someone so cute can be so annoying."

Bria giggles and I kiss her quickly. "I think his cuteness more than makes up for that."

"As much as I hate to pop this bubble, if we don't get out there he'll come in, and even though he's three, I don't want anyone who's not me looking at you." I hop out of the shower.

"Aw, honey, are you getting all territorial over me?" she coos.

I pull her tight to me. "One, I love that you call me honey,"—I kiss her nose—"and two, we said last night that I'm yours and you're mine, so you're damn right I'm going to claim you every chance I get."

She bites her lip. "Damn, Reed, now I'm wet."

I arch an eyebrow and slip a finger between her slick folds to find her practically dripping. I throw my head back and groan. My dick's standing at full attention to her heat.

"Damn, Bria, now I'm hard."

"A quickie?"

"Will you be quiet?"

"I can try." She smiles her mischievous grin. Damn that grin; it gets me every time.

I grab her hips and bend her over. "Grab on to the sink, baby." She does as she's told and I plunge into her.

We're both breathless but more than satisfied when Chris bangs on the door again.

"Uncle Reed! Aunty Bria!" he whines, and Bria giggles.

"I'll go keep him occupied while you clean up," I say with a kiss to her forehead.

"I left my bag in my car, and it has my clean clothes in it. Can you grab it for me?"

"No worries." With another kiss, I open the door and nearly bowl over Chris, who is readying his little fists again.

I scoop him up and close the door before he can cop a view of Bria, three-year-old or not.

"What were you doing with Aunty Bria?" he asks as I put him on my bed. He immediately starts jumping on it.

"We were having a shower."

"Why were you in dere together?"

"Saving water, buddy. How come you're calling her Aunty Bria?"

"Daddy and Uncle Jax told me to."

"Of course they did. Where is Uncle Jax?"

"He's at his house. He said to come get him when you and Aunty Bria stop sucking face. Why are you sucking her face? Does she like it?"

I laugh and start to get dressed. "Yes, buddy, she likes it, and it's something you'll do when you're older. Where's Pa?"

"Grown-ups are weird. Pa's making breakfast."

"All right, you go have breakfast and I'll get Uncle Jax." Chris nods and hops off the bed. I follow him out of the house, grab Bria's clothes, and drop them off to her.

"Thanks, honey," she says, rewarding me with a hot kiss before kicking me out so she can get dressed. I personally don't see the problem with me watching her get dressed; it's not like I can't control myself. Okay, so it's probably better I don't stay. Instead, I barge next door to rouse Jax.

I open his bedroom door. It hits the wall before bouncing back at me. I rip off his blankets and kick his feet.

"Get up, fucker."

He stretches languidly. "You and sis done sucking face?"

"Never, but we'll wait, and thanks for telling Chris that. I had to explain what it meant."

Jax bursts out laughing. "That's practice for when you two have little Reedlets."

Shit, I hadn't thought of having kids with Bria. Don't get me wrong, I want them; she'd be a great mum and the image of her belly round with my baby makes my dick twinge again—shit. I adjust myself and Jax laughs again.

"Like that idea, huh?"

"Man, you have no idea. The girl's a dream."

"Seriously?"

"She's it, 100 percent."

"I gotta tell ya, it's an awesome thing to watch."

"Huh?"

"Watching the great lady-loving Reed Ryan, my big brother, being brought to his knees by a woman? Granted, a very lovely, very beautiful woman, but a woman nonetheless. I wasn't sure it was going to happen for any of us."

And with that statement, Jax reminds me why there hasn't been a prolonged female presence around this family: we're not good for them.

CHAPTER THIRTEEN

BRIA

I finish getting dressed and go into the living room. Seconds later, Reed and Jax come in, and I walk into Reed's arms. He seems a little sombre and sad.

"Hey, sis," Jax says, and flashes me a panty-dropping smile.

"Hey, Jax."

"You ready for the circus?"

"Sure. It'll be nice to see the world you guys live in."

Reed doesn't say anything so I give him a squeeze and look into his eyes. "You okay?"

"Yeah, I'm fine." He kisses my nose. "Come on, Pa's cooking breakfast." He takes my hand and leads us over to the big house.

Chris comes flying at me when we enter the kitchen. I bend down to pick him up and he hugs me tightly around my neck.

"Aunty Bria!"

"Hey, handsome."

"Uncle Liam's racing today and we're gonna watch."

"We are," I say, sitting down. "Are you excited?" He nods.

I've chosen to ignore him calling me aunty along with Jax and Parker calling me sis. Admittedly, I love it and it makes my heart skip a beat, but I don't want to read too much into it, especially in the wake of Reed's weird mood. I thought he was fine in the bathroom, and then when he wanted to watch me get dressed, so what happened once he left?

Jay's bustling around the kitchen and turns, spotting Chris and me. A big smile breaks across his face. "Bria my girl, how are you, darling?"

"I'm good, Jay, thank you. How are you?"

"Still trucking, darling. Someone's got to keep these knuckleheads in line." He nods in the direction of Reed and Jax.

I laugh. "Funny, I thought that was Chris's job." I bounce him in my lap.

"We do it together, don't we, buddy?" Jay asks Chris.

"Yep." He nods.

"You keeping an eye on your Uncle Reed for me?" I ask Chris.

"I dare say you'll be around enough to keep an eye on him yourself," Jay says, and I shoot him a shy smile. I wonder if Reed's thinking the same thing, or if he doesn't want that to be the case anymore.

"How do you like your eggs?" Jay asks, breaking me out of my reverie.

"Er, scrambled will be fine, thanks, Jay."

He puts a plate down in front of Chris, his bacon already cut up. I pick up a fork and begin to feed him.

I look up at Reed and he has a strange look on his face, almost a cross between pain, want, and love, and I've never been so confused. What the hell is going on with him?

"There you go, sweetheart," Jay says as he sets a plate down in front of me.

I manage to feed both Chris and myself, and then we're hitting the road.

Reed is driving. I'm up front with him; Jay and Chris in his car seat are next, and Jax is in the back of Parker's SUV.

I look over at Reed. He shoots me a small smile and takes my hand. It's something, but I have no idea what's going on. Is he trying to get rid of me now that we've slept together? Were all the sweet words he was saying last night empty?

I squeeze Reed's hand once and then make myself comfortable.

CHAPTER FOURTEEN

REED

I know I'm acting weird but I can't help it. I want Bria so badly, but my family doesn't have the best track record when it comes to keeping women. It terrifies me to think of anything happening to her, but it also makes my heart ache at the thought of being without her.

Seeing the way she was with Chris this morning killed me. It killed me to see what our future could be like, how she'd be with our kids. Can I go through a relationship with her knowing I'm putting her at risk? And kids? Can I risk them having to grow up without a mother just like I did? I mean, sure, I'm a well-adjusted member of society, but we all need our mum. On the other hand, can I walk away from her? Can I function without her?

I care about this girl so damn much, but I don't want anything to happen to her and therein lies my dilemma. I know she's noticed my change in behaviour, but I'm so goddamn fucking torn on what to do here. Pa only had eighteen months with Nan; she died during childbirth and he was a mess afterwards, apparently. Pop fared better; he and Ma were together almost ten years before she died of ovarian cancer. I was only six at the time, but I remember how the life went out of our family afterwards. I know it's not a scientific thing and nothing may happen to Bria, but what if it does? I can't lose her, and with our track record, if I were a betting man the odds wouldn't be good for us. But I can't let her go; I won't let her go. Maybe we'll be lucky like Pop was with Ma. A decade's a long time, right? And surely any time is better than none. What it comes down to is I don't think I can imagine my world without her.

Bria sleeps the entire two and a half hours to the track and I'm glad. I kept her up late last night making love to her. Not that I regret a single second of it but I don't like the thought of her being tired.

I gently shake her to wake her up. "Baby, we're here."

She blinks, smiles a dazzling smile at me, and I lose my breath. She's so goddamn amazing. Why the fuck am I thinking of pushing her away?

My mind made up, I kiss her deeply and she smiles so big at me I feel like my heart is going to burst. "Morning, angel."

"Hi," she says shyly. I can tell she's wary of my reaction but her intent is clear. I can see the care in her eyes.

"We good?" she asks.

I kiss her nose. "Yeah, we're good. Come on, let me show you around." I get out of the car and race around to open her door.

She giggles. "There's that smoothness, Ryan." She winks at me.

I take her hand and lead her into the pits. For obvious reasons, we're down at one end and Devil are down at the other.

We walk into our garage and are met with wolf whistles and suggestive gestures. Bria blushes and hides her face in my arm while I give my brothers the finger. Pa covers Chris's eyes and ears.

"Nice of you to show up," Liam says, coming through the crowd. "Nice to see you again, sis," he says, kissing Bria on the cheek and slapping me on the back. "Warm-up is in an hour."

I nod. "Got it. All right," I say, bringing my attention back to Bria, "this is our garage. Welcome to the inner sanctum of Ryan Racing."

As I say this, Jax comes up and presents Bria with a Ryan Racing polo.

"So this is where the magic happens, huh?" she asks, pulling the polo over her head.

I lean down to whisper in her ear, "No, angel, that's my bedroom. Or did you already forget last night?" I'm rewarded with a blush.

It's then that I see her good mood vanish. I take her arm and lead her away from everyone else.

"What is it?"

"Devil Racing will be here, won't they?"

Ah, so that's it. "Yes, baby, they are."

She looks around. "Where?"

"All the way down the other end of the pits. They won't bother us here."

"But they could, couldn't they?" she says, and bites her lip.

I release her lip with my thumb. "Realistically they could, but so could an asteroid by landing right here on this very track." That gets a smile.

"Smart-arse."

I kiss her quickly. "I'm your smart-arse."

"Yes, you are." She grabs the back of my neck and kisses me unhurriedly.

Pa clearing his throat brings us back to earth. We break apart and Bria hides her blush in my chest.

"Hey, Pa," I say, running my hand through Bria's hair.

"Reed, I was wondering if our girl Bria there might do me a favour?" Bria peeks up through her lashes.

"Sure, Jay, what's up?" she asks.

"One of the mechanics can't make it today. He says he's sick but I reckon it's one too many beers. Anyway, Liam's a mechanic short, so I was wondering if you wouldn't mind looking after young Christian during the race?"

A smile graces her face and she jumps away from me. "That's no problem, I'd love to. I'd hate to deprive Liam of a top mechanic." She winks at Pa.

I pull her back to my front and grind against her arse a little. "Oh, he's already got a top mechanic in me. Pa's just there to make up the numbers." Pa scoffs and Bria laughs.

"If that's the case," Pa says, "then you better get a move on. Warm-up's in just under an hour."

"Got it. Come on, we'll get you and Chris set up here for warm-up and then you can go to the box for the race."

"You mean I get to see you get all hot and sweaty?" She bites my earlobe. I have to hold back a groan. "I can't wait." She dances away from me to go get Chris.

I really shouldn't be worried about anything happening to *her*. She's going to kill *me* before too long.

CHAPTER FIFTEEN

BRIA

Getting to see Reed work up close was a lesson in self-restraint I never want to repeat. Seeing him all hot and sweaty and covered in grease? Holy shit, it was hot; and he's all mine. I'm so glad he got over whatever was troubling him earlier. Especially since I've completely fallen for him.

He walks Chris and me up to the Ryan Racing box, leaving me with a kiss before going back down to the pits.

Chris and I watch as the teams set up on the grid, and it's then that Chris realises he left his backpack in the garage. He insists he needs it so we hurry back to the pits.

We're at the mouth of the garage when the air shifts around us. Instinctively, I crouch and turn slightly, gathering Chris in my arms, trying to shield him as much as possible as something explodes. The shock wave hits us and I barely manage to keep my feet on the ground. If I fall, I don't want to crush Chris, and if I land on my back, he's exposed to debris. It falls around us and I feel a sharp pain in my leg but ignore it, making sure Chris is protected. I have no idea how we manage to stay on our feet, but my guess is we were just far enough away. The explosions stop and I feel Chris shaking in my arms. I bring him closer to me.

"It's okay. We're okay. You're okay," I murmur. Smoke and ash fill the air. People screaming and shouting and sirens blaring swarm us. People rush around, heading towards the remains of the Ryan Racing garage.

The pain in my leg is getting worse and I think I can feel blood dripping but at the moment, it's not my primary concern. I hear the roar of a bike and look up to see Liam approaching.

"Bria! Chris!" he yells.

"We're okay!" I reply.

He gets to us and I stand up, hissing as I put weight on my leg. Chris once again is clinging to me like he did the other night at the diner.

"Shit, Bria, what are you guys doing here?" Liam asks.

"Chris left his backpack in the garage and wanted it. I thought we'd have time before the race started."

"Shit! Oh God, Bria, your leg."

"Oh yeah, it hurts."

"You've got a piece of metal sticking out of it!"

"Oh, well, that'd be why it hurts." My voice is eerily calm as I try to make light of the increasing pain pulsating through my leg.

"Liam!" I hear Reed yell.

"We're over here," Liam yells back.

I hear a rush of feet and then Reed comes barrelling out of the crowd trying to put out the fire of what once was the Ryan Racing garage.

"Shit, Bria, baby, what are you doing here?" He pulls me to him and I yell as my leg moves.

"What is it? What's wrong?" Reed asks worriedly.

"My leg… there's something stuck."

"Shit." He pulls me away and kneels down to examine my leg. "Liam, take Chris. We've got to get Bria looked at," Reed orders.

Liam tries to take Chris but he clings to me harder.

"Don't worry about him, Liam. He's fine. I can be looked at with Chris with me. It's fine."

"Angel, you need to have this leg looked at. You're bleeding like crazy."

"They can look at my leg while I hold Chris. It'll be fine."

"Baby, what were you doing here?"

"Chris left his backpack."

"You could've been seriously hurt, or killed."

"We're fine." My words are almost a mantra as I try to convince the guys as much as myself. He pulls me in for a kiss.

Jax, Jay, and Mav make their way through the crowd, a paramedic with them.

"Oh, thank God," Reed says. "Over here!" he yells. "She's hurt!"

"Bria?" Jay asks.

"I'm fine. It's just my leg."

The paramedic gets to me and I sit down for him to take a look.

"I would take this out here, but you're going to need stitches and for this to be cleaned, so I think it's best if we take you to the medical centre."

"Okay," I agree.

I get into a car, Reed never leaving my side, Chris still plastered to me. Surprisingly, it's Chris wrapped up around me that prevents me from freaking out. I think I need him as much as he needs me. At the medical centre, the metal is removed, the wound, which isn't all that bad, is cleaned, and four stitches later, I'm good to go. I'm given a prescription for some antibiotics to stop any infection.

In the time it's taken for me to get fixed up, Chris has fallen asleep.

"Are you sure you're all right?" Reed asks me for the hundredth time.

"Yes! Reed, I'm fine. My leg doesn't even hurt. The only thing that's annoying me is you constantly asking me how I am." I struggle to keep the bite from my voice.

"I'm sorry. It's just, I feel like this is my fault."

"Why? You didn't set off the explosion, did you?"

"No, but you were in the vicinity because of me, because I asked you to come here. I fell in love with you and now you're going to die." He hangs his head.

I jolt at his words, my brows furrowing. "You fell in love with me?" My voice dips low as I speak.

He looks up bashfully. "Well, yeah."

"You love me?" I repeat for clarification.

He nods.

"Come here." I beckon him to come closer. "I love you." The words fall free, natural and true. I can barely believe the speed in which they come so naturally, but I've always been a great believer in saying what you feel. Well, to a certain degree. There are always exceptions.

A beautiful smile crosses his face. "You do?"

"Well, yeah. I mean, what's not to love?" I tilt my head to the side and smile.

"God, Bria, this is so fucked-up. The first night we met you were showered in glass and now you've four stitches in your leg."

"Yes, okay, the circumstances aren't great, but it doesn't matter."

"How can you say that?"

"Reed, you just told me you love me and I told you I love you. That right there should tell you all you need to know."

"But—"

I put a finger to his lips. "No buts. I've already died once, so I look at all this as a bonus." I almost laugh at the shock registering on his face, but I hold it back when I see seriousness and panic racing directly after it.

"What?"

"When I was a kid, I was outside playing and was stung by a bee. It had never happened before so I didn't know what was happening wasn't normal. I kept playing and then collapsed. By the time Dad found me, my airway was closed. Luckily, we lived close to a hospital. They injected me with adrenalin, and I started breathing again. So you see, you can't kill me because I've already been there."

"Baby," Reed whispers as he cups my face.

"I'm okay. I'll be okay, and you're going to be stuck with me for a while, all right?"

"Okay."

He brings his lips to mine and kisses me slowly.

"God, Bria, when I saw you standing there with Liam I almost died. Then when you cried out when I pulled you to me... fuck." He runs a hand through his hair. "I don't want anything to happen to you, Bria. So quickly you've become such a big part of our family, and you've become my whole world, baby."

Emotion blooms in my chest. I've never met anyone, especially a man like him before. He shares so much of himself. I wipe away my tears. "I'm not going anywhere, okay? Nothing's going to happen to me."

"You don't know that."

"Neither do you."

"But all this shit with my family—"

"You and your family are more than worth the trouble."

"Are you sure? I won't blame you if it's too much."

"Reed, stop. I love you, I want you, and I want to *be* with you." I nudge him, attempting to lighten the mood. "It almost feels like you're trying to talk me into leaving you."

I shakes his head. "Never. I love you so much." He rewards me with a slightly disbelieving smile.

"Come on, you two," Jax says, cutting our moment short. "Let's go home."

"What about the garage?" I ask, trying to sit up, but it's difficult with Chris lying all over me. Jax takes pity and pries him off me; it's the first time he's let go of me since the explosion.

"There's a lot of damage. We lost a bike and a fair bit of tools, but insurance should cover it. The good news is the bomb was placed at the back of the garage, which minimised the damage,"—Reed shoots him a look—"which doesn't mean much with your leg, but for everyone else it was good. It was lucky Pop and Pa had bailed up Liam and were talking to him at race control, otherwise the injuries would be worse. I heard some of the firies as they were having a look around, and it sounds like the explosion was more designed to cause damage than kill and injure. That's why it wasn't like, total death and destruction."

"Oh, that's good."

"It is, but don't worry about it, angel. Let's get you home," Reed says.

I go to hop off the bed. "What do you think you're doing?" Reed demands.

I look at him, confused. "I thought we were going?"

"We are, but you're not walking."

"Then how am I supposed to get anywhere?"

"I'll carry you," Reed says like it's obvious.

I shake my head. "You're not carrying me."

"Yes, I am. You have four stitches in that leg and you're my responsibility. You. Are. Not. Walking." He puts his arms underneath my thighs and behind my back.

"Reed, no, not like this. Please."

He stops. "Fine, then get on," he says, offering me his back. "But if it hurts I'm carrying you the other way, okay?"

"Fine," I agree, knowing even if it does hurt I won't be telling him.

He grabs me underneath my butt, my legs swinging either side of him.

Jay, Liam, Chris, and Mav are in Parker's SUV. Jax drives with Reed and I curled in the back of Liam's Mustang, and Reed, true his word, carried me all the way to the car.

"Are you okay?" Reed asks once we're settled. "Are you comfy? You're not in any pain, are you?"

I cup his cheek. "I'm fine, honey. Please stop worrying."

"Okay." He kisses me on the nose and I snuggle into him, his arm thrown around my shoulders, his musky, manly scent invading my senses.

"Hey." I tap his cheek and he looks down at me, smiling his smile he reserves only for me. "I love you."

"I love *you.*"

"Oh man, this is good," Jax says from the front seat.

"What?" I ask, confused.

Reed brings my head to his chest. "Don't worry about my little brother. He's an idiot. Park dropped him on his head when he was a baby."

I giggle at their antics.

"Don't believe a word he says, sis," Jax says. "He's not thinking straight with his love-addled brain."

"I'm not love addled, you fuckwit," Reed swears. "I'm in love, and don't tell me you wouldn't do the same if you saw Bria first."

"I knew it!" Jax crows and throws his head back and laughs. "And by the way, that's my sister you're talking about, man. I don't think of her in any way but a strictly family." He winks at me and starts the car.

"You guys are nuts," I say before snuggling more into Reed and falling asleep in the arms of the man I love.

CHAPTER SIXTEEN

REED

It doesn't take long for Bria to fall asleep in my arms and I couldn't be happier. She loves me and I feel like I'm on top of the fucking world! The girl of my dreams, one I didn't even know I was looking for, loves me. I don't even know how it happened and I don't care, because she fucking loves me. I grin from ear-to-ear the entire trip back home, my hand running through Bria's hair. God, I came so close to losing her today. If she and Chris were a bit quicker walking back to the garage, or the bomb was thirty seconds delayed in going off, that would be it.

Maybe that's a sign our luck is changing?

Regardless, I hate the fact she's hurt; the scar on her leg is going to remind me every day for the rest of our lives how close she came to danger, but the main thing is that we *will* get the rest of our lives together. I guess four stitches is a small price to pay for that. I don't even care my brothers are giving me a hard time. I have no doubt that if they found a girl like Bria they'd behave exactly the same way. There's one thing us Ryans know, and that's how to hold on to a good thing when we find it.

We get home and I gently lift Bria out of the car. She stirs and snuggles further into me. *God, this girl.* I carry her into my room and have visions of doing this, only she's wearing a white dress and my ring, not a Ryan Racing polo and denim shorts. I place her gently on the bed and take off her shoes.

"Reed?" she asks in a sleepy voice.

"Shh, baby, go back to sleep," I say, smoothing the hair back off her face.

"What time is it?"

"Just after eight."

"I need to take my antibiotics."

"Okay. I'll go get them for you."

She starts to get up. "I can do it."

I gently push her back down. "I told you last night that I'll take care of you."

"Mmm," she moans, and wiggles against the bed.

"Baby," I warn.

"What?" she asks innocently. "My back was itchy."

I lean over and quickly kiss her. "I love you. Stay here and I'll go get your tablet."

I get Bria's medication, some water, and some cookies; she can't take her tablet on an empty stomach.

I walk back into my room to find Bria naked on my bed. I swear I almost bust my pants with the way my dick reacts to her.

"Jesus, angel, you ought to warn a guy before he walks into something like this."

"Why? Like what you see?" she all but purrs.

I climb over her and settle between her legs. "I fucking love what I see." I grind my denim-clad erection against her.

She moans and presses against me. "I want you, Reed." She nips my shoulder with her teeth.

"Tablet first, then sex." She pouts. "I don't want that leg getting infected. Who knows what kind of germs are floating around the track."

"Fine." She rubs against me as she sits up.

"Good girl." I hand her the cookies.

"What's with these?"

"You can't have your pill on an empty stomach." As she starts eating, I move down her body and stop when I get to the apex of her thighs.

"What are you doing?" she asks breathlessly.

"Eat your cookie," I say, spreading her legs and blowing on her clit.

She moans and thrusts her hips towards my face.

"Finished?" I ask, and suck on her thigh, right near her pussy.

"Uh-huh," she moans and I hand her the water and her pill.

"Bottoms up," I say, and move down her body again. I watch as she swallows the pill and chases it with the water.

"Good girl." I lick up her slit. "So sweet." I do it again, before sucking her clit into my mouth. She bucks against me and her hands grip my hair. I work down to her opening, sticking my tongue in and making her pussy even wetter.

"God, Reed," she pants, squirming against the bed.

I go back to her clit and slip a finger inside her, curling it so it hits her G spot. She tightens against me, so I add another finger and bite down gently and send her over the edge.

"Reed!" she yells, and I feel a hundred feet tall.

While she's catching her breath, I tear off my clothes, and am ready and waiting for her when she opens her eyes.

"Hi," she says shyly.

"Hey, baby." I run my knuckles over her cheek.

"That felt really good."

"I bet." I smirk.

"So I had my tablet...." She wiggles against me.

"I saw that," I reply, and refuse to move. I know what she wants and I'm not giving it to her just yet. She wiggles again and again but I don't budge.

"Reed," she whines.

"I wanna hear it, baby."

"Hear what?"

"What do you want?"

"You." She wiggles again and damn if it isn't driving me crazy.

"What do you want me to do?"

"I want you to make love to me."

"Done." I slide into her and we both sigh. I capture her lips as I slowly slide in and out of her, tilting her hips so I grind against her clit.

We've done the hard and fast, the rabid passion, but this, the slow and sweet, is making love at its finest.

I move to kiss her neck, kissing, licking, sucking, and nipping as I go. She moves to give me more room and I cup her breast, squeezing and pinching her nipple.

She arches against me.

I thrust into her with a little more force and she moans louder and tightens around me. I pull back to study her face; sweat beads on her brow and her eyes are closed.

"Angel, look at me."

She opens her beautiful brown eyes and all I can see in them is love.

"I love you."

She reaches up to cup my face. "I love you."

I thrust into her one more time and we're both coming hard.

I collapse on top of her because I have no choice. I do try to keep as much of my weight off her as possible though. As soon as I'm able, I roll us so she's lying on my chest, our bodies still connected. Her finger draws circles on my chest and I play with her hair.

We remain quiet, enjoying being with each other. I think Bria is almost asleep until my stomach growls, and she laughs.

"Guess your appetite hasn't been quenched, huh?"

I roll her onto her back and pin her hands to the bed, quickly hardening inside her again.

"Angel, when it comes to you I'll never have enough."

I'm starving but nothing comes before me loving my woman.

By the time we've finished for the second time, I'm practically ravenous.

I go into the bathroom and get a cloth to clean her up. I love doing this for her, and that she lets me do it.

I throw the cloth back into the bathroom and sit next to her on the bed. Running my hand over her hair, I ask, "How are you feeling? How's your leg?"

"I'm more than good." She smiles.

"Are you hungry?"

"A little."

"Good, because I'm starving. Do you want to go over to the diner? Best burgers in town!" I throw her a cheesy grin.

"Sounds like a plan." She goes to get up.

"Uh-uh," I scold, and go to get her clothes.

"Reed, I'm perfectly okay to dress myself."

I lean down and kiss her. "Shh, I'm taking care of you."

We dress, or I dress us, and give her another piggyback over to the diner. We enter through the back and when we come into the dining room where my family are gathered, we are met with cheers and whistles again.

Chris, who has woken up, rushes to Bria and pulls on her leg. Luckily, it's the uninjured one.

"Just be careful, buddy. Aunty Bria hurt her leg," I say, dropping her onto a chair at the table we've taken up.

"You're hurt?" he asks her, and his chin wobbles.

She scoops him up and puts him on her lap. "I'm okay, buddy. It's just a little scratch. I'll be fine. How are you? Are you okay?"

He nods and snuggles into her lap while I go and order us some food.

I get back to the table and Chris is still on Bria's lap, setting up for the long haul. As much as I love the kid, this really won't do. I lift him up and hand him to Pop. I've got to admit he goes pretty easily; I think he's too tired to argue.

I then pick Bria up, take her seat, and pull her back down on my lap, my chin resting on her shoulder, my arms tight around her waist. My family have amused smiles on their faces, the fuckers. I kiss her neck and she snuggles into me. Jax brings a tray of shots over and hands them out, but I take Bria's.

"Dude," he says, "that's for sis."

"Dude," I mimic, "she's on antibiotics. They don't mix."

"Oh," he says.

"But thanks for the thought," Bria says in her sweet voice.

Then Mav comes over with another tray with two glasses of milk: one for Bria, one for Chris. He sets it down in front of her and winks.

Pop stands and we all quiet down.

"We've had quite a week. An attack here, the bombing of the garage at the track, but most importantly of all, we welcome a new and already very loved member to this family." He nods to Bria.

"She may not have been with us very long, but she has slotted in seamlessly and taken to us like she was born into this family. So, all things considered, I'd say we ended this week ahead."

"Hear, hear," we yell, and down our shots.

Yep, my girl is well and truly stuck with us now.

CHAPTER SEVENTEEN

BRIA

Oh. Holy. Fuck. Nate's toast? Total tear-jerker. I shoot my milk—how cute, by the way—smile, and try to hide the fact there are tears in my eyes. Behind me, Reed gives me a squeeze and kisses my cheek.

In my pocket, my phone rings. I fish it out and see it's Grayson calling.

"Hey, lady," I answer.

"Lady? What the fuck, Bria! I had to hear about the explosion at the track on the news. Please tell me you weren't anywhere near it."

I swallow awkwardly. "Er, okay, I won't tell you."

"Jesus fucking Christ, Bria, first the diner and now this?"

"Hang on a sec," I tell her. "I'm gonna take this outside," I say to Reed, who looks concerned.

"Is everything okay?"

"My best friend heard about the explosion and she's a little upset."

"A little upset?" I hear Grayson yell. "You're goddamn right I'm fucking upset."

"Can I talk to her?" Reed asks.

"Yeah, put him on, I'll give him a piece of my mind," she says.

"I don't think that's a good idea." I bite my lip.

"Angel, give me the phone. Your best friend has concerns and I am willing and able to address them."

"You don't have to do this," I say, handing him the phone.

"Hello," he says into it, "this is Reed Ryan. Who am I speaking with?"

"I'm Grayson Dean, Bria's best friend, and *you* are putting her life in danger." The way she's shouting, I can hear her clearly. The phone's volume is loud but my BFF is louder.

"Hi, Grayson, it's nice to talk to you. Bria has told me lots about you."

"Oh, don't give me your player charm, Reed Ryan. I've heard all about you. You riders are all the fucking same, scum of the earth."

"Hey now," he says, trying to placate her.

"Is Bria hurt?"

"She has a small cut to her leg that required a few stitches. She was looked after by the race organisation's doctor, who cleaned the wound, stitched it, and prescribed antibiotics to prevent infection."

"How many stitches?"

"Not many."

"How many fucking stitches does she have, Reed?"

He sighs. "Four."

"Four fucking stitches. You motherfucker, how dare you put her in danger!"

I go to grab the phone from him but Reed holds up a finger.

"It kills me that Bria was anywhere *near* that explosion and I damn near lost it when I saw she was hurt, but don't you dare accuse me of putting the woman I love in danger. If it were up to me I'd lock her away and keep her to myself, but I know that's not a possibility; at least, not one she'd let me entertain." He winks at me.

"You love her?" Grayson asks. Even through her angsty pissed-off shout I can hear the shock.

"I do."

"You've told her this?"

"Many times."

"And she loves you back?"

"By some miracle."

"Oh please, I've seen you and your brothers around. What's not to love?"

At this, Reed chuckles and I tuck my head in between his neck and shoulder and hug him tightly.

"Listen, Bria and I are having dinner with my family at our diner. Why don't you come down? You can have a good meal and see for yourself that Bria's okay."

"Is this meal on you?" I hide a smile.

"I'll speak to the owners. They're friends of mine."

"Fine, I'll be there in fifteen minutes. But be warned, Ryan, I won't be impressed by your playboy charm."

"I have no doubt. We'll see you soon, Miss Dean." He hangs up the phone and hands it back to me. "She'll be here soon." He smiles his wicked smile.

I'm not entirely sure he knows exactly what he's invited upon us.

The hurricane that is Grayson Dean sweeps into the diner eight minutes later.

"And how many speeding tickets should we expect in the mail?" I ask.

My BFF might be tiny but she's fierce, and she takes a seat at our table in between Liam and Jax, making herself at home.

"Pfft, please Bri, you know I can talk my way out of a paper bag," she says.

"Fine, but just remember, you're the one who wants that pair of Jimmy Choo boots. A speeding fine will put a major dampener on that."

"Oh please." She waves a hand in the air.

Jax laughs and Liam tips his head. "The biker ankle boots? Pointed toe, silver buckles and riveting?" Grayson nods. "If they were my style, I wouldn't let a speeding fine get in the way of them either."

Grayson arches an eyebrow at him. "A racer with taste? And who might you be?"

"Liam Ryan." He sticks his hand out for her to shake.

"Oh, the star. Well, it's nice to meet you, Liam. Pity you couldn't race today. You've had MacCoy's measure the past few races. I was looking forward to seeing his response."

"I think I'm in love," Jax mutters.

Grayson turns her attention to him. "And you are?"

"Jax Ryan." He takes her hand and kisses it.

"The charmer, I see."

"No, that's just the Ryan gene," I say, and the Ryans all snicker.

"I can see why you've all but disappeared on me, Bri. They are quite a bunch up close."

"They are indeed. Now let me introduce the rest of them to you. Liam and Jax you've met. Next to Liam is Mav, then Nate and Chris, Jay, and Parker is in the kitchen," I say, going round the table, "and my ever-comfy chair is my boyfriend, Reed. Ryans, my best friend and roommate, Grayson Dean."

Grayson focuses her attention on Reed and the others chuckle. I smile and lean into him further. Grayson's just about to say something when our food arrives.

"But I didn't order yet," I say, confused.

Reed kisses my cheek. "I know, angel. I did."

"But how did you know what I wanted?"

"I remembered what you ordered the first time you came here and took a gamble that that's what you'd like."

"You remember her order from four days ago?" Grayson asks disbelievingly.

"It's what I ordered," I say, picking up an onion ring and popping it in my mouth.

Grayson's eyes narrow and Reed laughs. "You can scowl at me all you like but you can't scare me away from my girl."

"Your girl?" she scoffs.

"Yes, she's our girl," Nate says, "and since Bria clearly has no objections to being called that then I really don't see what reason you can have for questioning my son or his feelings for Bria."

"Okay," Grayson says cheerily, and picks up a menu. "So who do I see about getting some food around this place?"

I think we all sigh in relief before Mav voices what I know they're all thinking. "I have no idea what the fu— what the eff that was, but you are one crazy chick."

"Thank you," she says happily.

"What can we get you?" Park asks.

"I'll take a triple cheeseburger with mac and cheese, chili fries, garlic bread, apple pie, and a chocolate sundae. Oh, and a Diet Coke, thanks."

We pause for a minute before Park says, "Right," and gets up to place the order.

"So Bri, show me this leg."

I lift my leg to show Grayson the bandage.

"Careful," Reed says. "You don't want to pull a stitch."

I playfully elbow him in the side. "For God's sake, Reed, it's fine."

"It's my job, remember?"

"Oh, I remember," I purr.

He growls and tickles my sides. I squirm in his lap, his dick stirring to life beneath me.

Out of the corner of my eye, I see Grayson watching us like a hawk.

Reed pulls my face towards him, cupped between his hands and kisses me.

"Come on, let's eat. I'm starving." He turns me round in his lap.

In between bites of burger, Reed and I feed each other our sides, sharing as we did that night at Mike's. Only this time, neither of us is content to let the other do the work.

"You two are too fu—" Grayson remembers Chris. "Too effing cute. How do you stand it?" she asks my family.

"Personally," Jax says, "I happen to find it both amusing and heart-warming."

"It's sickening, is what it is," Grayson argues.

"That too," Mav agrees.

"Leave them alone," Jay scolds. "If there's one thing us Ryans know, it's when we're on a good thing, and there's no doubting Reed has got himself a very good thing in our girl Bria."

"Thank you, Pa," Reed says. "And as for the rest of you, you're jealous." He points to his brothers and they laugh.

Grayson gets along with everyone great, a little too well in the case of Jax, who spends the evening flirting with her.

Reed is constantly touching me, running his hands over my thighs or up my sides and casually grazing my breasts. It's driving me crazy but I can tell from the smug look on his face he knows what he's doing and is doing it on purpose.

Not wanting him to get the upper hand, I begin to surreptitiously grind myself against him. I grin when he hardens beneath me.

"Angel," he warns.

"What?" I ask and flutter my eyelashes at him innocently.

Just then, the most gorgeous guy I've ever seen—*sorry,*

119

honey—walks into the diner and my mouth drops.

Grayson notices and asks, "What is it?" but I can't answer, so she turns in the direction I'm looking. From the corner of my eye, I see her mouth drop as well. The guy in question is taller than Reed, maybe six four, but not as built, probably somewhere in between him and Liam. But that's not what's got Grayson and me speechless. No, this guy is a *dead* ringer for Jamie Dornan. Jamie Junior walks straight over to our table, seemingly towards Grayson. It's only when Liam gets up that I realise who he was heading for.

"Hey, sweets," Liam coos as he embraces Jamie Jr.

"Love," Jamie replies.

Behind me, Reed shuts my mouth.

"Who is that?" I whisper to him.

"Do my eyes deceive me, or do the Ryans have female company?" Jamie asks.

"Mase, this is Reed's girlfriend, the lovely Bria Adams." Liam points to me. "And this is her best friend, Grayson Dean. Ladies, my boyfriend, Mason Evans."

"Oh, so you're sis," Mason says to me.

"I seem to be." I shake his offered hand. "It's nice to meet you."

"You need to get the fuck out," Grayson exclaims. Thankfully, Parker took Chris off to bed a little while ago. "It's not fair that there is this much handsomeness in one place."

Liam and Mason chuckle while Reed squeezes me tighter, and Jax leans over to her. "I'd be more than happy to take this party elsewhere."

"Not so fast, junior," Grayson says, pushing his face away.

Reed and I both laugh; Jax smiles but doesn't look deterred. Lord help her.

We sit, eat, and chat well into the night before I start yawning and Reed decides it's time I go to bed. I'm "allowed" to walk around the table to hug Gray before Reed offers me his back again and insists I hop on. Him carrying me this way reminds me of our first date at Mike's and riding his bike, so I don't mind that much. Okay, I still think it's over the top, but if this gorgeous, loving man wants to look after me, who am I to argue?

Reed walks us over to his house and into his room, gently lowering me onto the bed before kneeling down to take off my shoes. He then pulls me up, undoing my shorts, taking off my shirt and bra and throwing an old Ryan Racing shirt over my head before pulling back the covers so I can get in. I watch as he takes off his jeans and shirt and climbs into bed in only his boxer briefs. He pulls me to him and I rest my head on his chest, my fingers tracing the patterns inked into his skin, his arms around me, one at my hip, the other running through my hair.

"So Grayson's a trip," he says with humour.

"She can be a handful but that's mostly a front. When she was with Rome, she was so soft and caring. The end of their relationship really did a number on her."

"How long ago did it end?"

"Four, almost five years ago."

"Has she dated since?"

"Not seriously. She's been with guys, but none for more than two weeks."

"She really loved him."

"They loved each other, but there wasn't room for her and Devil in his life and he chose Devil."

"I'd say that's total bullshit, but knowing Hunter, he'd want his riders 100 percent devoted to him."

"Have you guys ever thought about taking on riders outside the family?"

"Not really. I mean, there's enough of us to keep the team going, but maybe when Liam decides he wants to retire we will. The same with Mav and Jax in their disciplines. We're not really a big team, nowhere near a factory team despite being successful. The guys don't get paid as such. They don't get a salary, but their bills are paid and they get a small amount of spending money each month, but that's it. We can't afford the massive salary a non-family member would demand."

"So now that you don't race, you work at the diner, the garage, and with the team?"

"Yep."

"And you're happy doing that?"

"For the moment. Eventually I'd like to take over Ryan Racing from Pop, see if I can make us financially competitive with the factory teams. I don't think it would take much; a little networking, a little promotion, and I think we could do it. I'm slowly talking Pop around, but like most things, you need money, and we don't have it."

An idea starts forming in my head. I'll need some help from Grayson, but I think I can pull it off. I snuggle further into Reed and fall asleep in his arms, our future slowly building in my mind.

CHAPTER EIGHTEEN

REED

I wake to Bria's mouth wrapped around me and I barely have time to think before I'm coming hard. She licks me clean and makes her way up my body to me.

"Good morning," I say and kiss her nose.

"Good morning." She smiles a shy, sweet smile.

"So, not that I mind, but what did I do to deserve that wake-up?"

"Just my way of saying I love you and thank you for looking after me yesterday."

"No need to thank me, angel. I told you, it's my job."

"I know. I just wanted you to know I appreciate it. You're not the only lucky one in this relationship."

I pull her closer to me and nuzzle her neck, inhaling her sweet, fruity scent.

"I never gave any thought to settling down or the type of woman it would take to get me to do that, but even if I had, you're so much more than what I could ever come up with."

"Reed," she says quietly, leaning back so she can look me in the eyes.

"I've been with my fair share of women," I tell her. She freezes in my hold, but she needs to know. "I don't have a stellar reputation when it comes to women, none of my family do, well, except for Chris and Liam." She chuckles and I smile before continuing. "I know there might be some backlash from some of the women around. They'll be jealous and disbelieving and I wish I could shield you from that, but I imagine some of this is going to come from girls on campus." The last thing I want is to sound arrogant. The women and everything that comes with racing was something I happily went along with and enjoyed. But, I also know the women in the circuit well enough to know they can be bitches when they want to be. My line with them was always set: I wasn't interested in commitment. Of course, I never planned for Bria.

She looks unfazed. "Honey, I told you before, you don't need to worry about me. I know what we have here and I know how you feel about me. I'm not worried what anyone thinks or says about us. I only care about you and me."

"Every time you say stuff like that to me I'm always so surprised."

"Why?" she asks, hurt.

I'm quick to reassure her. "Because you're just so amazing and understanding, and I can't believe someone like you could want to be with someone like me."

"You're not so bad yourself you know," she says, running her thumb over my cheek, "and I'm not the only one who can't believe you'd want to be with someone like me. There are a million girls who'd claw out their eyes to be with you, yet you chose me."

I offer her a smile. "I'd seen you around before, saw how fucking cute you are, but it wasn't until we actually spoke, and then the way you protected Chris… hell, it was enough to tell me I never wanted to let you go."

"Is that why your brothers call me sis?"

At this I blush, possibly a first for me, and hide my face a little.

She pulls on my hair so she can see my eyes and I nod. "Yeah, they know one day I'm gonna marry you." I pause, waiting for a reaction. Her eyes soften as she listens and waits for me to continue. "I think they knew it almost before me. Chris certainly did, and even though Park was the only one here at first, it's like some kind of bulletin flashed through all of them alerting them to the fact I'm no longer on the market."

"I love your family," she says and my heart almost bursts. My family and I are as close as can be and any woman in any of our lives needs to know, understand, and be okay with that. It's a bonus if they get along like a house on fire. Luckily for me, Bria and my family do.

"If you don't know they love you, then you're blind, lady. They think you walk on water."

Bria giggles and I tickle her gently.

"What are you doing next weekend?" she asks.

"Besides being wherever you are, nothing."

She kisses me sweetly. "Well, in that case would you like to come home with me? I haven't been home in a while and I owe my parents a visit. With exams coming up soon, now's the best time."

"You want me to meet your parents?"

She nods and smiles her beautiful, breathtaking smile.

I roll her to her back and settle between her legs, my previously semi-hard cock now rock-hard. "I'd love nothing more." I kiss her gently.

"Really?"

"Absolutely."

"You're really all in, huh?"

"Baby, if you can't tell I am,"—I thrust inside her—"then I'm doing something wrong."

She giggles, and her movements make thinking impossible.

CHAPTER NINETEEN

BRIA

Reed and I barely got out of bed on Sunday, and he doesn't want to let me out this morning. We've just caught our breath after another round of lovemaking. The man has incredible stamina.

"I have to go."

"I don't want you to." He hugs me tighter and throws a leg over mine, effectively trapping me with his body.

"I have to get to class."

"Education is overrated."

I snort. "Not all of us can ride motorbikes and look good doing it."

He snuggles into my neck. "So I look good, huh?"

"Shut up." I elbow him. "But I really have to go."

"Fine," he says, releasing me and throwing his arms and legs out wide on the bed, "but at least shower with me."

"*Will* we shower?"

"Eventually." He wiggles his eyebrows at me.

"At least you're honest."

"Is that a yes?"

I groan and go to the bathroom. When I get to the door, I look back at Reed, who's lying on his side watching me.

"Enjoying the view?" I ask.

"Absolutely," he says and sends me his panty-dropping smile, complete with dimple overload.

"So are you going to lie there and watch or are you going to join me?" I've barely finished my sentence before Reed rushes at me, picking me up around my waist and spinning us into the bathroom.

He gets a waterproof bandage out and carefully puts it over my stitches before picking me up again, my legs wound tightly around his waist, and walking us into the shower.

He carefully and lovingly washes my body, his hands all over me electrifying me and making me think if he were to take me right now I'd probably come instantly. When Reed's done with me, I return the favour and come to the conclusion that washing him, getting to rub my hands all over him, may be even better than him washing me.

He proves me right by giving me two insanely intense orgasms before shutting off the water.

"You're going to have to help me walk." Exhaustion drips from every syllable.

A smug smile crosses Reed's face. "No worries. I've got you."

He reaches out to grab a towel before wrapping me in it, then proceeds to sweep me off my feet and gently places me on his bed. I lie there while he grabs a towel for himself, and I watch as a drop of water slides down his chest.

Reed laughs as I lick my lips.

"You okay there, angel?"

"I think you broke me."

With his brows dipping in concern, he asks, "Is it your leg? Are you okay? Do you need anything?" He sits beside me on the bed.

I laugh and reach up to cup his cheek. "I'm fine. My leg is fine. I've just never come so hard in my life. I'm still tingling."

"Oh." His smug smile returns. "Well, if that's the case...." He leans down to kiss me.

He's deepening the kiss when I pull back. "I meant what I said earlier. I really do have to go."

Reed pouts. "I don't want you to go."

"I don't either, but I'm a few weeks from exams, then graduation. I don't want to stuff this up, not this close to the end."

"Will you come here after class?"

I smile gently at him. "There's nowhere else I'd rather be." His answering smile lights the whole room.

"So quickly," he murmurs.

"So quickly what?" I ask, confused.

He cups my face. "So quickly you've become my whole world." He presses his lips against mine. It's chaste from what I'm used to, but it doesn't stop the tingles from spreading through my body.

This time he breaks the kiss. "Okay, you've gotta go. I don't want to be the cause of you failing and having to retake the semester and spend *more* time away from me."

We get up and dress before a quick breakfast with Liam and Mason, and then I'm out the door.

My afternoon class is cancelled so after swinging by my room to grab some clothes—*I wonder if Reed would give me my own drawer?*—I head to Wheels, getting there just after lunch.

Reed happens to be passing by the door as I walk through it. He grabs me by the waist and hugs me tightly before pulling back to kiss me. His lips are soft and familiar.

"I missed you," he says once we break apart.

"I've been gone four hours." I roll my eyes.

He grins and over exaggerates his pain "I know, and it's been torture," he says, rocking us back and forth.

Liam comes out of the kitchen, pauses, and upon seeing us, exhales. "Thank God you're here, sis. He's been unbearable." He comes over and gives me a kiss on the cheek before moving towards a businessman at a table.

"Unbearable, huh?"

Reed just shrugs. "I want to be with you always. I'm not going to hide that fact."

I soften immediately. "Reed…."

"Come on," he says, releasing me and leading me to a booth. "Have you had lunch? You know you can't have your antibiotics on an empty stomach; have you taken them?"

I sit and pull him down with me. He slings an arm around my shoulders and I curl into his chest.

"No, I haven't had lunch or taken my antibiotics, and yes, I know I can't do that on an empty stomach, so if I could get a club sandwich that would be great."

"Caramel shake?"

I nod.

"On it. I'll be back soon." With a quick peck, he's gone.

I watch him walk through the swinging doors to the kitchen and then hold them open a second later as Chris comes sprinting through the restaurant straight for me.

"Aunty Bria," he yells, scrambling up into the booth before hugging me around my neck.

"Hey, buddy," I say, patting his back gently. "How are you?"

"Good," he says, releasing me.

"What have you been up to?"

"I was with Pa. We were watching races."

"That sounds like fun."

He nods. "It was. Uncle Liam's going to smoke 'em next weekend."

"That's right, buddy," Liam says as he walks past and puts his hand out for a high five. He then heads to the bar.

I pull out some of my textbooks while Chris goes and gets his backpack from Parker. Apparently, it survived the explosion.

I watch as a guy comes into the diner and heads straight for Liam. He sits down right in front of him and begins asking questions. When Liam shakes his head and refuses to answer, the guy leans forward, trying to get in his face. I can see Liam is trying to be polite, but he's having a hard time trying not to lose it.

I've always been fiercely protective of people I love. It goes with the territory of wanting people I care for to be happy and safe. I'm therefore not surprised when I ask Chris to stay at our table, giving him the important mission of saving our table, while my feet lead me to Liam.

"Come on, Liam, you must have something to say about the explosion of your garage at Mechanical Field on Saturday," the guy, obviously a reporter, says.

"As you no doubt know," I say, cutting Liam off, "the explosion is currently under police investigation, so Mr Ryan and the rest of the staff and family at Ryan Racing aren't at liberty to discuss it."

The reporter swings to me, looks me up and down, and finds me lacking. I admit my usual outfit of jeans and a hoodie isn't professional, but neither is this guy asking questions he knows can't be answered.

He flicks a hand at me, dismissing me. "Go away, girlie. Why don't you go back to the shops or something?"

Anger flashes in Liam's eyes and I put my hand on his arm, halting whatever he has to say.

"I'm afraid I can't do that. As Ryan Racing's PR rep, you've made my afternoon shopping trip impossible now."

That gets his attention. "PR rep, you say?"

"Yes, sir, and if I may ask, which publication do you work for that would be willing to put a very serious police investigation in jeopardy?"

He flounders. "What did you say your name was?"

I extend my hand. "Bria Adams, and if you have any further and legitimate questions for Mr Ryan and the Ryan Racing team, you can go through me."

"Huh," he says and scratches his chin. "So, does the Ryan Racing team have a statement they'd like to put out regarding the weekend's events?"

I stand a little taller. "Ryan Racing is shocked at this weekend's events but is looking forward to getting back on track next weekend. They are cooperating fully with race officials and the ongoing police investigation."

The reporter sighs at my generic words. "That's it?" he asks.

"You know that's all we can give," I reply sharply.

"Fine." He grunts and slides off the stool, and walks out of the diner.

"Our PR rep, huh?" Liam asks, an amused look on his face.

I shrug. "It's what I'm studying, so I took the opportunity to put my education to use." I grin, my heart picking up speed a little though, hoping I didn't offend him.

"Well, you did a damn good job. I've never seen Bob get shut down so easily."

"Have you guys put out any sort of statement about the weekend?"

"I don't think so. We've just been answering 'no comment' when anyone calls."

I throw my head back. "Ugh, that is a total no-no. You *never* 'no comment.' Who's your PR rep?" I ask.

Liam shrugs. "We don't have one."

"How do you not have one?"

"We just do it ourselves."

"That explains so much."

Just then, Reed and Nate come into the dining room and head towards Liam and me. Reed puts my club sandwich in front of me and goes to make my shake.

Nate squeezes my shoulder and sits on the stool next to me. "I heard Bob was here," he says.

"He was," Liam replies.

Nate looks around. "Where is he?"

"Sis took care of him."

Nate looks at me, confused. "What do you mean?"

"I mean," Liam says, "meet our new PR rep, Miss Bria Adams."

"Huh?" Nate asks.

"She stepped in when she saw Bob hassling me, shut him down too."

"It was nothing really," I say.

"We really should put out a statement, Pop."

"I haven't the faintest idea how to do that," Nate admits.

"Do you have a website?" I ask.

"Yeah, Mav updates it, designed it too," Liam says.

"Then it's simple. We put it on there. That's going to be most reporters' first port of call."

"How do you know all this?"

"Because my girl is awesome," Reed says, placing my shake in front of me and coming to stand behind me and kissing my cheek.

I smile at Nate. "I'm a Journalism / PR student at Booker."

"So you know about all this media bullshit?" he asks.

"Been training for it for years."

"We can't pay you much."

"You just did." I take a bite of my sandwich.

"Seriously?"

"She's family, Pop," Reed says behind me, and I sink into his arms a little more. I love that I've been accepted into this world of men so easily and quickly.

I give Nate a reassuring smile. "I don't mind helping out. I'm graduating soon and I'll be looking for a job. Why not this one? Granted, I'm not fluent in all things racing, but I'm willing to learn."

"I'll teach you, baby," Reed whispers in my ear before biting the lobe gently. I have to hold back a moan.

"You sure you want to do this?" Nate asks.

"Hey, I offered. I came over here. No one forced me. Plus, this is an awesome opportunity, for both me and Ryan Racing."

I look at Reed as I say that and see he's joined the dots. I'm doing what I've been trained for *and* trying to make his dreams come true.

"Fucking hell, Bria," Reed says and crushes me to him, "you are so much more than amazing. You're—you're everything. I love you so much, baby."

"And I love you." I turn back to Nate. "So, you ready to do this?"

He nods.

"Well, come over to my office." I lead him back to the booth where Chris is colouring quietly.

"Are you sure you want to do this?" Nate asks me once again as we sit down.

"Absolutely. It'll be a learning experience for both of us. There will be missteps, from both sides, but you guys need this. If you want Ryan Racing to be more competitive with the factory teams, we need to get you guys a presence."

"We can't pay much."

"Free meals is fine by me. I was told you guys have the best burgers in town so I think I'll consider us even." I flash Nate a smile. "But more than that, I know Reed and I have only been together a few days but I love him and see a future with him. I consider him and all of you my family. Family helps family."

"My boys call you sis?" he asks, and I smile.

"They do."

He nods. "Then call me Pop." He returns my smile.

"Right, let's get down to business, shall we?" I ask, and he nods.

Just then, Reed comes over with my sandwich and milkshake that I left over at the bar. "Thanks, honey," I say, and lean up to kiss him.

He takes a seat beside me and slings an arm along the back of the seat.

"The first thing we have to do is get a statement out about the explosion. Because it's under police investigation, we can't say much but 'no comment' is a no-no. It looks like we're trying to dodge questions. We have nothing to hide so if asked, either don't answer or give some generic answer."

"Like what?" Pop asks.

"Like 'it's under police investigation and we're cooperating fully' or even more basic with 'we're just looking forward to racing,' something like that. We don't need to be pulled into all that sh— stuff," I say, remembering Christian sitting next to me. "Our focus is on racing and getting Liam that title."

Across from me, Pop looks impressed.

"Damn, baby," Reed says, discreetly taking my hand and moving it over his crotch so I can feel his erection pressing against his zipper. I give him a squeeze and he groans under his breath.

"What sort of contacts do you have in the media?" I ask.

"Hang on, I'll go get 'em," Pop says as he gets up. "I'll call Mav and Jax as well, get 'em down here."

"They should be here soon," Reed says. "It's Monday."

"Right," Pop says. "Let me go get those details."

As he does, I pull out my laptop and start it up.

"Do you have Wi-Fi?" I ask Reed. When he doesn't answer, I look over at him and find him staring and smiling at me.

"What?"

"You're so professional, it turns me on," he whispers close to my ear.

"I know, I felt it," I say, and laugh.

"Bria, baby, you have no idea what this all means."

I cup his cheek. "I do."

He shakes his head. "This, right here," he says, tapping the table, "this is my dream. You're making my dreams come true, even ones I only had a couple of days ago."

"The way I see it, I'm building my family's dreams, building our future, all of ours, forever."

Reed pulls me to him, pressing his lips against mine. Our tongues connect and it takes everything in me to remember our surroundings and pull away. Once again, his mouth is next to my ear. "Fuck, angel, I need to be inside you. Right. Now." I'm nodding before he finishes his sentence.

"Buddy," Reed says to Chris, "can you tell Pop that Aunty Bria and I will be back soon?"

Chris nods without looking up from his colouring.

"Come on," Reed says, pulling me up and pushing me in front of him to hide the evidence of his arousal. We run, giggling, through the diner, ignoring the knowing looks from Liam and Parker.

~

After our afternoon interlude, we run into Jax and Mav as we're cleaning up; we only made it as far as Reed's kitchen table.

"Brother, sister," Jax says, a large grin on his face. Both he and Mav are dressed similarly in black singlets and basketball shorts, their skin glowing red from the workout they just came from.

"Hey, Jax, Mav," I say and wave at them, my head resting on Reed's chest.

"It smells like sex in here," Jax says. "Were you two partaking in a little afternoon delight?" He wiggles his eyebrows. "And in the kitchen too. I hope you sanitised everything."

"Seriously, man?" Mav asks.

Jax holds up his hands. "Hey, I'm not the one who had sex in the kitchen. I'm just asking if they're being hygienic."

"Shut up, you idiot," Reed says, slapping Jax on the back of the head. "Come on, Pop and Bria have work for you guys."

"Us? Why?" Jax asks.

"Up you hop," Reed says to me, offering me his hand. "Bria's Ryan Racing's new PR rep, so they're getting everything set up."

"Oh, nice," Mav says, nodding.

Jax gives a cheesy grin and does a little dance. "Oh yeah, we're moving to the big leagues now!"

Reed shakes his head as we walk out the door.

"Do either of you have Facebook, Instagram, or Twitter accounts?" I ask.

"I have Facebook, but no to the other two," Mav says.

"Personal or professional pages?"

"Personal."

"Okay. Jax?"

"Just Facebook and Instagram."

"Personal?"

"Yeah."

"I'll take a look at your Instagram and then we'll set up the others and streamline them. Mav, Pop said you update the Ryan Racing website?" He nods. "Okay, so if we can, it'll be good to link them there. We'll have to set all this up for Liam as well."

I say all this and Reed starts to turn around.

"Where are you going?"

139

"You keep talking like this and I'm gonna chain you to my bed."

I laugh and pat his head. "Stop! You're going to have to get used to me saying this sort of stuff."

"Fine," he huffs, and heads back to the diner. "Sorry," Reed says, leading me to the seat of the booth. "Bria needed to change the dressing on her leg."

Pop and Jay both nod before Pop says, "Reed, go give Park a hand."

He nods and kisses me.

"Here," Pop says, and hands me a tattered notebook. Inside are the contact details for dozens of journalists and publications.

"Oh great, thanks. I'll type all this up and then send out a press release."

"What will it say?" Jay asks.

"Much what I said to Bob. That we're shocked at the explosion, we're cooperating with race officials and police, and we're looking forward to the next race. I'll also include that I'm now our PR rep and any and all questions and requests are to come through me."

Pop and Jay look at each other and smile.

"Yeah, we got a good one," Jay says, patting my hand.

"Thanks, Jay."

"Pa," he corrects, and I beam.

"Pa. I also want to set up social media presences for the guys and the team as a whole."

"Well, that sounds very new age to me," Pa says.

"Not really, it's just an instant way to get news and

information to your fans. I'll then have Mav put links up on the website. Speaking of… Jax!" I yell, and he saunters over. "Let me see this Instagram of yours."

He types in the address and I have a look. Most of the posts are harmless, but his username, @hotbmxboy, isn't going to cut it.

"I'm changing your username," I tell him.

"To what?"

"@jaxryanofficial. It'll be your username for Twitter and Facebook as well."

"Will Liam and Mav's usernames be as boring?"

"Yep. @liamryanofficial and @mavryanofficial to go with @ryanracing."

"Fine," he sighs. "I'll be boring."

"It's not boring. It's appropriate. We're going to be shining the spotlight on you, all three of you, and we need to make sure you're presenting a face sponsors will love."

"Oh yeah, baby, now we're talking!"

"Who you calling baby?" Reed asks as he walks past.

"Er, no one," Jax says meekly.

"Yeah, just remember that." Reed leans over to kiss me before walking away. I watch him for a minute before looking around and noticing the diner's getting busy.

"If you need to help out here, I'm fine to do this by myself. It's just a lot of filling in forms," I say to Jax, Pa, and Pop.

"Thanks, darling," Pa says, and kisses the top of my head.

I spend the next couple of hours setting the accounts up, entering the reporters' contact details in a spreadsheet, then typing up and emailing the press release. I look up to see the

Ryans all lounging around socialising, the patrons all very male.

I get up and stretch, and Reed notices my movement. He comes over and rubs my shoulders. "You done, baby?"

I moan and move my neck from side to side. "Yep, all done. God, Reed, that feels so good." I'm sure he's smirking behind me. "I know you're smirking back there."

Reed draws me back into his arms and rests his chin on my shoulder. "I don't smirk, baby. I was simply enjoying your reactions."

"Sure. So what's going on?"

"The Monday night footy shows," he says, like it's the most obvious thing in the world. I guess it is if you're a general football fan, but I only pay attention if my team, St Kilda, are being featured. I think I'll reveal that chestnut a little bit later on.

"Oh, of course!" I exclaim, "How could I not realise?" I bat my eyelashes at him.

"So fucking sweet," he mutters under his breath.

"Is it okay if I stay?"

Reed comes to stand in front of me and takes my face in his hands. "Baby, I'd be mad if you didn't. If footy isn't your thing, feel free to study or whatever. I just want to be with you, near you, wherever you are."

I beam at him. "Do you mind if I call Grayson?'

"Not at all. Food's served afterwards so if you want anything between now and then, get it now."

"Some cheese fries?" I ask.

He kisses my nose. "Anything for you. Another shake too?"

I smile shyly and nod. I love the way he takes care of me and is always looking out for me.

I call Grayson and invite her over. She arrives about the same time as my cheese fries.

"You know," she says as she slings her bag onto the table and plops down in the booth next to me and Chris, who's eating his dinner. He'll go to bed before the programmes start. "Normally I'm not a footy fan, but seeing all these good-looking men, it's not a hardship to sit and watch."

"I thought you might be convinced to come over."

"So you're a part of this now, huh?"

I nod. "I am. Reed and I are official, making plans for the future. The guys call me sis, I call Nate and Jay Pop and Pa. They've taken me in. I love them, all of them."

She nods. "And they love you, all of them, not just Reed—who left a massive hickey on your neck, by the way."

"I know, about all of it."

"I have to admit I had my doubts, but I'm glad to be proven wrong."

"I know. It's all happened so fast, but it feels right. Everything just clicks, you know?"

She nods.

"I started working for them today, doing PR for the team."

"Really? That's awesome! What's the pay?"

"They're not paying me, as such. I'm family, they're family. We look after each other."

"You make it sound like the mob."

I laugh. "Not the mob, just love."

"Fair enough," Grayson says.

"So in light of my new job, I need your help. I need you to give me the rundown on the National Racing Series."

She smiles, takes a breath, and begins her lesson.

CHAPTER TWENTY

REED

I wasn't lying when I said I just wanted to be with Bria, near her. This girl has my heart and soul and I never want them back.

She and Grayson spend the game chatting in the booth we're now calling Bria's office. She deserves so much more, but at the first possible moment, we're getting office space, just for her. Whipped? Absolutely. Do I care? Not in the slightest. When a guy gets a girl like Bria, they'd understand.

The night's programming ends, but if somebody asked me what was discussed, I couldn't answer. I spent most of it watching my girl. I swear I almost shot my load when she told me forever. I have the same plans. I can easily imagine one day calling her my wife and see her belly round with our child and watch them grow. Beautiful little boys—the Ryans always have boys—who have their mother's blonde hair and brown eyes and my love for bikes. Boys who, together with Chris, can help take Ryan Racing from a family-run team to a major player in the world of action and motor sports. With Bria working on our PR, I have no doubt together, we can build Ryan Racing into a powerhouse.

I'm still bowled over that she wants to work for us, and for nothing, really, when I don't doubt she could demand a much better job elsewhere. But I'm not going to question it. I want to build RR with her, for her, for our family, both present and future. She said she's on the shot, so I wonder if she'd consider not getting it when she's next due? Maybe she'd want to be married, or at least engaged before we start trying, but that shit can take months or even years… and it's not like I'm not going to propose eventually. A pregnant Bria…? Shit, that's the dream right there.

Once the diner has cleared out, I take her back to my house, although it's really ours now as I have no intention of her sleeping anywhere else and certainly not without me. I remind her to take her antibiotics as the thought of her getting sick kills me, squeezing my heart in a vise.

She puts her bag on my, now our, bed and I remember the drawer I cleaned out for her today while she was in class. She actually has two drawers and half my wardrobe.

"If you want to keep some stuff here," I say in what I hope is a nonchalant voice, "I cleaned out two drawers for you. There's also some room in my wardrobe if you need to hang stuff up."

"You cleaned out drawers and your wardrobe for me?" she asks in what I think is a disbelieving voice, but I can also hear the underlying excitement.

I shrug. "Of course. I told you I want to be wherever you are, and as I'm not sure if I'd be allowed to stay with you in your dorm, it makes sense that you have room here, in our room," I say as I come up behind her, moving her hair off her neck and kissing, nipping, and licking softly.

"Our room?" she asks in her breathy, turned-on voice that gets me hard instantly.

"Yep, our room. We're a thing now, a couple, and couples share spaces. This, previously being my space, now becomes ours."

"Mmm," she moans and I chuckle.

"Come on," I say and slap her arse. "Let's get ready for bed."

We move around each other with a familiarity you wouldn't think a couple of almost a week would have, but I've come to realise Bria and I are not a typical couple.

I'm in bed waiting for her when she comes out of the bathroom wearing my Ryan Racing shirt. It's huge on her, coming down to almost her knees, but it's never looked better.

She hops in and I pull her to me, her head automatically resting on my chest, her hand drawing circles.

"So earlier you mentioned you and me together forever. What does that entail?" I ask.

She bolts up, a worried look on her face. "Why? Do you not see the same?" She bites her lip.

I release it. "Relax, angel. I'm just curious as to what

your forever entails. You know, marriage, kids, even location. I just want us to be on the same page."

"Oh." She slumps back on my chest and I run my fingers through her hair. "Um, well I guess I want to be married," she begins.

I pull back to look at her. "Hang on, you guess you want us to be married, meaning you don't really care if we are or not?"

She shrugs and to be honest, my stomach drops, but I step up. I'll take anything she willingly gives me.

"Fine, no marriage. We can make that work."

"Reed—"

"I just want you, us, Bria." I kiss her head and squash the desire to growl that I want nothing more than to see my ring on her finger, but I hold back. I flick off the light and go quiet.

Her voice cuts through the darkness. "I want a small wedding, just immediate family, my parents, your brothers, Chris, Pa, and Pop. My parents have this gazebo in their yard, and I've always dreamed of having the ceremony there."

I roll over and see her lying on her back, tears glistening in her eyes, captured by the sliver of moonlight shining into the room. I pull her to me. She clings to me and continues to talk.

"I want two, maybe three kids. Ideally I'd like all girls, or maybe two girls and a boy. I don't care where we are, if we have to move or not. I assume Ryan Racing would dictate most of that, but I think we can run it from here with no problems. I don't think I'd like to be too far away from your family though."

I sigh and kiss her forehead. "You don't have to share all this with me, you know. I was being pushy."

She sits up to look me in the eye. "It's really what I want. I swear, Reed, when I said forever I meant forever, until the end of time, till death do us part."

I nodded. "Why did you feel the need to hold back?"

She shrugs. "I don't know. I guess I didn't want you thinking I was one of those girls who's already started planning our wedding."

I cup her face. "As far as I'm concerned, you can book the fucking thing."

"I can?" she asks in a small voice.

"Absolutely. Go dress shopping tomorrow if you want, because I *will* be proposing and we *will* be having that wedding in your parents' garden. You'll wear a pretty white dress, I'll wear a suit, and then I'll put my ring on your finger and we'll have babies. Lots of little boys. I'm sorry, angel, I can't make your little girl dream come true. Ryans only have boys, and you will be a Ryan." She sniffs and I hug her to me, her tears dripping on my bare chest. "And then we'll build Ryan Racing into the powerhouse I know it can be, and raise our boys, with blonde hair and brown eyes like their mama, and I'll teach them how to ride and we'll grow old and watch them fall in love and have babies of their own."

By now she's full-on sobbing. "How does that sound?"

She nods. "It sounds like a dream."

I smile and wipe her tears. "It's our dream and we're going to make it happen."

She nods. "I love you so much, Reed."

"And I love you, angel. Now come here." I crush her to me. "No more tears, okay? We have a future to build, and I can't do that if you're crying. It kills me to see you cry, baby."

She nods and wipes her face.

"There's my girl."

"You really want all that?" she asks.

I nod. "Got the kids' names picked out and everything; might be working on a dog too." She laughs and it's the best sound in the world.

"Is that what you want too?"

She nods. "Although I really would like at least one daughter and maybe a cat."

I release a breath I didn't know I was holding. "I'll see what I can do. Maybe we'll just have to have twins, a boy and a girl."

"That's fine with me, as long as it's your children I'm carrying."

"Jesus, Bria." I kiss her head. "So we're doing this? Marriage? Kids? The whole lot?" The reality of this conversation and the meaning behind it hits me hard. I knew our conversation wasn't empty words, but this... fuck me, we're making it happen.

There's no fear looming in the distance waiting to swallow me whole. The speed, the seriousness, the whole for-fucking-ever... all it does is make me grin and want it all so bad that I want to drag her out of bed now and start making real plans.

"The whole lot, pets included."

"I promise I'll give you the dream proposal and your ideal ring." I'm impressed with myself for holding back, but I need to make this right.

"I don't care as long as I have you."

"Forever, baby."

I bend down and kiss her. "So what do you say we start practicing for those boys now, huh?"

I'm so desperate to get inside her, I don't even wait for her answer, instead crushing my lips to hers and silencing whatever she was about to say. It doesn't matter anyway; I'm gonna get my girl pregnant in two months' time, and nothing's gonna stop me.

CHAPTER TWENTY-ONE

BRIA

I wake to find Reed wrapped around me, his head resting on one of my breasts, a hand cupped around the other. I take a minute to study him in his sleep, this beautiful man of mine. His hair is all over the place, probably a result of me running my hands through it last night. His long, dark eyelashes are flat against his cheeks while his full lips, probably like mine, are bruised and swollen.

I can't believe this man, this enigma, wants to marry me, have babies with me, grow old with me. I don't know why I said I wasn't bothered if we got married or not. Of course I am. I guess I was trying to protect that tiny vestige of my heart Reed Ryan hadn't got to. Needless to say, he well and truly captured that last night and several times earlier this morning.

But what did he mean when he said we were practicing for our boys *now*? I mean, what the fuck? I'm twenty-two and haven't even finished uni yet. I know our whole relationship has developed fast, but babies? I thought I'd be well into my career before that happened, twenty-seven at *least*. But the way he was talking made it seem like he wants to start trying straight away. I'm not totally against it, but being a mum at twenty-three is not something I ever planned on. Maybe he didn't mean now; maybe he just wants us to practice for later down the track, *way* later down the track. I do love him, but that love can keep for a few years yet.

In his sleep, he nuzzles my breast and I have to bite back a laugh. I know they're not spectacular but Reed seems to like them, judging by the marks he's left on them. In the end, that's the only thing that matters. Some of the girls in my dorm have chests I'm sure their plastic surgeons are very proud of, and take every opportunity to thrust them in anyone with a dick's face. *Hmm, have any of them been with Reed?* I discount that thought for two reasons. One, I'd like to think Reed has better taste than that, and besides, I *really* don't want to know who or how many girls he's been with, and two, if they had been with him, they'd be bragging all over campus. Reed Ryan is not a slouch between the sheets, and I get wet thinking about all the things he did to me last night. I shift slightly to help ease the throb between my legs; I can definitely feel where he'd been last night. Not enough to stop me from having him again though.

All these thoughts have me worked up. How long will it take for Reed to wake once I start playing with him? His erection is at my hip, so I reach down and grab him, grasping him firmly and moving my hand up and down.

In his sleep, he groans. "Bria," he mumbles, but stays asleep.

I move a little faster, twisting this time, but still Reed sleeps. I'll need to remember this for when we have kids. I won't be the only one getting up at 2:00 a.m. for feeds.

I reach down and grab his balls, squeezing them gently, and finally his beautiful green eyes open.

"Holy shit," he exclaims in his sleep-laced voice.

"Good morning," I say, pushing him to his back and latching on to his neck, leaving a fresh mark to join a couple from last night.

"Mmm," he moans, thrusting into my hand. He comes all over it, and like the first morning we spent together, I lick him off my hand.

"You know, if you had let me inside you, we could've practiced more for those boys of ours."

I stiffen. "Yeah, about that…."

"You want their names, baby? I got 'em right here." He taps his head.

"You mean for when they're born, like, *way* down the track right?"

"Yeah. I mean, you've still got that shot thing and that'll be good for a while, and then it might take time for my guys to do their job, and then you've gotta cook the kid, so we're probably looking at *least* a year before you pop him out."

"A year?" I ask, my voice getting high and squeaky.

"If I could get it done earlier I would, but contrary to

popular opinion, I'm not God, angel. I don't have a say on when these things happen."

"I'm only twenty-two, Reed."

"So?"

"I haven't even finished uni yet."

"So do you want to wait until you graduate? When's that? December, right?"

"I've only just started working for your family."

"If you're worried about maternity leave, don't. We'll take care of you." He goes to pull me into his arms but I put a hand to his chest and stop him.

"What?" he asks.

"I can't do this."

"What?" he asks again, his brows dipping.

"I had plans, Reed, dreams of my own. I've studied for four years so I can graduate with honours and have a career. A baby would put a *major* damper on that."

"What are you saying?"

"I'm saying this is all happening really fast."

"What does that mean, Bria?" His anger comes through loud and clear.

"It means I need to stop."

"For good?" Anguish replaces the anger on his beautiful face.

I grab his hand. "No, not for good, but I need time to think, to process everything. I want a career, Reed. I don't want to be just a baby machine."

"But you said last night, the two girls and a boy…."

"I know, and I do want them, and I want them with you, but I'm only twenty-two."

"Do you love me?"

"With everything I've got."

"And you want to marry me."

"Absolutely."

"But you don't want to have babies with me."

"I *do*, just not now. I'm not that girl, Reed."

"What girl?" His voice is low with an edge of anger. I'm fucking this up, but deep down, I know it's not right for me.

"The type of girl who gets married and immediately starts popping out the kids. That's not me."

"So what does this mean?" he asks, defeated.

"I just want us to take a breath. We've gone from strangers to planning our wedding in a week, Reed. That's just crazy."

"But I love you."

"I know, and I love you, but even you've got to admit this has been fast."

"I don't give a fuck," he says, grabbing my shoulders.

"I just need a minute."

"Are we breaking up?"

"No!" I rush to reassure him. "I just need to catch my breath. You blew me away, Reed Ryan, and now I just need to get my bearings back."

"So we're not breaking up?" he asks again, seeming to need clarification.

"No, honey, we're not. I love you, you love me, but you've gone speeding off up the track. Just give me a minute to catch up, okay?" I put my hand over his on my shoulder, and give it a squeeze.

"Okay." He nods. "I can do that."

I smile and squeeze his hand again. "Thank you. Um, do you know what Mav, Jax, and Liam's schedules are like today?"

I really don't want to do this now, but it can't wait.

"Um, they um," Reed mumbles and my heart constricts at the pain I'm causing him. "They, er, have morning workouts and then Mav and Jax usually go to our training compound and tool around and um, Liam might go as well sometimes."

I feel like a total bitch for asking for this, but it has to be done. "Do you think you could call them and ask them to come here instead? They need media training, and since I don't have class today, I was hoping we could do it now."

Reed nods. "Right, I'll text them and ask."

We dress silently and go over to the diner for breakfast. It's a sombre affair. I've hurt Reed and I *hate* that fact, but I have to stay true to me too.

A little while later, the three youngest Ryan brothers traipse into the diner.

Jax slinks into the booth and Liam pushes him over. "What's up, sis?" The name causes my heart to clench. "Reed said you wanted to see us."

"Well, you know I've come on board as Ryan Racing's PR rep, and in that role I'm in charge of media relations. Our relationship with the press is crucial and so is the need for you to know how to talk to them, behave with them, and control the image you project to the public."

"Media training," Mav surmises.

"Exactly. The plan here is to make you guys more professional, and in doing so we'll hopefully attract the attention of sponsors and the like, which will increase cash flow and only mean good things for the team and family as a whole." It's easier to talk if I keep it professional, but seeing Reed so down guts me.

Liam and Mav nod and Jax shoots me a cheesy grin.

"This is really your thing, huh, sis?" Jax asks.

"What I've spent years and countless dollars training for."

Liam kisses the tips of his thumb and index finger and points to the sky.

"You think?" Mav asks.

"Who else?" Liam asks. "*How* else?"

"Eh, point taken." Mav tilts his head.

"Fits," Jax adds.

I watch the exchange utterly clueless. "What was all that about?" I ask.

"It's something we do to remember our ma and nan," Reed says, his voice flat, "if we want to thank them for something."

"So why did you do it just then?" I ask.

"Because they must have been working overtime when they sent you to us."

His words cut me to the quick and it takes all I have not to break down and bawl right there.

"Right." I clear my throat. "Well, if you guys are good, we've a lot of work to do."

"Right you are, sister-boss," Jax says and pushes Liam out of the booth. He sweeps an arm out. "Lead the way."

We grab Pop on our way to the big house, taking Chris with us, and get settled. I take a deep breath.

"So, PR 101…."

CHAPTER TWENTY-TWO

REED

It takes all my self-control, while Bria talks us through her PR spiel, not to throw her over my shoulder, carry her to our room, and make sweet, sweet love to her all day. But I don't even know if I'm allowed to do that anymore. I thought we were all good last night when she started talking about kids. I mean, she brought them up! Sure, I was *thinking* about them but she was the one with the plans. I'm so far out of my league here. I thought chicks liked when you started talking about weddings and babies and shit. Figures I would pick the one that doesn't.

Her sweet voice lures me back to the present, and I've gotta hand it to her, the girl knows her stuff. It drives me crazy that when she refers to Ryan Racing it's always we and us, not you.

She's a part of this, one of us, in a professional way anyway. But is that what she really wants? "A minute to catch her breath." What the fuck does that even mean?

"The first thing you've got to keep in mind with the media is they're going to try to look for a way to twist your words and read into your answers, make things that aren't a big deal big, etcetera, etcetera." We all nod. It's killing me to sit here and pretend nothing's wrong.

"The best thing to do is give short, simple answers, and no more 'no comments.' it makes it seem like you have something to hide. A reporter might ask a question you don't like. For example: do we think the rivalry with Devil Racing is affecting our performance? We all know it's bull, but they want to get a rise out of you. They want a reaction. A simple 'we're focusing on our own race' will suffice. Please refrain from taking shots at Hunter David and Devil Racing or anyone else, got it?" Again, we all nod.

"I'd prefer you not duck questions. It'll only draw attention to an issue you don't want to talk about. Just keep it simple, short, and about us, how *we're* racing, what *we're* focused on; no one else comes into it. They don't affect us and we're not going to give them free publicity."

We all look at each other, nodding and smiling. She gets it and it kills me a little more. This girl was born to be a Ryan, to marry one and give birth to a whole heap, but it feels like she's pulling away. Fuck, I know she didn't even say that but it doesn't stop me from rubbing my chest to ease the ache that's taken up residence.

"Specifically in relation to the explosion, we're not

allowed to say anything to the media. It could be seen as interfering in the police investigation. In this case, we say we're shocked and look forward to getting back on the track. We're cooperating with race officials and the police. If any charges are laid and the case proceeds to court, we'll also be limited in what we can say, but I'll be here and we can cross that bridge when we get to it. Most of the reporters know this, but they'll still try and get something out of you."

"Like Bob the c— clown," Pop says, spying Chris in the corner playing.

"Right. For the most part, I'll be with you, but I can't be everywhere all the time. The most serious press requests will go through me and I will be there." For us, but will she be for me? It doesn't escape my notice that not so long ago, I never would've reached this stage in a relationship, or even been involved in a relationship to begin with. I know I need to give her the space she's looking for, but it's so fucking hard.

"You sure you're okay with not being paid?" Pop asks. "This is a big role you've taken on, a lot of work."

My girl, and she still *is* my girl, flashes Pop a kind smile. "Ryan Racing is a family business, right?"

Pop nods. "And I'm family, right?" My heart soars at her words.

Again, Pop nods. "So there we go."

"But—" Pop begins.

"No buts, I'm family. These guys"—she gestures to me and my brothers—"don't get paid, do they?"

"No, but—"

"So why am I different? Reed and I have a future. I have a

future with Ryan Racing I hope, so I don't see the difference." It warms me that despite her pause button, she thinks we still have a future.

"Pop," I say.

He turns to me. "You know she deserves to be paid, Reed."

I nod. "She does, and so do these guys. Look." I stare straight into her eyes, leaving her in no doubt. "I *will* be making Bria a part of this family. She'll be mine to love and look after, so let her return the favour. We have no problems using Liam, Mav, and Jax's talents, no problem using Park and me before them, so let's use all of our family's talents. PR is Bria's." Because she *will* be a Ryan, I add silently. I know my good thing and I'm not letting her go. I'll give her a minute, but I refuse to let her get away.

"Fine," Pop agrees, "but this means you're stuck with us, all of us," he says to Bria.

She beams. "I think I can handle that." I smile at her and squeeze her hand.

She throws us some practice questions and does some more fine-tuning before Pop has to go back to the diner for the lunch rush.

"Pop," she says in a quiet voice, "I wonder if you could take Chris with you. This next part is a bit… sensitive."

"Oh right, come on, buddy." He holds out his hand, which my nephew dutifully takes.

"Okay," Bria says after they've walked out the door, "this bit is probably not suitable for young ears."

"You gonna be talking to us about sex?" Jax asks and wiggles his eyebrows.

"I am," Bria says, deadly serious.

"Uh oh," Mav says under his breath.

"You guys might think that I'm trying to ruin your fun. I swear I'm not, but you guys, all going well, will have a spotlight thrust upon you and that comes with certain… benefits. I'm not saying don't partake in these benefits, but be careful. Unless those benefits are illegal, in which case I will cut off your balls and keep them in a jar by my bedside, you got me?" We nod solemnly.

She continues, "Okay. Girls. Liam, I apologise for this, and Reed, if you get any ideas, I will kill you."

"No worries, angel," I say and kiss her cheek. She's the only girl for me and so she has nothing to worry about.

"Please, for the love of God, don't tape anything, or have sex in a public place where people can see you. We don't need that getting out. Sponsors don't tend to like those sorts of things. Also, use condoms. Don't trust that the girl you're with is clean and on birth control. This next bit might sound odd, but go with me. Use condoms you've bought yourself. A pinprick is almost undetectable but easy to do. We don't need some girl coming out of the woodwork claiming you knocked her up then left her and your child to fend for themselves. On that same line, take your used condoms with you. Don't leave them in her rubbish, or somewhere she can go and pick them up. If taking it with you isn't an option, and I know this is gross, wash it out and then toss it. We don't need some nutjob using a used condom as a turkey baster."

"Oh fuck," Jax says.

"I know, and I'm sorry, but if all goes well, your profile

will start building and some women will see you as a pay cheque. I don't want that to happen to you, to the child, or this family. I love Chris, and I know you guys do too, but we don't need another Emma situation but with a bigger media spotlight."

"Fair enough," Liam says, and Jax and Mav nod.

"Liam, I know you don't hide your sexuality. I certainly wouldn't hide a man as fine as Mason either, sorry, honey,"— she pats my knee and I grab her hand and lace it with mine— "but I don't think we need to flaunt it. I don't want anything to detract from your racing. What do you think?"

"Fine with me," he says.

"I don't want to ignore or hide it, but it's not a big deal. You're gay. It has nothing to do with how you perform on the track. You're not a gay rider. You're the series-leading rider, end of story."

"Sounds good, sis."

"Okay, so now the awkward part is out of the way, here's the stuff we can have fun with."

Jax lets out a whoop.

"I set up professional Facebook, Twitter, and Instagram accounts for you three and Ryan Racing last night. These accounts are not for personal use. No talking to friends or flirting with girls, giving out personal information, or confronting keyboard jockeys. These are a way to give fans a glimpse into your life in a manner we control," she says when she catches Jax and Mav grinning at each other like idiots.

"Please keep swearing to a minimum. Obscene, insulting, derogatory, and inflammatory material is not to be posted and/

or commented on. I'll be updating the Ryan Racing pages and checking on yours. If you're not sure, don't post it. Once it's been posted, even if you delete it later, people will still see it, screenshot it, and share it from there. I don't want you to be angels but I do want you to be sensible. What we're aiming for here is to give people a glimpse into your lives outside the contrived media spotlight, a behind-the-scenes look if you will. Post stuff like you doing your morning workouts, without your shirts if you want." Jax and Mav wiggle their eyebrows. "This is all about self-promotion, so promote," Bria says.

"Post videos of you training, trying new tricks, or even just tooling around, stuff that makes you look good but at the same time, down to earth and normal. People like to relate to their idols. They like to feel a part of something."

We nod.

"But don't go over the top. We're not the Kardashians, so the world doesn't need to know what you're doing every minute of every day. Just be sensible. We're going to build something here. We're going to make something of this team and give those bigwigs a run for their money, but we can't do that if I'm putting out fires you guys start. If you're not sure, ask me. If a reporter is hassling you, refer them to me. This is my job now. Any questions?"

Jax raises his hand and Bria shoots him a glare. "Not that I doubt your commitment to our cause, dear sister-boss, but have you considered how you're going to tear yourself away from our big bro over there long enough to deal with our shit?"

"First of all," Bria says in a stern voice, "there will be no shit for me to deal with, only business, right?" All three of my brothers nod like the good boys Bria wants them to be. "Good. And second, I'm a talented woman. You don't need to worry about Reed and me."

So it's just me who'll be worrying about us. Great idea, leave it to the manwhore. Not that I *was* a manwhore, but you know… I should be glad she's still talking about us, right?

Jax shoots me a cheesy grin. I flip him the bird and mutter, "Fuckstick," under my breath.

"So you guys are good with all this? Think you can do it?"

"Don't worry, sis," Mav says as he gets up. "We got this, and if not, we've got you."

She nods. "I'm always here."

"Except when you're in Reed's bed," Jax says.

She looks over at me and smiles sadly.

Quietly the three of them file out of the house.

"Angel," I say quietly.

"I think I should go," she says, and my heart breaks.

"You don't have to."

"I think it's best if I do." She gets up and I follow her.

"Please, Bria."

"It's not over. We're not breaking up. I still love you. I just need a little time and space, some time for my head to catch up to my heart."

I take her in my arms. She doesn't fight me, and I don't know if it makes it easier or harder. "I love you so much, Bria. You're my whole world."

"And you're mine."

"So why are you doing this? Why are you pulling away from

me?" I'm on the cusp of sounding whiney. Fuck, who am I kidding? I'm already there, but this woman makes me behave irrationally.

"I'm not pulling away from you. I'm just getting myself together. We'll talk soon." And with a quick kiss, she's gone.

CHAPTER TWENTY-THREE

BRIA

The rest of the week passes in a blur. A miserable blur. The more I sit around and sulk, the more I realise how ridiculous I'm being.

A super-hot, super-loving guy wants me to have his kids. What's the big deal? Reed won't leave me hanging, nor will he expect me to give up my career to raise our kids. And really, twenty-two isn't like *young,* young. If we wait until my shot wears off in November, by the time the baby comes, if I were to get pregnant straight away, I'll be twenty-three, and it might be nice to still be young and have a family. Pop and Pa must have been fairly young when they had kids and that worked out well, and my parents were only a few years older than I am now when they had me…. It's not like I can't see myself with a baby; I can. Yes, everything with Reed has happened fast, but none of it is anything that I don't want, and that's the kicker. I *want* Reed, I *want* to be a part of his family. I *want* to have his children, *our* children, and if it happens sooner rather than later, then so be it.

Grayson and I are lounging on the couch, me trying to work up the courage to go and see Reed, when a knock on the door gets us out of our stupor. It opens, inviting possibly the most annoying girl in the world into our space.

"Ladies," Jane Spencer says in her sugary-sweet voice.

"Jane," Gray and I all but grunt.

"We were thinking that it's been a while since we all went out and caught up and with exams just around the corner, now is really the time."

"Who and what are you talking about?" Gray asks irritably.

Jane ignores the tone of Grayson's question and soldiers on, "Me, Melody, Kimmy, Lana, and Amy were thinking we should go out for dinner, just to catch up."

"Why?" Grayson asks with genuine confusion.

"Because we're friends, silly," Jane says as if she's stating the obvious.

"Oh right, how could I forget?" Gray rolls her eyes.

I smother a laugh. "And where were you thinking for this catch-up?" I ask.

"Well," Jane says, moving to the edge of her seat, "we've been in this town for four years, and it suddenly occurred to us that none of us have seriously made a play for one of the Ryan boys, which is crazy because they're seriously H.O.T."

169

"Uh-huh," I say through clenched teeth. There's no way in *hell* one of those plastic bitches is getting within a metre of *my* family without me.

"Anyway, we heard Reed has a girlfriend now, which is absolutely ludicrous. I mean, he's a Ryan. Everyone knows they have major mummy issues and will never settle down." It takes everything I have to restrain myself.

Beside me, Gray takes my hand and squeezes tight. I squeeze back to let her know that it's okay. That I'm okay. I know what Reed and I have, and some bimbo won't convince me otherwise.

"So anyway, we thought we'd go there tonight and see if we can't snag us one."

"Huh," Grayson says, nodding.

It doesn't escape my notice that there are five Ryans and five in Jane's little group. Clearly Gray and my roles will be to make sure their cars get home safely.

"Sounds like fun," I say, and Gray's head whips to me. She opens her mouth and I squeeze her hand in warning.

"Yeah, fun," she agrees, without any sign of enthusiasm.

"Great!" Jane says and bounces in her seat. "We were thinking of leaving here at six."

"Perfect, we'll see you then," I say, and smile sweetly at her.

She beams at us then dances her way out of our room.

"What the fuck are you playing at?" Grayson asks me once the door's closed.

"It's Monday night."

"So?"

"So the Ryans are having their usual Monday night review tonight."

"Oh," she says, and I can tell she gets it. "You, my friend, are an evil genius."

I rub my hands together. "I'm just working with what God gave me." We burst out laughing.

"But are you okay going there? I thought you and Reed…."

"I just needed a minute, but I'm good now, and if you think I'm going to let the love of my life be around those Barbies while I sit around here making myself miserable, obsessing over Reed and my relationship, then you don't know me at all," I say, getting up.

"That's my girl."

"Eh, I'm more Reed's, but I'm sure he won't have any objections to sharing me," I say and we burst out laughing. It's time I went home.

CHAPTER TWENTY-FOUR

REED

I haven't seen Bria in almost a week. Every day she'll send me texts telling me she loves me and every day I tell her how much I miss her, miss *us* and pray that she comes back to me, that "her heart catches up to her head". Whatever the fuck that means. I've been miserable without her and moody as fuck. My brothers have wisely steered clear, but Chris keeps asking where Aunty Bria is. It slays me every time he does. I find myself smelling her clothes, her sweet, fruity scent trapped in the fabric, torturing me. I've even driven past the uni a couple of times, hoping that I'll get lucky and see her, but I never do.

I'm hit with more reminders as the door to the diner opens and in walk five overly made-up girls wearing scraps for clothes. My heart stops as behind them are Grayson and Bria. She's even more beautiful than I remember. I shoot her a quizzical look as she stands there, making no effort to come to me. My fears are eased when she smiles, shakes her head, rolls her eyes, and shrugs. Next to her Grayson shoots me a wicked smile and winks.

Jax and Mav's heads have whipped up at the new arrivals. I turn to each of them and make a slashing motion against my neck. Bria may have needed time to "get herself together" but I know my girl, and these aren't friends of hers. My brothers look at me quizzically—apparently there's a lot of that going around—before they notice Bria and Grayson and nod.

I go over to greet them.

"Ladies," I say. Bria makes no effort to greet me but throws me her mischievous smile so I go with it even though I'm dying to go to her.

"You're Reed, right?" one of them asks me, twisting her bleached-blonde hair around her finger.

"I am, and you are?"

"Kimmy." She comes and presses herself to me. I shoot Bria a look and she laughs. Okay then.

"I heard you have a girlfriend," Kimmy says.

"I do."

She laughs as do the four other girls with her. "That's funny."

"And why's that?" I know my reputation's not great, but geez, ladies, cut me some slack.

"Because," another one says, sidling up to my other side, "you're Reed Ryan, notorious playboy. No woman can ever give you all you need." She runs her finger down my chest. I grab her hand and throw it away from me. I can feel the steam coming out of my ears.

Just then Mav and Jax come up to the group, shoving the Barbies aside and embracing Grayson and Bria.

"Hey, sis, hey, Grayson," they say, and hug and kiss them both. I don't miss the extra attention they give Bria.

"Sis?" the second Barbie asks Bria.

"Bria's Reed's girl," Jax says, like it's the most obvious thing in the world, and I smile.

"*You're* the new girlfriend?" she asks Bria.

"Yeah, Jane, I am," Bria says as she pushes through the crowd to me and her rightful place.

"Hey, angel, I missed you so fucking much," I whisper before bending down to kiss the shit out of her. "And for the record," I say when we break apart, "Bria's not the *new* girlfriend. She's the *only* one I'll ever have." I'm dying to do more than kiss her, but I'll wait. I don't want to scare her off again.

"Bullshit," Jane says.

"Afraid not," Jax says. "My big brother is in love and off the market."

"Hey, Bria girl," Pa says as he passes by. He gives her a kiss on the cheek and clasps Grayson's hand.

"Get it now?" Mav asks.

That seems to snap them out of their trance and they turn their attention to Mav and Jax. Their eyes light up when Liam and Chris come out.

"Aunty Bria! Aunty Grayson!" Chris shouts, and runs into Bria's arms as she bends down to pick him up. Liam greets both the girls with a kiss, and Jane's eyes light up.

Bria sees her and chuckles. So does Jax.

He slings an arm over Grayson's shoulders. "Let's go somewhere more comfortable, shall we?" Grayson shoots him a look.

"A table, I meant a table," he insists, holding up a hand.

Bria goes to follow them but I grab her hand and tug her to me. "I hate to be the needy chick in this relationship," I say and she chuckles, "but what does this mean?" I refuse to let myself get carried away, not when there's this much at stake. This girl is my heart and I refuse to fuck things up again.

"It means I'm here to talk footy with my family."

"Yeah?"

"Yeah," she says and leans up to kiss me.

"But—"

"Let's talk about it later. The shows will be starting soon." She pulls me over to the table with the others. I can't believe she's here, but that's all that matters; the rest can come later.

I pull out a chair for her but when Jane, Kimmy, and the other evil Barbies try to sit down, Chris loses it.

"You can't sit here," he says.

"Excuse me?" one of the background Barbies says.

"You can't sit here," he repeats.

"You've got to be kidding me," Jane says as she sidles up to Liam.

"You heard the kid," Mav says.

Liam laughs and sits down, ignoring Jane's attempt to catch his eye. She takes this as a personal affront and huffs off to a nearby table. We all high-five Chris. Mav goes and grabs Chris's dinner while Jax gets drinks and nibbles before the game.

"So, your friends are nice," I say to Bria.

She snorts. "No, they're not, but Gray and I wanted to have a little fun."

"You two are evil geniuses," Mav says, putting down Chris's mac and cheese.

"As much as I'd love to take credit, it was all Miss Adams here," Grayson says as Bria makes sure some of Chris's dinner makes it to his mouth.

"So fucking perfect," I whisper into her ear, and she smiles. God, I missed her.

With Bria's help, Chris manages to eat most of his dinner, then curls into her chest and falls asleep.

"I still can't get used to seeing Chris with a woman," Mav says, watching him sleep.

"I know. It's weird, isn't it?" Jax asks.

"But not surprising," Liam adds.

"Nah," they agree.

"Fuck that was freaky," Grayson says.

"And what's that, darlin'?" Jax asks her.

"The way you're all so in synch with each other."

"It's all part of the Ryan charm," Jax says and winks at her.

"We should get him to bed," Bria says. I nod and help her up.

Jax, Mav, and Liam get up and kiss Chris on the forehead, as do Pa and Pop when we walk past them.

"We're just putting him to bed," I say to Park as we pass the kitchen.

"How much did he eat?" he asks.

"Most of it. Bria made sure it went in his mouth, not on the floor."

"Thanks, sis," he says and kisses her on the forehead. "I'll be there in a minute. Just gotta prep the rest of this food. Shove it in after *360*," he reminds me.

"I got it, Park. We've done this before, remember?"

"Except for the times you forgot and then the food isn't done until after midnight."

"That was one time!" Beside me, Bria giggles.

"Come on, let's get the kid to bed." It feels so normal, so *right* for her to be here.

I open the door for Bria and she lays Chris down gently, brushing his mop of brown hair off his face.

"Do you think our kids will be this cute?" she asks.

"Er…." I stumble.

"It's okay, Reed. I'm not going to run again."

"Are you sure? I *really* don't want to think that I've got you back only for you to pull away from me again."

She gets up and wraps her arms around my neck, my hands automatically finding her hips. Man, does she feel good.

"I'm so sorry I pulled away from you. I've been miserable the past few days but I needed to get my head in the right space."

"And did you?"

She nods.

"What happened?"

"I freaked. We slipped into domestic bliss so quickly, and then when you started talking about having babies straight away…."

177

"We don't have to, you know. If you want to wait, I'm fine with it. Whatever you want. I'm at your mercy."

She smiles and my heart warms. "I don't want you at my mercy. I just had to reconcile myself to being in a couple and opening myself up to couple things."

"Like having my babies."

"Like having *our* babies," she corrects.

"And are you reconciled?" I ask. "Opened up to these 'couple things'?" I make air quotes.

She nods. "I am."

"And?"

"And I've come to the conclusion that anytime you want to let your guys loose to do their job, my egg will be ready and waiting for them."

I swear my heart bursts out of my chest. "Yeah?"

"Uh–huh. I love you, Reed Cooper Ryan. I love your family, and I want to be a part of it and have my own part of it."

"You want babies with me?"

"I really do." She cups my face. "I love you, Reed Ryan, and I can't wait to be a part of your family, whenever you see fit to do that. I think the biggest problem was getting my head around all this happening so soon and being afraid you were going to chain me to the bed and make me keep popping out the kids."

I open my mouth to interrupt but she places a finger on my lips. "I know you wouldn't ever do that to me, but I was scared. I don't want to be just a baby-making machine. And the more I thought about it, I realised that that's not what you want for me either. I want to have a career. That *together* we're going to grow Ryan Racing."

"Yeah, we are." I bring her closer to me.

"Plus, I'm a talented woman and can have it all," she jests, wriggling her brows and laughing.

I grin. "So true," I say, kissing her neck.

"And if not, then we can always get Jax to babysit. He owes us for all the heart attacks I'm certain he's going to give me."

I laugh.

"I missed you so much."

"I missed you so much, too, and I'm sorry if I hurt you. I didn't mean to and it's the last thing I ever wanted to do—"

I press a finger to her lips. "It's okay, baby, you did what you needed to do and you're here now, back where you belong, so don't worry about it."

In his sleep, Chris cries out, and Bria rushes to his bed, pushing his hair off his face and kissing his forehead.

"And our kids will be cuter," I say, picking her up and wrapping my arms around her again. "Park's a good-looking fella but he's got squinty eyes and wonky ears. Now me, I'm pretty damn perfect and any flaw I have will be fixed by your perfectness."

"My perfectness?" she scoffs.

"Uh-huh," I say and move her hair out of the way so I can kiss her neck. God I missed her *so* much.

"I'm not perfect," she says breathlessly.

"Maybe not, but you are for me—to me. Do you know how many girls would go apeshit over what those girls were doing in the diner?"

"I'll admit I didn't like it, but I know what we have and

I'm confident in that. If these past few days have taught me anything, it's that what we have is solid and can survive anything we throw at it, even if it's ourselves."

"You should be. You're the only girl for me, Bria. You'll be my wife and the mother of my children, and I can't wait to spend the rest of my life with you."

She turns in my arms. "I can't wait either."

Our kiss starts off slow and passionate but quickly turns heated. I've just moved her against the wall when Park walks in.

"Not here, fuckstick," he says, and shoves me off Bria.

She laughs. "Sorry, Parker, we got carried away."

"Yeah, yeah, thanks for looking after him."

"No worries. Chris is adorable."

"Yeah, when he's sleeping. Anyway, you guys should get back. The shows are about to start."

"We'll check ya later," I say and slap Park's shoulder.

"Don't forget—"

"After *360*, I know."

"I got him, Parker, don't worry," Bria says.

"Thanks, sis, it's good to have you back." He kisses her on the cheek and then we're heading back to the diner.

"Does Park miss out every Monday?" she asks.

"Nah, we take turns. This is his Monday."

"I love how Chris is the centre of your world."

"We're big on family obviously, and the kid had such a fucked-up time with his mum we just want to make sure he knows he's loved."

"Well, you certainly do that."

"Like my pop says, we know when we've got a good thing. Chris is a good thing for this family, as are you." I bring her in front of me, her back to my front, and latch on to her neck again.

She squeals and tries to escape my arms but I hold on tightly and start tickling her. For as long as I live, I'm never gonna let her go. Eventually we manage to make it back to our table, which is thankfully still Barbie free, and I pull her on my lap. She rests back on me and I wrap my arms around her and rest them on her stomach. I seriously can't wait until it's round with my child. But maybe I should tie her down first, make sure she can't get away again. Which means I'll probably need to start looking at rings.

I smile at the thought.

Out of nowhere Bria shouts, "That was *such* a shit call! That was so a hold!"

"What the fuck?" I ask, snapping out of my matrimonial bubble.

"There was a blatant hold on Roo and the fucking umps did nothing as per usual and those chumps"—she motions to the panel on the screen—"don't see anything wrong with it!" Bria exclaims angrily.

"You're a footy fan?" I ask, surprised.

"Nah, just the Saints. Oh, come on, give us a break!" she yells.

Beside us Grayson laughs. "She's a diehard Saints fan. She didn't tell you?"

I shake my head.

"Fucking typical." Bria hits the table in frustration.

"Dude, you are one lucky motherfucker," Jax says with a smile on his face. "Not only is she hot and kind *and* Chris loves her *and* she's going to keep our arses out of media jail"—he gestures to Liam and Mav—"but she's a footy fan? Share the love man, c'mon!"

"I'm sorry?" I flash him a cheesy grin.

"Yeah, really sorry I bet."

"Oh, yeah!" Bria cheers as they show Josh Bruce going up for a speccy and high-fives all of Pop and Pa's friends. She makes her way back to me, straddles me, takes my face in her hands, and kisses me deeply, her tongue invading my mouth.

"Happy?" I ask when she releases my mouth.

"Dude, you have no idea," she says breathlessly, whether it's from our kiss or the excitement of the mark, I don't know, but I'd like to think it was us.

"Oh, I think I do." I hold back my desire to thrust my erection against her, but I'm pretty sure it nudges her anyway.

She pats my face fondly. "Oh, honey, I'm afraid you're going to have to hold it. My boys were on fire and I've got to hear this. I can't possibly leave."

I groan. This is going to be worse than sitting through her media training. One thing I do know, I better get that ring quick.

CHAPTER TWENTY-FIVE

BRIA

Reed and I barely made it out of bed the next day. I begrudgingly got up the following day because I had class and had to go so I could have Friday off and we could get to the NRS's next stop. I want to get there early so I can scope out the media scene and see how it operates. It shouldn't be too bad. I've been studying the names and photos of the journos I'll have to deal with, and then it's just a matter of a few press releases to recap each session and the day overall.

On our way back to Booker, Reed and I stop in on my parents for our rescheduled visit. I did call to warn them I was coming home and bringing someone with me and their interest is piqued. I have dated in the past, but mainly local boys who my parents already knew so I've never had to do the whole bringing-home-the-boyfriend thing. Plus, it's not like Reed has ever been brought home so, as always, we're in this together.

I direct him to my family home and he pulls into the drive. It's about 200 metres from the road to the house, and then he turns off the engine and we sit.

"You okay?" he asks.

"I'm fine, honey. It's just I'm looking at the house I grew up in and for the first time, it's more than that. It's the house I'll marry you in."

"Jesus, Bria, now I'm hard and about to meet your parents," he groans.

I laugh. "Sorry." I pat his cheek. "Do you want me to do anything?" I reach for him.

"You're not getting me off metres from your parents. Just give me a sec." He closes his eyes, rests his head against the headrest, and exhales a large breath.

After a moment, he says, "Okay, let's go."

He comes around, opens my door, and we walk hand in hand to the house. I don't even have to knock before the door is opening and my mum rushes out.

"Darling!" she says and hugs me tightly. Reed lets go of my hand and smiles fondly, watching Mum and me.

"Hey, Mum," I say.

"I missed you," she says.

"I missed you too."

She reluctantly lets me go and notices Reed standing next to me. I retake his hand.

"Mum, this is Reed Ryan, my er... I would say boyfriend

but boyfriend isn't enough," I say, looking up at Reed. "My everything?" I ask him. He smiles at me and shrugs. "We'll go with my everything."

I look back at Mum and she's beaming.

"It's nice to meet you, Mrs Adams," Reed says, extending his hand for her to shake.

She ignores it and spreads her arms wide for a hug. Reed smiles and embraces her.

"It's lovely to meet you, Reed. Welcome to the family." I think my heart explodes. I'm so glad Mum has accepted Reed so quickly. She doesn't know how long we've been together but I spoke to her a few days before we got together so she probably has a vague idea.

They let go and we walk into the house where Dad is in the living room.

"Dad," I say, getting his attention.

"Hey, baby girl," he says and gets up to give me a hug.

We break apart and I grab Reed's hand again.

"Dad, this is Reed Ryan."

"Her *everything*," Mum chimes in.

Dad raises an eyebrow and I smile shyly.

"Looks like you and me are going to have to have a little chat," Dad says to Reed.

"Yes, sir," he replies solemnly, but they shake hands and Dad smiles.

We all sit and I curl into Reed, my feet tucked up beneath me, my head on his shoulder, his arm around me resting on my hip.

"I love you," I whisper.

"I love you," he replies and kisses me chastely.

Mum and Dad watch on with smiles on their faces.

Reed speaks up. "Mr and Mrs Adams," he begins.

"Aaron and Lacey, please," Dad says and Reed nods.

"Aaron and Lacey, I know Bria and my relationship has evolved fast. It may seem a bit crazy to you that we're this serious so soon but I want to assure you I love your daughter with all my heart. I promise I'll do everything I can to take care of her and keep her safe and happy for the rest of my life."

Dad raises an eyebrow at Reed's forthrightness. Mum just smiles.

"Glad to hear it, son," Dad says.

"Why don't you tell us about yourself, Reed?" Mum says.

He smiles and relaxes, squeezing me quickly.

"I'm the second of five boys. My family own a diner and garage in Booker, and I work there as well as with our racing team."

"Racing team?" Mum asks.

"Ryan Racing?" Dad asks. "That's you?"

"Yes, sir, my family."

"Do you race?" Mum asks.

"Not anymore, ma'am. I retired a few years ago."

"Injury?" Dad asks.

"Politics," Reed replies. "My younger brother Liam is racing in the National Racing Series for us now, and my two youngest brothers, Mav and Jax, are working towards Extreme Games invitations."

"What do they do?" Mum asks.

"Freestyle motocross and BMX."

"Tricks on bikes," I tell her.

"Are they good?"

"Liam is leading the standings and Mav and Jax should be getting their invites soon."

"The invites in themselves are an indication of talent," I tell her. "Only the best of the best get invites."

"And there's a future in this, a living for you and my daughter?" Dad asks.

"Yes, sir, even more so with Bria on board."

"On board?"

"I'm doing Ryan Racing's PR. That's where we were yesterday and today, with Liam and the team."

"And she's doing a fantastic job. She's got my brothers and the team set up on all kinds of social media, got press releases out, and sat us all down for media training the other day. She's the ultimate professional and I have no doubt she's going to help us get far."

"Well that's wonderful. Let's get some lunch shall we?" Mum says and we get up to go into the kitchen. Apparently, she's unfazed by our relationship.

Mum has prepared a fantastic meal and afterwards I take Reed out to the garden. It has three terraces leading up to the gazebo.

"It's beautiful," he says, standing behind me, his chin resting on my shoulder.

"Good enough for a wedding?" I ask.

"If this is what you want."

"I just want you." I snuggle into him.

"You got me, angel, anywhere, anyhow."

I turn in his arms. "I love you and I can't wait to marry you one day."

"I can't wait to marry you either," Reed says, and excitement shoots through me.

"You're something else, Reed Ryan."

"I could say the same of you, Bria Adams, but all that matters is you're mine." He leans down to kiss me.

We're interrupted by my dad. We break apart and I smile at him from my spot against Reed's chest.

"It's time you and I had a chat," he says and Reed nods.

"Be nice," I warn before giving Reed a quick kiss and heading inside.

CHAPTER TWENTY-SIX

REED

I watch Bria go into the house and turn and face Aaron, squaring my shoulders.

"No need to worry, son. I can see you love my daughter. I just want to chat."

I release my breath. "I do, sir. She's unlike anyone I've ever known."

He nods. "She's a special girl."

I smile. "She's so much more than that. I don't know if there are words."

"You might be right."

"I wanted to talk to you as well," I say, biting the bullet.

"You asking for her hand?"

"I will be. Not right now, but soon, and I wanted to ask for your blessing."

"Not my permission?"

"No, sir. With all due respect, I'm not going to ask for your permission because Bria knows her own mind and is no one's property. The decision to marry me rests with her, but I would like your blessing for me to ask her." I twist my hands nervously.

Aaron smiles and I relax. "You seem like a good man, Reed, and you respect my daughter. That's all a father can ask for. You'll learn that when you have your own kids. You are planning on having kids, aren't you?"

"Yes, sir, we are. Bria wants two or three. I'm leaning towards three or four, but I won't be the one carrying them so I'll leave it up to her."

"Having kids is one of the best things you can do. You realise your life is no longer about you, it's about something bigger, it's a life the two of you are creating. It's truly magical"

"Bria's going to be a wonderful mum. She's already a fantastic aunty to my nephew."

"He calls her aunty?"

I nod. "He does. Chris, my nephew, loves Bria. He doesn't take well to women, issues stemming from his own mother, but he took to Bria immediately."

"Your parents like Bria?"

"There's only my dad and grandpa. My nan and ma have both passed, but both Pop and Pa consider her a daughter and granddaughter, and my brothers call her sis. We've well and truly taken Bria in."

"You've had some trouble lately."

I nod. "We have, and unfortunately Bria's been caught up in it." I grimace and clench my fists.

"I can tell you're not happy about that."

"Absolutely not. I hate that she's in the same postcode as danger, but I will do my best to make sure she's not exposed to any more."

"That's all I can ask. I know all this has been out of your control, but I trust you with my girl, Reed."

"Thank you, sir. It means a lot to me."

"She told you about young Roman?"

"Yes, sir."

He shakes his head. "I know he rides for your rivals, but he was a good boy. This, what he's doing, who he's turned into, isn't him."

"Knowing Devil as I do, I know how they can take over and change your priorities."

Aaron nods.

"So you keep an eye on the bikes, huh?" I ask.

"Colt, Roman's father, and I are good friends, grew up next door to each other. I keep an eye out to see if he'll get to ride, but I think now it's probably too late. If we can, Colt and I get together to watch the race."

"We're racing again next weekend. Would you like to come along?"

"I'd like that."

"I would invite Mr Thomas, but with the connection to Devil, I don't think that would be a good idea."

He smiles sadly. "I appreciate the sentiment." He slaps me on the back. "Come on, let's get back to the women."

We go back in and Bria comes to me. I hug her and she stares up at me.

"Okay?" she asks.

"Perfect." I kiss her nose.

"Bria," Lacey says, "you should show Reed around town before it gets dark. The Thomases are coming around for dinner."

Bria looks at me, panicked. "Er, Mum, I don't think it's a good idea for them to meet Reed. Ryan Racing and Rome's team don't get along."

Lacey bites her lip. "Bria," she says softly, "they've asked to see you. And besides, Rome hasn't been home in five years, hasn't spoken to them in nearly that long. They have nothing to do with racing."

"What do you think?" she asks me.

"It's fine. The Thomases have no more control over what their son does than your parents do you, or Pop, me. They're not Hunter," I say quietly.

"Are you sure?"

"I'm not making your parents pick sides. They're friends. It'll be fine."

"Okay, let's go." She takes my hand and leads me out the door.

CHAPTER TWENTY-SEVEN

BRIA

Fuck. Me. What do the Thomases want with me? I know they don't know of my connection to Ryan Racing but I know this goes beyond just wanting to say hi to a friend's daughter.

I take Reed around to all the spots I frequented as a child, a lot of them with Grayson and Rome.

We end up at a park down the street.

"You okay?" Reed asks. He's sitting on a swing and pulls me between his legs.

"This thing with the Thomases, it's got me worried."

"For me?"

"And Grayson. They can't know of my connection to you, but if by some chance they do, I don't want to put you in an awkward situation or inflame tensions."

Reed opens his mouth to speak but I hold up a hand. "I know you guys wouldn't ever hit Hunter and Devil, but they could use me against you."

"Baby, they're your parents' friends. Hear what they have to say. It could be nothing."

"Fuck, Reed…."

He takes my face in his hands. "It'll be okay. I'm here with you. My whole family is with you, no matter what happens."

I bend down to kiss him.

"We better get back," he says, and I sigh.

The Thomases are already at the house when Reed and I get back.

He squeezes my hand. "Just hear them out. I'm here with you, okay?"

I nod. "Thanks, honey." We walk into the house.

My parents and the Thomases are in the living room. I see Colt and Anne and all the good times I had with Rome and Grayson come flooding back. Anne gets up and gives me a hug, a sad smile on her face.

"Hey, Anne," I say.

"Bria darling, how are you?"

"I'm good."

"A man in your life, I see."

I smile. "This is Reed Ryan."

"It's nice to meet you, Mrs Thomas," Reed says.

"You too, Reed. You be good to our Bria, now."

He smiles and chuckles. "I fully intend to, ma'am."

"Colt," I say and hug Rome's dad.

"How you doing, Bria girl?"

"I'm good. This is Reed Ryan." The two men shake hands.

"Ryan as in Ryan Racing?" Colt asks.

"Yes, sir."

"The same Reed Ryan who retired a few years back after all that nasty business with Hunter David?"

"Yes, sir."

Colt shakes his head. "He's no good. The racing series doesn't need someone of his type involved with it. They made a mistake choosing him over you."

"That's kind of you to say, sir."

"You know my boy?"

"No, sir, but my brother Parker has seen him on occasion. He says he has real talent."

"It's a pity he doesn't get to show it. Spent the best years of his career hanging on the coattails of that no-good demon."

This is fascinating conversation and the rest of us are loath to interrupt. It's as I have this thought, Reed and Colt seem to realise we're all listening.

"I'm sorry, we're hogging the conversation," Reed says politely.

"Let's go on through," Mum says, smiling kindly.

Reed takes my hand as we walk into the dining room and pulls my chair out for me. I give him a quick kiss before sitting down.

Mum has made lasagne, garlic bread, and salad, and Reed wolfs it down. My mum is a pretty awesome cook, so I'm quick to clear my plate. We go back into the living room after dinner and I know the dance is done; the moment of truth is here.

"So as you know, we asked to see you," Anne says to me. I nod. "I do."

"And I bet you're wondering why." Again, I nod.

"First off, we want you, both of you," Anne says, gesturing to Reed and me, "to know that we don't approve of Hunter David, his actions, or anything to do with Devil Racing."

"Okay," I say, not knowing where this is going.

"Roman has been in touch with us."

"That's great," I say, still not knowing where this is going.

"He seemed like his old self," Anne continues. "He apologised for everything that's happened during the past five years, all the heartache, the pain.... Roman's back, Bria."

"I'm glad." And call me slow, but I'm still not putting the dots together. I'm genuinely glad Rome has reached out to his family again but I don't know what that has to do with me.

Anne smiles. "He's asked that we get in touch with you and—" She pauses. "—Grayson," she says tentatively.

"Anne—"

She holds up her hand. "Bria, I know the position I'm putting you in, both with Grayson and the Ryans, but he's sorry and he's reaching out. He wants to make things right."

Okay, so now that I know where this conversation's gone, I really wish it could go back.

"Bria," Colt says, getting my attention, "trust me. I know what you're feeling and thinking but please, hear us out, hear *him* out."

"Is he here?" I ask, panicked, looking at Reed. He's solid, showing no emotion. He sees me staring and squeezes my hand reassuringly.

"No, he's not here. He's still in Booker," Anne answers.

I release my breath. "Okay, good."

"He's not a bad man, Bria."

"What does he want?" I ask in a small voice.

"He wants to get back to the old Roman."

"Just like that?"

"He said he wants to leave Devil, that there's some stuff going on there that he doesn't like or support and he wants out." She glances at Reed.

"That'll be tough," Reed says.

"He knows," Colt says, "but he wants to try."

"So why does he want me and Grayson?"

"He wants his friends back, Bria. He wants to know if he leaves Devil, that he'll have something to come back to."

"I can't put Grayson through that again," I say. "He broke her heart and she still hasn't gotten over it."

"Just think about it. That's all we're asking. He's a good boy, Bria, and deep down he's still the boy you grew up with. He lost himself for a while but he's back now and he wants to come home. You and Grayson are his home."

Tears slip down my cheeks and Reed wipes them away.

"What do you think?" I ask him.

"I think it'll be tough to leave Devil and when he does, he'll need support, friends."

"You think I should meet him?"

"If you want to. I can't tell you what to do, baby. I'm sorry."

"What about your family?"

"Roman's not Hunter. We've never really heard of him,

so I don't think there'd be too much hostility, but if you decide you want him back in your life, we'd deal."

"You really think they'd be okay with it?" I can already feel myself leaning towards meeting with him.

"We can bring it up tomorrow at dinner if you want."

"I want to make sure they're okay with it. I know Rome himself hasn't personally victimised you, but he's part of an organisation that has made your life hell."

Reed smiles kindly. "He's your friend. They'll be fine and if they're not, they'll answer to me, okay? Nobody upsets my angel." He winks at me.

"Okay, but no visible bruises. I don't want to have to explain that to the press."

He chuckles and pulls me to his side.

"So can we tell Roman to call?" Anne adds hopefully.

I nod. "But," I start, "if any of the Ryans are uncomfortable, I won't take it any further."

Anne nods. "And Grayson?"

I huff out a breath. How the fuck am I supposed to bring this up with her?

"I'll figure that out once I've met with Rome, *if* I meet with Rome."

Anne relaxes. "Thank you, Bria."

I just nod. I feel like shit, tied up in knots and totally and completely torn as to what to do. I saw first-hand what a perfect couple Rome and Grayson were. I was also there through the utter devastation she felt when Rome left. I know deep down they're meant to be, but how can she trust him again? How can she forget the pain and the heartache he put her through?

These questions swirl through my head making it pound.

"If you'll excuse me," I say.

"Are you okay, baby?" Reed asks, concern written all over his face.

I nod. "I just need some air."

I go up to the gazebo, a place where I plan to have one of the happiest days of my life, and wonder if I'm giving Grayson hers or tearing it away.

CHAPTER TWENTY-EIGHT

REED

"We're sorry," Anne says after Bria's gone. "We didn't mean to cause trouble."

"It's okay," I say. "Bria and I haven't talked much about your son but she has told me about his relationship with Grayson."

"They were perfectly suited for each other, thought the other hung the moon, much like you and Bria."

I smile. Personally, I think the world revolves around Bria, or at least mine does, but I get the point.

"Do you think he can do it?" Colt asks.

"Get out of Devil?"

He nods.

"It'll be tough, *really* tough. Hunter doesn't give up

easily, to that I can testify, but if he's strong and determined he'll make it through. But be prepared."

"For what?"

"I can't say for sure, but threats maybe, vandalism, physical violence definitely. Does Roman have his own apartment?"

Anne shakes her head. "He lives with other guys in Devil."

"He'll need somewhere to go. I don't know his job situation, but if he's working for Devil, then that'll disappear too. I imagine you'd welcome him home but if he wants to stay in Booker, that's something he'll need to think about."

Colt slumps in his seat. "It's a lot to handle."

I nod. "It is, but at least Roman has you and possibly Bria."

"Do you think your family will mind?" Anne asks.

"They'll be sceptical, but it's not in our nature to hold grudges. Time and time again Hunter hits us. He's slashed tyres, stolen merchandise, tried roughing us up at our diner, and I'm sure you've heard about the explosion at our garage the other weekend. We've never hit back, never tried to, and never will. We didn't do anything wrong. This is all Hunter."

"And the guys who are on his team?"

"There're a few guys on the team we know do Hunter's bidding. As far as we know, Roman isn't one of them, which frankly is surprising considering he's been around Devil for so long. What *is* going to be of concern for us is how all this affects Bria, and I assume a lot of *that* will have to do with how this all affects Grayson."

"Jesus," Colt curses quietly.

"I know it's messy, but I understand why he did it. Roman was seventeen, eighteen when he went to Devil?" I'm met with nods. "At that age all you want to do is ride. Get on a bike, impress some people, and bang, you're the next Mick Doohan. That's what Hunter promises guys, all of them talented, but young and impressionable. He promises that if they pay their dues for a few years, eventually they'll get that ride. The lucky ones are let go, the useful ones, for whatever reason, are kept around. Seeing as though Roman isn't thick with Hunter, I can only guess it's because he has real talent."

"Could he still have a career?" Colt asks.

"I don't know enough about him to say but anything's a possibility."

"Thank you for this, Reed. I know it's not a great topic," Anne apologises.

"It's fine. Roman's your family and Bria is mine, just as much as I am part of hers. But if you'll excuse me, I better go check on her."

I'm met with smiles and nods on my way to the garden and up to the gazebo, where Bria is deep in thought.

"You okay?" I ask.

She looks up and when she sees me, smiles.

I fucking love that I can put that look on her face.

"Eh." She shrugs.

I tug her up from her seat, sit down, and pull her on my lap.

"You wanna talk about it?" I ask as she snuggles into my chest, my arms holding her tight.

"Yes and no."

"All right." I kiss the side of her neck.

"Fuck," she exclaims after a while. "What do I do, Reed?"

"I wish I could tell you, baby, but it's something you've gotta work out yourself." She swings around so she's sitting sideways.

"I've been sitting here, in the place where I intend to tie myself to you for the rest of my life, and I know Gray and Rome have the same love we do, but how do I know it's going to stick? That she can trust him again? That *I* can trust him? How can she forget the pain and heartache? I don't want to get them back in touch if he's only going to do it again. She won't survive it, Reed. She barely survived it the first time."

I rub up and down her back. "I know, baby, it's not an easy decision to make, but maybe it'll be easier once you meet with him again."

"You sure your family won't mind?"

"The only thing they'll worry about is how it affects you. We're here for *you*, Bria."

She rests her head on my shoulder. "Will you come with me to meet with Rome?"

"If you want me to. I'll do anything you want me to do, anything you *need* me to do."

"Thank you," she whispers.

"You don't need to thank me. This is all part of my promise to always take care of you."

"I don't want to hurt her, Reed."

"I know, baby, but hear him out and then give her the rundown. Let her make the decision. I know you want to be there to protect and mother everyone; it's part of who you are, but every now and then you have to let people make their own decisions."

"Fuck!"

"I know, but I'm here and we'll get through this together, okay?"

"Okay." She snuggles further into my chest and we sit in silence contemplating the future for two people just like us, but in a wildly different situation.

CHAPTER TWENTY-NINE

BRIA

I get my first text from Rome on our drive back to Booker the next day.

Rome: Hey, Bria, it's Roman. Mum gave me your number. I'd really love it if we could get together sometime.

I read the message and sigh.

"You okay?" Reed asks and grabs my hand.

"I just got a text from Rome."

"What did it say?"

"He'd love it if we could get together sometime."

"What are you going to do?"

"I want to run it by your family. You never know, they might be able to offer some advice for him." I shrug.

"You're not worried about their reaction?"

I shake my head. "Not so much. I know they love me and support me and they're smart enough to realise Rome isn't Hunter." It's true. I know whatever I do the Ryans will support me.

Reed squeezes my hand. "We do support you, no matter what."

"I'm going to tell him I have to talk with a few people and I'll get back to him."

Reed nods. "Sounds good to me."

I text Rome.

Me: Before we meet, I'd like to talk with a few people. I'll get back to you.

He texts back almost immediately.

Rome: Grayson??

Me: No. I don't want to bring her into this just yet. I'm with Reed Ryan and I want to run it by his family.

Rome: The Ryans are good people. I hope this doesn't disrupt your relationship. I just really want my friend back.

"What's he saying?" Reed asks.

I read the message to him.

My phone beeps with another message from Rome.

Rome: I know I have no right to ask this of you and I fucked our friendship up once before but I'm so sorry Bria.

After reading the new message out, I ask, "What do you think?"

"I think at the very least I want to hear what he has to say."

Reed nods and smiles.

"What?" I ask.

"I knew that would be your decision."

I turn to face him. "And why's that, oh wise one?"

"Because that's the kind of person you are, angel. Loving and caring."

"You're still going to come with me to meet with him, right?"

"As long as that's what you want me to do."

I nod. "I do."

"Then I'll be there." He lifts our entwined hands and kisses the back of mine. It amazes me how such a simple touch can quieten my nerves even just a little.

When we're ten minutes from home, my thoughts drift to Gray. "What if Grayson finds out we're talking before I have a chance to explain? She'll never forgive me." I'm silently freaking out. Okay, not so silently.

Reed pulls into his driveway and shuts off the car. He turns to me and cups my face.

"Baby, it'll be fine. If Grayson finds out, you'll explain to her that you wanted to check everything out before involving her. She'll realise that you're only trying to protect her. Let's cross this bridge if and when we come to it, okay?"

I nod, even though thoughts are still running through my head a thousand miles a minute.

"Hmm," he says, and I know he doesn't believe me.

He gets out of the car, comes around to my side, opens my door and throws me over his shoulder.

"Reed!" I squeal and pound his back. "Put me down!"

"Nope," he says as he walks us into the house.

"Reed!" I pound harder this time with a giggle.

"Stop it, you'll fall."

"So help me God, if you drop me, Reed Ryan, I will cut off your balls."

I hear laughter and look to see Liam and Mason sitting in the living room.

"Hey, bro, sis," Liam says.

Reed grunts out a "Hey" but continues to walk us straight to his bedroom. He lays me gently on the bed and undresses me. Every thought in my head flies out as he kisses his way down my body, and proceeds to "distract" me.

"Better?" he asks, wiping his mouth.

"Huh?"

"All those thoughts that were running through your head, they gone now?"

Oh, *that's* what that was about. I lean up to kiss him.

"Yes, thank you, honey."

"It'll all be okay, Bria."

"I know," I say with a yawn.

"Go to sleep, baby. I know you probably didn't get much sleep the past few nights and dinner's not for a while," he says, running his hands up and down my back, lulling me to sleep.

~

I wake to find Reed kissing my neck, his hands all over my body.

"Mmm." I moan and rub myself against him.

"Have a good nap?" he asks from behind me.

"Very good." I feel him smile against my neck. "What time is it?"

"Just after five. Dinner's in about an hour. How are you feeling?"

I blow out a breath. "Okay, just anxious, you know? I want everything to work out. I want Rome to genuinely want to change, and I want him and Gray to work things out, to be as happy as we are, but I'm terrified none of that is going to happen. I'm terrified Gray is going to get hurt and she'll blame me and be devastated."

"I know, baby, but we just have to have faith that everything will be okay."

I snuggle closer to him. "It's just there's so much I can't control, and it's so fucking hard. I want everything to be okay *so* badly." Tears sting my eyes but I refuse to cry.

"I wish I could guarantee everything will be all right."

"I know, and I love you for it."

"I hate seeing you so torn up."

Just hearing him say those words makes me feel better, a little bit of anxiety lessening knowing he's right beside me.

"Come on, let's get cleaned up. We don't want to keep your family waiting," I say, getting up.

"Don't worry. One thing you'll learn about my family is when it comes to food, they wait for no man." But he follows me into the bathroom regardless.

CHAPTER THIRTY

REED

I timed waking Bria up just right and was able to take her again before we went over to the diner. Shower sex with Bria is amazing, but then, any sex with Bria is mind-blowing. I can't wait to have a lifetime of loving with her and only her, which is something I never thought I'd want. I tuck her under my arm, hers around my waist, and we walk over to the diner.

"What do you want, baby?" I ask after the greetings are out of the way.

She stops to consider for a moment. "Nachos?"

"And to drink? Caramel shake?"

"Hmm, no. I'm feeling something fizzy. Lemonade?"

"No worries." I kiss her nose before putting in our order. I go back to the table and as usual, I lift Bria up, take her seat, and pull her back down on my lap.

"There are other chairs, you know," she says with a playful smile on her face.

"Baby, I'm the only chair you'll ever need," I say, nuzzling her neck, and she giggles. I fucking love when she giggles. So light-hearted and carefree.

She gasps and her eyes widen when our meal is delivered, and one of my brothers—I'm not sure who but my money is on Mav—gags.

"What the hell, Reed?" she asks when the giant platter of nachos is put in front of us.

I shrug. "When you said you wanted nachos, I felt like them too. I knew we'd be sitting at the same spot so I combined our orders."

"You're too cute," she says, grabbing my face and squeezing my cheeks between her palms.

I kiss her quickly on the nose.

We eat our meal and then she relaxes back on me, her head on my shoulder.

"Was my boy well behaved over the weekend?" Pop asks Bria.

She nods and snuggles into me more. "He was the perfect gentleman."

"Gentleman? Can't have been Reed," Park says, and everyone laughs.

"I can be polite," I argue, and the laughter continues.

"Poor baby," Bria coos and leans over to kiss me. "No, seriously, Reed was extremely well behaved. My parents loved him," she says.

"The good old Ryan charm," Pa says.

"You see any embarrassing photos of sis?" Jax asks.

"A few."

"What?" Bria screeches.

"Your mum showed me."

"Oh, my God!" She buries her head in my neck.

"You were adorable, angel. Still are."

"I'm going to kill her."

"Nah, you're perfect."

She unburies her face and rolls her eyes at me. "Smooth, Ryan, real smooth."

I lower my voice. "You wanna bring up Roman now?"

She blows out a breath. "I suppose." She sits up straighter.

"Something came up while we were home," Bria tells my family. I see them perk up and become more alert at the perceived threat. I smile at their eagerness to protect my girl.

"Oh?" Pop says, his jaw tense.

"My parents' friends joined us for dinner, Colt and Anne Thomas. Their son, Roman, rides for Devil Racing."

"Okay," Mav says, waiting for the other shoe to drop. Mav's the quiet one amongst us, the thinker.

"Rome joined Devil five years ago, when he was seventeen, and cut everyone off, including me and Grayson, with whom he was in a serious relationship. He broke her heart and hasn't spoken to us in all that time."

"But?" Mav asks.

"But he's recently gotten back in touch with his parents and has reached out to me."

"What does he want?" Liam asks.

"He says Devil has been doing things that he doesn't agree with and he wants out."

"So what does this have to do with us?" Jax asks.

"I know your history with Devil and while Reed has told me Rome hasn't come onto your radar, I wanted to make sure it was okay with you, *all* of you, before I meet up with him."

"And then what?" Park chimes in.

"I want to talk to him, make sure he is sincere in his desire to leave Devil and return to the life he had, or was on track for, before he got involved with that scum. If he is, I would welcome him back into my life again."

"You wouldn't be meeting with him alone, would you?" Jax asks, alarmed.

"Reed would be coming with me."

"Getting out of Devil isn't going to be easy," Liam says.

"She knows. So do his parents," I say.

"What do you think?" Park asks me. "You had the most trouble with Devil."

"I think as long as he's genuine then I don't have a problem with Bria reconnecting with her friend. What do you know about him?" I ask Liam.

"Roman Thomas?" he asks, and Bria nods.

"He's been around Devil for a while, a lot longer than most guys, but he's not one of Hunter's main guys. From what I've seen and heard, he has a lot of talent for mechanics, which is why Hunter's kept him around so long."

"What is he going to do once he's out?" Pop asks.

"I have no idea. That's just one of many questions I'll want to have answered," Bria says. "So is it okay with you all? I don't want to cause trouble between you and Devil or even me and you guys."

"I think I speak for us all," Liam says, "when I say that as long as Reed's with you and this guy is genuine, we don't have a problem." Everyone nods.

"But it's not going to be easy for him to leave Devil," Mav says, "especially if Hunter finds him useful."

"If he is genuine, what can I do to help him?"

"Just be there for him," Mav says. "He'll need a job and probably a place to live, but that'll be stuff he has to do himself. Getting away from here might be the best idea. If he's hanging around and not with Hunter, it could get ugly."

"Fu—far out," Bria says, remembering Chris sitting next to her.

"It's gonna be rough for him, Bria," Mav says. "Real tough. Tough enough that he may even decide that it's easier to stay."

"Will they hurt him?" she asks in a small voice, and I hug her tighter to me.

"More than likely," Park says.

She nods. "I'm sure he's probably thought of this, knows it himself."

"It's also about preparing you, sis," Mav says.

"And Grayson," Jax adds.

"Okay, thanks guys."

"We're here for you," Liam says. "We're here for Grayson too, and would be for Roman himself if it wouldn't cause more problems for him."

Bria sniffs and wipes her eyes, and I turn her so she's

sitting sideways on my lap and hug her even tighter.

"Thank you, all of you," she says and tries to smile.

"You okay, angel?"

She nods. "It's just a lot, you know?"

"I know, but we'll get through it together, taking everything one step at a time. Okay?"

"Yes."

"Can we have ice cream now?" Chris asks, clearly bored of the adult conversation, and everyone laughs, the tension broken. God love that kid.

CHAPTER THIRTY-ONE

BRIA

I slept well last night. Reed made sure I was too tired and otherwise occupied to think about what was going to happen in the coming days and weeks, not only for me but Grayson and Rome himself.

I sent a text to Rome after dinner, asking him to meet me and Reed at Mike's on Tuesday arvo. It's off the beaten track, so not many people make it there, and by two it should be late enough that whatever customers Mike does have are hopefully gone.

"How are you feeling about today?" Reed asks on Tuesday morning.

I shrug. "I'm nervous."

He rubs my back. "Don't be. I'll be right there with you."

"I know, and I'm glad. I'm not sure I can be objective." I lean back so I can look him in the eyes. "I'm relying on your instincts."

He nods solemnly. "No worries, I got you."

I hug him tightly. "I know, thank you," I say and kiss his chest.

"You ready to shower now?" he asks and I nod.

He turns on the shower and sits on the bench, my legs wrapped around him, the water running over us. Neither of us really bother to move, just enjoying our closeness in our bathroom cocoon. It's only when Liam bangs on the door that we snap out of it.

After our shower, Reed dresses in his usual ripped jeans and baseball tee and slaps a Ryan Racing cap backwards on his head. If he's trying to take my mind off this meeting with Rome, then mission accomplished, but if he wants me to be able to concentrate, then that's going to be a more difficult feat.

"What?" he asks me, coming over and wrapping me in his arms. I take a deep breath, his manly, musky scent calming me.

I look up at him and wind my arms around his neck. "You really are too good-looking sometimes."

His green eyes sparkle with amusement and love. "*Too* good-looking? Is there such a thing?"

"There is when I'll be trying to talk to Rome and all I can think of is how hot you are."

He lowers his head so his forehead rests on mine. "That will be a problem. What if I promise to behave myself and you can reward me tonight?"

217

I pretend to consider for a moment. "*Can* you be good?"

"For you, I'll be anything you want me to be."

I melt and don't even pretend to be unaffected by his sweet, sweet words. "Fine, I guess I can go along with that."

"Good." He kisses my nose before releasing me and slinging an arm around my neck. I sling one of mine around him, sliding my hand into the back pocket of his jeans and giving his fine arse a squeeze.

He chuckles and we walk out to his car, a Mustang like Liam's.

He opens my door for me, then sprints around to the driver side.

He takes my hand before he starts the car. "I'm right here with you. If there's anything you don't like or if you're not comfortable, just tell me and we'll leave, okay?" I nod.

"It's gonna be okay, Bria. Just hear him out." Again, I nod. He cups my face and looks straight into my eyes. "I love you and I won't let anything happen to you."

I smile at his protective words. Warmth spreads through my chest and I try to blink away my tears. Geez, all this emotion overload is turning me to mush.

"You good? You ready?"

"I am." I square my shoulders.

"There's my girl." With a kiss to my forehead, he starts the car.

The drive to Mike's is silent, both of us preparing for what's to come. We pull into the car park and I spot Rome's old dirt bike. I smile. He used to tool around with Grayson and me on the back of that thing for hours.

I look over to the tables and spot him instantly. It's pretty easy, seeing as he's the only one here.

Reed comes and opens my door, and we walk hand in hand over to Rome.

"Bria," he says, and stands when we get near. It's clear he's relieved I showed, as though he thought I wasn't going to.

"Hey, Rome," I say, and stop a metre from the table.

"It's so good to see you. Thank you for coming. I know it can't have been an easy decision. Roman Thomas," he says, extending a hand to Reed.

"Reed Ryan." They shake hands.

"Will you sit?" he asks, and gestures to the bench seat in front of us.

We sit. Reed sits sideways, one leg on either side of the bench, and pulls me between them.

"I heard rumours Reed Ryan had settled down. Doesn't surprise me one bit that you were able to tame him, Bri," he says, playing with his fingers.

"What do you want, Rome?" I ask quietly, my stomach is in knots. I feel like I'm about to spew.

"I want out," he says simply.

"What does that have to do with me?"

"I want my old life back, Bri. I want out of Devil and away from Hunter. I want to go back to the way things used to be with me, you, and Grayson."

"You want her back?" Anger laces my question. Immediately, Reed rubs my back, trying to calm me.

Rome runs a hand through his shaggy chestnut curls. "I

know I fucked up beyond comprehension and broke Grayson's heart, but I love her, Bri. I never stopped."

"You didn't just break her heart, Rome, you broke *her*. You have no idea how devastated she was and still is. No idea of the amount of damage you did to her. She's not the same girl you first fell in love with."

"I know, but please, Bri—"

"Why now?" I ask.

"Huh?"

"Why, after all this time, have you decided that you want out? What changed?"

"Hunter changed."

Reed scoffs.

"Look," Rome says, his attention on Reed, "you gotta know I never approved of his rivalry with you, never agreed with the way he went about things."

"Didn't do anything about it though, did you?" Reed spits and I grab his hand and squeeze, this time calming him. "All those times he pushed too hard and sent me, him, and whoever else happened to be in the way into the gravel. All those times he was openly doing drugs, putting lives at risk. You never once went to the race organisation, did you? Never thought to put a stop to him. Even now, you let him get on the bike. What happens when he kills someone?"

Rome hangs his head. "I was scared," he says in a small voice.

"Oh, please," Reed scoffs. "I gave up my entire career to stop that dickhead and it still wasn't enough. If you or someone on your team had backed me up, we could've put a stop to him."

"He said he'd blackball me."

"That would've been hard to do when he himself was blacklisted. No one would've listened to him. Besides, Hunter may be a psycho but we all know he has a nose for talent. Someone would've picked you up."

"So why are you leaving now, Rome?" I ask, trying to get back on track.

"Because of you." He looks right at me. I hold his stare and I can see remorse, pain, but more importantly, honesty in his blue eyes.

"What?" Reed stiffens next to me.

"I was at the diner that night, Bri."

"What ni— Oh," I say, putting two and two together.

"I was supposed to just wait outside for Drew and Dean, but then I saw you run and grab the kid. I knew nothing was going to stop them from beating you,"—he looks to Reed— "and your brother to a pulp or worse, except the chance of getting caught. That's why I smashed the windows, so they'd get spooked and run."

"You did that?"

Rome nods. "After that, we started getting reports that Reed was spending a lot of time with a blonde-haired chick. We thought it might be just his usual fling, but then you kept going back to the diner and he would kiss you in public, so we thought it might be something more serious. When he took you to the race, Hunter thought it'd be a great opportunity to hit the Ryans where it hurt. All of them had clearly taken to you and Hunter was ecstatic. Reed Ryan *finally* had a weak spot."

Reed growls and clenches his fists. I pat his thigh and try to calm him down.

"Hunter already had the idea to hit you at the track, but when he saw Bria, that cemented it. He got one of the guys to mix up something, just enough to destroy your garage but not take out the whole building. Hunter wanted to do it while he was out for warm-up. He gave it to Bobby and told him to lob it once he was gone. I went with him and when I saw you and the kid—"

"Christian," I correct.

"Christian, right. Parker's kid?" Reed nods.

"Right, well when I saw you two were still in the garage, I grabbed Bobby and managed to convince him to let me do it."

"You?" I stutter.

Rome hangs his head. "Yeah. I locked Bobby in a closet and told Hunter he'd freaked and bolted. I told him I'd do it. Hunter wanted me to do it right away but I told him people would see me, so I did it before the race when no one would see me or be hurt."

"Which is all well and good, fuckstick," Reed bursts out angrily, "but Bria and Chris went back to the garage."

"What?" Rome asks, shocked.

"They were almost there too, when your little explosion went off."

"Oh, my God, Bri, are you okay? Was the kid hurt?" he asks frantically.

"Luckily for you, Chris was unhurt, but Bria was hit by shrapnel."

Rome looks distraught. "Fuck, Bria, I'm so sorry! Was it bad? I didn't think anyone would be around, fuck!" he exclaims.

Anger at his involvement rushes through me. He put Chris and me in danger. But as much as I want to throat punch him, his reaction now is not fake. Remorse mars his features, and I can't help feeling sorry for him making such stupid decisions and being caught up in the nightmare that is Hunter. "Rome," I say, and reach out for him. His head is in his hands.

He lifts his head and I see tears in his eyes. "I'm so sorry, Bria. I never meant for that to happen, I truly didn't. Hunter, he wanted to hurt you but I thought this way I'd be able to protect us both. Are you okay?"

I nod. "I'm okay, just a little bit of metal in my leg."

"And four stitches," Reed adds.

"What?" Rome asks.

"Really, Rome, it wasn't anything major. I'm fine now. The stitches have dissolved and I've only got a small scar."

"Fuck!" Rome yells and pulls on his hair. "How did this happen, Bri?" he asks me, despair written all over his face.

"I don't know, Rome. Life doesn't always turn out like we think it will."

"Everything is so fucked up." A tear falls from his eye.

I look to Reed and he nods. I'm not even going to ask how he knew what I was after, but he gave it to me. I get up, go around to Rome's side of the table, and put my arms around him. He folds into me and grabs me by the waist, sobbing into my shoulder. I pat him on the back and try to console him.

"You really want out?" I ask him when he starts to calm down.

He nods and sniffs. "I can't do it anymore, Bri. I miss the old me. Hell, I miss you. I miss Gray. I miss having you guys in my life. I miss the time we could've spent together, all three of us—or four now," he says, looking at Reed. "I hate the person I've become, what I've done, what I haven't done. This isn't me, Bri, you know that, right?"

I nod. "I do."

"So what happens now?" Reed asks.

Rome releases me and wipes his face. "I don't know."

"You live with guys from Devil, right?" Reed asks, and Rome nods. "Do you have somewhere you can go?"

"Home." He shrugs.

"Anywhere else?"

Rome shakes his head.

"You know when they figure out you're not with them, they're going to come after you?"

"Yeah." Rome sighs. "I know, but anything is better than staying there." He takes a deep breath. "There's something you should know, though," Rome says, looking at Reed.

"Oh yeah?"

Rome nods. "Hunter's planning on hitting the garage, your garage. He's going to destroy it."

"What?" Reed all but shouts.

"He knows you guys store everything there, all the racing bikes, Jax and Mav's bikes, everything, and he's going to destroy it."

"That motherfucker," Reed curses. "When? How?"

"He's going to wait until it's the most inconvenient for you."

"Of course he is. How?"

"Hunter doesn't have a lot of imagination—"

"This I know," Reed interrupts.

"He's going with an explosion and fire again."

"Fuck. Me," Reed says, and cracks his knuckles. "You dead serious about getting out?" Reed asks and stares Rome in the eyes.

He nods. "I am."

Reed lets out a breath. "Okay, this is what you're going to do."

CHAPTER THIRTY-TWO

REED

"You're going to go back to Devil."

Bria squeaks and I know she's going to hate it, but for Roman's sake this is how it's gotta be.

"I know you're not gonna like this bit, angel, but it's what's best for Roman."

She looks into my eyes and I see nothing but love and trust. She nods; that's my girl.

"You supposed to be going with them to the race this weekend?" I ask Roman, and he nods.

"You won't be going."

"Okay." I see Bria relax a little.

"Find a reason to delay your departure and for Christ's sake, make sure you're alone. Pack all your shit and then come to the diner. My brothers, Mav and Jax, have a place nearby with a spare bedroom and they're about to leave for big air training. You can stay there. You'll need to leave your car and bike at our garage. There's enough storage room there that we can put them inside so no one knows you're with us."

"Okay, sounds good." Roman nods.

"One other thing." He stills. "You need to find out as much as you can about the hit on the garage, and then we're going to the police."

"Yep, okay."

"You think you can handle this?"

"It's time, man, past time."

"They're going to come after you."

"I know."

"They're going to hurt you." He really needs to understand the reality of the decision he's about to make.

"I know."

"If I find out that you're playing us...."

"I'm not playing you."

"I don't give a shit about me, but if you break my girl's trust, Hunter David will be the least of your worries."

He smiles and turns to Bria. "So when's the wedding?"

"Shut up, Rome." She shoves him playfully.

He grabs her hand. "But seriously, Bri, you've got a great guy here. I've heard about his reputation, but I can tell you guys have the real deal."

Bria smiles. "Thanks, Rome."

"Are you—" He stops and clears his throat. "Are you going to tell Grayson you saw me? That you're helping me?"

Bria bites her lip; I know this is a major point of concern for her.

"I don't know," she says truthfully.

"Please, Bri. I know I fucked up, but I love her."

"I know, and she loves you, but I can't just open her up to all this. I need to know you aren't going to bail on her again."

Roman nods. "That's fair."

"Let's just get you settled and then we can decide what to do about Grayson, okay?"

"Okay."

Just then, Bria lets out a yawn. I know she's probably had a tough time sleeping lately. The past few days have been an emotional roller coaster and it doesn't look like it's ending anytime soon.

"We should get going. It's been a long few days," I say, getting up and extending a hand to Bria.

She stands, as does Roman, and they hug.

"Thanks for coming to see me, Bri."

"Just don't make me regret it, okay?"

He nods. "I won't."

I write down my number. "Don't save it under my name. Actually, it might be better if you get a new number altogether."

"I'll do that."

"If you need something, let us know."

"Thanks, Reed. I know you have no obligation to help me, but thanks."

I shrug. "You tried to protect my girl. For that reason alone, I can respect you. Just don't…."

"Fuck up again. I get it."

I shoot him a wry smile. "Good. We'll be at the track Saturday, but either my older brother Parker, or my pa will meet you at the garage on Saturday and then take you to the littles' house."

"The littles?" he asks.

"Mav and Jax's house. They're the youngest so we call their house the littles'. Mine is the middles', and so on."

"Right."

"Take care, Rome, and I can't help it."

"I know, but let this one"—he gestures to me—"do all the worrying. I think he can handle it."

She bobs her head.

"We'll be in touch," I say and shake his hand. He takes it and gives me a nod and I hope to God he's not playing us.

"Come on." I hold my hand out for Bria. She takes it and I pull her close as we walk back to the car. "I have a reward to claim," I whisper in her ear.

She giggles and slaps my chest. I catch her hand and bring it to my lips. She stops, looking up at me, showing me nothing but love.

"Thank you for being here, for helping my friend."

"I gotta admit, it was touch and go for a minute there."

She blows out a breath. "I know. It was a lot to take in. *Way* more than I thought it would be."

I spin her round, tuck her into my side and walk her to the car, "I know, but hopefully we can put an end to all this bullshit once and for all and get your friend back."

"What am I going to do about Grayson?"

"I honestly don't know, but at some point, you are going to have to clue her in, let her make her own decisions."

She expels a heavy breath and rests against the car. I cage her in. "I know, but what happens if he hurts her again?"

"I think that's the last thing he wants. I saw how he looked when he talked about her."

"How was that?"

"Like how I look at you." She melts against me. "Let's go home. I think we both need a little stress reliever." I wink at her as I bundle her into the car.

CHAPTER THIRTY-THREE

BRIA

I must have fallen asleep on the way home because the next thing I know Reed is unbuckling my seat belt and lifting me from the car.

"Reed?" I ask sleepily.

"Shh, angel, you fell asleep. We're home now."

"Mmm." I stretch in his arms.

Liam opens the door. "How'd it go?" he asks.

"Let me put Bria to bed and I'll tell you."

"I'm okay. Put me down."

"You sure?"

"I had a nap, Reed, not major surgery." I laugh.

"Fine." He heads to the living room. "See who's free. I want to tell this story as few times as possible," he says to

Liam, then sits on the couch and folds me into his lap.

Liam's phone beeps. "Park, Pop, and Pa are on their way over. Mav and Jax will look after the diner."

Reed nods and plays with my hair. He seems to like running his hands through it so I wear it down a lot more.

Thirty seconds after the text, the elder Ryans come through the back door. They all greet me before taking a seat.

"So how'd it go?" Liam repeats.

"Pretty good, I think," Reed says. "We chatted, Roman explained a few things, and I think he's genuine in his desire to leave Devil."

"Good," Pop says, and it doesn't surprise me one bit that they've taken Rome's cause as their own.

"He told us he was the one who smashed the windows of the diner that night." I can see their anger rising before Reed continues, "But he did it because he knew the two inside wouldn't stop until we were seriously injured. He also saw Bria with Chris and wanted them to be safe."

"But it's okay for them to be showered with glass?" Park asks.

"Better than the alternatives. There's a lot of dangerous shit in the kitchen, Park. One wrong move and we could've been headed face first into the fryer or grill. Roman stopped them in the most effective way."

"Whatever," Parker mumbles.

"There's more," I pipe up. "Rome was the one who caused the explosion."

"He did what?" is the general reaction.

"I know it's shocking, but the original plan was to cause

it during the warm-up, which, if you remember, was when Chris and I were in the garage, and all of you were close too. He opted to do it when he did because the garage was empty."

"That's little consolation," Parker says.

"I know," Reed butts in, "but you have to think of it from his point of view. Plus, when he heard Bria was injured, he was distraught."

"You don't think it was an act?" Pop asks.

Reed shakes his head. "He's one hell of an actor if it is."

"So why now?" Pa asks.

"Because of Bria. Hunter wants to go after her." Reed holds me tighter like that's going to protect me.

"And that's not a convenient excuse?" Parker asks. I really hope he's playing devil's—no pun intended—advocate and not voicing his true thoughts.

"If you saw Rome when he first left for Devil," I say, "you'd know he wouldn't give a shit if me or Grayson or even his parents were in the firing line. He wanted in, no matter the cost. Now, he's actively doing things to circumvent Hunter and his desire for destruction."

"He did seem like he really wants to get out," Reed says.

"So what now?" Pop asks.

"There's one more thing," I say with trepidation.

"More?" Liam asks.

I nod. "Hunter's going to go after our garage."

"And you're trusting this guy?" Parker fumes.

"Just calm down, okay?" Reed says tersely. "Roman told us about the plan. That's a start."

"Is it the end?"

"No. I've sent him back to get as much info as possible and then we're going to the cops."

"He's willing?"

"He is," I say. "Look, I know this news is upsetting. Hell, it was for me too, but I think Rome really does want out. Did he stay too long? Yes. Is he an idiot for going in the first place? Yes, but he's willing to put himself on the line to stop Hunter. I know you guys have no reason to trust him, no reason to help him, but he's my friend and I'd like to think that if the positions were reversed he'd help me. You guys don't have to be involved if you don't want to. We just wanted to run everything by you, keep you in the loop, and be honest and open with you."

"If he's part of your family," Pa says, "then he's part of ours. If this boy wants to leave and have a better life, then who are we to deny him that? If you and Reed trust him, that's good enough for me." Everyone else nods.

"Thank you," I whisper and tears pool in my eyes.

"Jax and Mav are going out to Bucky's for training after the race this weekend, aren't they?" Reed asks.

"Yeah," Pop says. "They'll leave from the track."

"We thought Roman could stay there, at least for the time being."

"It's a good idea," Liam says. "Unless he wants to go home?" he asks, looking at me.

I shake my head. "He doesn't want this following him there."

"Fair enough," Parker says.

"So you're all okay with this? I promise I understand if

you don't want to deal with any of this."

Pop shakes his head and repeats the same sentiment, "If he's your family, he's ours."

I get up and hug them all before snuggling back into Reed's lap. My tummy rumbles.

"And on that note I'm going to feed my girl and then we're going to chill because she's had a roller coaster few days."

I smile. I can't imagine anyone taking as good care of me as Reed.

We all go over to the diner where we fill Jax and Mav in on everything. Mav nods while Jax crows.

"He can have the fucking place if it gets rid of that douche."

"I don't think that will be necessary, but thank you anyway," I say.

"Oh, sis," Jax says, slinging an arm around my shoulders, "you really are the gift that keeps on giving."

"And why's that?" Reed asks, removing Jax's arm and pulling me into his side as we sit at my booth.

"One," Jax begins, "because she tamed you, giving me endless opportunities to rag on you. Two, she's a mega PR ace, who's going to make me rich and famous and keep me out of media jail."

"Please tell me you're not actively doing anything to land yourself in media jail," I implore.

Jax brushes my concern away. "No worries, sis, I'm all angel." He winks at me. "But third, and this is the kicker, you're delivering us the guy who's going to shut down Hunter

David. Doesn't get much better than that."

"I can think of a few things that are," Reed whispers in my ear and bites down on the lobe. I moan quietly.

We eat dinner and head back to his house. Reed then disappears into the bathroom. I'm not going to lie and say I don't think it's strange but there are some things a girlfriend doesn't need to know about. You know what I mean?

I'm lying on my stomach when Reed finally comes out. He climbs on top of me, nibbles on my ear, and kisses my neck.

"Relaxed?" he asks.

"Getting there."

"So this stuff with Roman?"

I huff out a breath. "I just can't think about it anymore. I keep running scenarios through my head over and over and it's driving me crazy. The race this weekend gives me the perfect opportunity to think about something else."

Reed kisses the back of my neck and I shiver. "That's what I thought." He gets up. "Come with me."

I roll over and take his hand. "Where are we going?"

He leads us to the bathroom where candles burn on every surface and the bath is filled with a thick layer of bubbles on the top.

"Reed," I breathe.

"Shh," he says, pressing a finger to my lips. He reaches for my top and lifts it off, undoing my bra a second later. Those are quickly followed by my shorts and panties. Reed quickly strips and then steps into the bath and offers me his hand. I step in and we sit, my back pressed to his chest, me seated between his legs.

Reed cups water over my shoulders, the water running over my breasts and chest, then down my back. I relax further into him. He begins to massage my shoulders and I let out a moan.

"That feels *so* good."

"You've had a few big days."

"That's an understatement."

"Do you regret being with me?" he asks in a neutral voice, as if preparing for the worse.

I turn to face him. "As long as I live, I will *never* regret being with you. How can you regret being with your soul mate?" I offer him a smile. The ease in which I can talk to him, even when sharing the mushy stuff that would usually leave my face glowing comes easily.

"It's just, if it weren't for my family, you'd be able to accept Roman into your life so much easier."

"No, I wouldn't. He'd still be facing all their retribution and he'd have no one to help him."

"I'm sorry. I know you don't want to talk about it—"

"But this is new to you and you worry about me. It's okay, Reed, I get it," I finish for him.

His hands move from my shoulders to my breasts and I hiss. "What? What is it? Did I hurt you?" Reed asks, panicking.

"It's fine. They're just a little sensitive. It happens when I'm about to get my period."

"Oh, sorry."

"It's fine, Reed. It's a normal bodily reaction."

"I've never had to deal with this stuff before."

I smile, and I catch a glimpse of his blush. "Well, you

better get used to it. You'll have to deal with it for another thirty or so years, and we'll need to get familiar with it if we're going to have those sons of ours."

He nuzzles my neck. "I like the sound of that."

"More practice?" I ask.

"Definitely more practice," he says and for the rest of the night the only thoughts I have are of Reed and me and the love we share.

CHAPTER THIRTY-FOUR

REED

"I need your help," I say to Pop once Bria has left for class. With everything going on last week, I haven't had an opportunity to broach this subject.

"If you've done something to upset that girl of yours again, I'd suggest you fix it right quick," he replies.

"The opposite actually, but thanks for the vote of confidence."

Pop looks up with a sly smile on his face. "The opposite, huh?"

I nod. "I want to ask Bria to marry me."

"So you'll be needing a ring then, I imagine."

"Yeah, I wanna go shopping for one today but I'm not sure what I'm looking for or where to begin really."

"And you figured my age and wisdom would come in handy."

"May as well get some use out of it," I joke.

"It'll do more than that. Follow me." He puts the paper he was reading down and leads me to his room. He goes straight to his bedside table, pulls out a small velvet box and hands it to me.

"It was your nan's. Pa bought it, cost him his life savings, which probably wasn't much but it was all he had."

I open the box and find a ring with a plain gold band and a solitaire diamond. It's a pretty decent size too.

"I gave it to your mother and now it's yours to give Bria."

"Shouldn't Park have it?"

"Pa and I decided whoever was the first to settle down would have it. What you two have is real."

I nod, still looking at the ring. As a child, I never paid much attention to the jewellery my mother wore and knowing this adorned not only her hand but also my nan's... well, to say it holds a lot of sentimental value is an understatement.

"I know it's not much or very flashy, but I'm sure if you wanted to have it remodelled Pa would have no objections."

I shake my head. "It's fine as it is. I don't think Bria would want anything flashy and she'd kill me if she knew the history of this ring and I had it changed. It's just... doesn't it bother you? Growing up without a mother, raising us without one, you losing your wife?"

"Of course it bothers me."

"How do you deal with it? How did you deal with it?"

"Worried the same thing will happen with you and Bria?"

"I can't imagine my life without her, can't imagine this family without her. What am I supposed to do if something happens to her? She's already come under attack twice simply as collateral damage. What happens if Hunter realises she's connected to both Roman and me? He's already fixated on her because of me, but add all this Roman shit to the mix?"

"What are you going to do? Turn your back on her friend? On her? On us? You can't protect her from everything, and she wouldn't want you to. Bria knows what is going on with our family and Hunter. She knows what Roman will likely go through, and still she's here. She's a woman worthy of that ring. Your mother would've done the same given the choice. All you have to do is love her and be with her. Make a life for yourselves, give me some more grandchildren, and Chris some cousins. That's all you have to do, Reed. All you *can* do. If you do it, then that'll get you through the—touch wood— bad times. Don't let this worry or sheer bad fucking luck ruin a good thing, because make no mistake, Bria is a good thing. A very good thing."

I'm shocked. I'm not sure I've ever heard my pop talk for so long or so passionately.

"Geez, Pop, tell me what you really think." We laugh.

He clips me across the back of the head. "You're a smart-arse, aren't ya?"

"I learned from the best." I shoot him a cheesy grin.

"So what does this Roman do for Devil?" Pop asks, our moment clearly over.

"Apparently he's a mechanical genius. Had to be something for Hunter to keep him round this long, and he's not riding, so…."

"Must be one hell of a mechanic."

I shrug.

"Always got room for one of those."

"You want to take him on?"

Now it's Pop's turn to shrug. "Maybe after all this shit has blown over, we can take a look at the guy. Couldn't hurt."

"No, it couldn't."

"That girl of yours," Pop says, smiling wryly, "she has a way with us, doesn't she? Got us firmly in her corner and protecting her back."

I smile. "You know I wouldn't have it any other way."

"No, I know, but Bria, she just walked in and bam!" He snaps his fingers. "She's one of us."

I nod. "I know."

Pop kisses his thumb and index finger and points to the sky.

"Yep." I nod.

"Took them long enough," he says with a grunt.

"Worth the wait though."

"No doubt. I mean, Mase is great and him and Liam fit, but we have a responsibility to make sure there are plenty of Ryans long after I'm dead and gone."

I chuckle and slap his shoulder as we walk into the diner. "Bria and I have talked about that. Are three enough for you?"

"You working on it already?"

"Not yet, but soon."

Pop shoots me a smile. "Good. She'll be a great mama, that one."

"She's a great everything." My phone buzzes in my pocket.

Unknown: This is Rome. This is my new number, and only you, Bria and my parents have it.

Me: Good, I'm working out the details for Saturday. I'll let you know. Find out anything?

Roman: Working on it. Will let you know. Thanks again.

We get to the diner and I go over to Pa.

"You ask that girl of yours to marry you yet?" he asks in greeting.

"Not yet, but soon."

"Your pop give you the ring?"

"Yep." I pat the pocket where it sits.

"You going to change it?"

"Bria would have my balls if I changed it."

"She's a good girl, that Bria."

"Are you planning on staying here this weekend?" I ask.

"I was intending on it. Not as young as I used to be."

"Ah, but still as sharp as ever," I say and he chuckles. "Anyway, I've organised with Roman for him to go to the littles' on Saturday. Think you'd be able to give him a hand? I've told him to come here to unload his stuff and then go to the garage to store his car and bike."

"No problems."

"Thanks, Pa."

"You're doing a good thing, Reed, both for this boy and your girl."

"I'd do anything for Bria."

He smiles. "We all would."

My phone buzzes in my pocket again.

Roman: He's planning next week, before the final race of the season. Got pics of his stockpile.

So now we know.

CHAPTER THIRTY-FIVE

BRIA

As I drive away from the diner on my way to class, I decide to tell Grayson about Rome. I can't keep this from her and she has a right to be there for him if she wants. I drop by our room before class but she's already gone. It's probably the best for her, that way she doesn't miss a whole day of classes. I go to my own classes and then head back to wait for her.

I wake to the door closing and Grayson dumping her backpack on the floor.

"Hey," I say sleepily.

"Come back for a catnap?" she asks jokingly.

"Well, I have to admit it is convenient." Although why I'm tired is beyond me. Maybe all this shit is stressing me out more than I thought.

"So how is your hunk of a man?"

"He's good. Busy, but good."

"How's the PR stuff going?"

"It's okay for now. The weekend is a different story but at the moment, I've got a handle on it."

"You'll have a handle on it on the weekend too."

"Thanks."

"So did you stop by just to crash or did you actually want to see me?"

"You know it's not like that, Gray."

"I know. I just miss my best friend."

"I know, and I miss you too." I pat the couch. "But I do have something to tell you."

"Are you pregnant?" she asks accusingly.

"No! Well not yet anyway." I blush hotly.

"Have you guys decided to start trying?" Her eyebrows shoot up.

"Not in so many words. I'm on the shot, as you know"—we're shot buddies, getting them together—"but when this one's up, I probably won't be going back."

"Holy shit."

"I know, but that's not what I wanted to talk to you about."

"What?" She crosses her arms and leans against the kitchen bench.

"Will you sit, please?"

"What is it, Bri? You're freaking me out."

"Fine," I huff. "Rome's getting out of Devil."

"What?" she gasps.

"Come on, come sit down." She falls onto the couch.

"His parents asked to see me when I went home, and told me he wants out. Reed and I met with him yesterday."

"How is he? How did he look?"

"He's fine, a bit anxious, but with what's coming that's understandable. He still looks like the old Rome, just a little more worn and weary." Beside me, Grayson sniffs.

"Did he ask about me?" she probes in a small voice.

I bob my head. "He did."

"What"—she swallows—"did he say?"

"Are you sure you want to hear this?" I ask.

"Yes and no. On one hand, I hate him and think he's a bastard who can burn in hell, but on the other...."

"He's the boy you fell in love with."

"Yeah." She shrugs one shoulder.

I take a deep breath. "He says he knows he fucked up. I think 'beyond comprehension' were his exact words. But he loves you and he never stopped." At this, the dam breaks and she begins sobbing. I grab her and cradle her in my arms. After a while, her crying slows.

"Fuck," she curses.

"I know."

"After all this time?"

I answer with a shrug.

"You think he means it?" I can see the hope in her eyes.

"I hope he does. Reed thinks he does."

"How would he know?"

"He says Rome looks the same way when he talks about you as Reed does with me."

"Really?"

I take her hand and give it a squeeze, offering a small nod.

"So what now?" she asks.

"Reed's helping him get out. Most of it will take place on Saturday while Hunter's guys are at the track. Either Parker, Pa, or Jay, will help him get his stuff and move his car and bike."

"Where's he staying?"

"At Mav and Jax's. They're going to do some big air training and will be away for a bit. He's storing his car and bike at Wheels' garage."

"Why are they helping him?"

"Because they're good people."

"No, I know that, but Hunter and Devil…."

"I know, but it's okay. Rome explained some things and it's all good."

"What things?"

I exhale. I really didn't want to go into all this, but she asked.

"Rome was at the diner the night of the fight, outside waiting for the two guys inside. When he saw me, he knew he had to end it so he smashed the windows."

"That's it?"

I shake my head. "No, there's more." My stomach rumbles. "Do we have any of those sweet potato chips? I'm starving."

She gets up to get them. "So what else? Keep talking, lady."

"Fine. Rome was the one who threw the explosives at the track." Gray gasps and drops the chips.

"I know it sounds bad, but hear me out. Hunter had another guy who was going to do it during the warm-up. Both Christian and I were in there at that time and Reed and his family weren't far away either. Rome managed to delay the guy and do it himself. He did it when he did because no one was around. It was only bad luck that Chris and I were heading back there."

"Still, you can't excuse that behaviour," Grayson says, *finally* handing me the chips.

"No, but apparently Hunter is going after Wheels' garage. Rome told us about the plan and is finding out as much as he can about it. Then he's going to the police with Reed."

"He is?"

I nod.

"So what now?"

"Whatever you want, it's up to you. I just wanted to give you the opportunity to decide for yourself."

"What do you think?"

"It's up to you, sweetie."

Hope and anxiety swirl in her eyes. I can only imagine how she's feeling. "Do you think it's real?"

"I think so. Reed has threatened him that if he fucks up again, he'll have to answer to him, so…."

Gray chuckles. "That guy…. You did good, Bria."

"I know, and look, Rome knows he fucked up and that if you forgive him and he does it again, he deserves everything that will come to him, namely eight angry Ryans."

"But they don't even know me."

"I get the feeling Jax wouldn't mind rectifying that, but you're my family so that makes you their family. It's the same reason they're helping Rome in the first place."

She gives me a small smile and I know she's scared. I take her hand again.

"You don't have to jump in and pick up where you left off. You don't even have to be together if you don't want to. Take it slow, make him work for it, and make him earn it. A few gifts wouldn't go astray either." I wiggle my eyebrows, which gets me a smile and a watery laugh.

"I'm not going to tell you that you and Rome belong to each other because you know that, but whether you get back together or how fast you take it is all up to you. He's waiting on you. The next move is yours, Gray, but if you do decide to reach out, you need to know getting out of Devil won't be easy. Rome's probably in danger. He might even get hurt, and you need to be prepared for that. They might even go after you."

She offers me a tentative smile. "Okay."

"Here's his number. Only me, Reed, and his parents have it." I write down the number he texted me earlier. She sits and stares at the piece of paper.

"You don't have to do anything, you know. Rome doesn't even know I've spoken to you about him."

"I know, it's okay."

"Just take it slow, a few texts, maybe some coffee, somewhere out of the way. You know, that sort of stuff."

"How long?"

"Until Hunter's gone? I don't know, but hopefully soon."

"What will he do in the meantime?"

"Lie low. We don't want Hunter to come after him or us, so that's another reason I hope it's all over soon."

MEGAN LOWE

"Us?" she asks.

I shrug. "For all intents and purposes, I guess I'm a Ryan now, in everything but name."

"Does that bother you?"

"That I'm a Ryan? Or in everything but name?"

"In everything but name."

I shake my head. "No. I know what Reed and I have and when he's ready, we'll take the next step. I mean, we haven't even been together a month yet, so there's no rush." I grin.

She nods, still a little shell shocked by the whole conversation.

"There's no rush for you and Rome either. Take your time. He hurt you and that's a lot to overcome. Don't hide from that. He needs to know how badly he fucked up."

"Okay." She inhales a large breath. "It's just a lot, you know?"

"I know."

"I just need… I don't even know." She gets up and starts pacing, pulling at her hair.

"How about we go over to the diner and get some dinner. I'm sure Jax will be happy to take your mind off things."

She shakes her head. "I think I need to be alone."

"No worries," I say, getting up, "but if you need me, call me. No matter what the time, I'll be here."

She nods. "Thanks, Bri."

I hug her. "You're welcome. Just take your time, okay?"

"I'll be fine."

As I close the door to our dorm, I hope with everything I have that's the case.

251

CHAPTER THIRTY-SIX

REED

By the time Saturday rolls around everything is in place. I've been coordinating with the police on Roman's behalf, passing all the information he's given me to them. He's told Devil he thinks he has food poisoning and can't make it at all this weekend. Most of the guys left Friday, so he started moving his stuff with Pa's help. Bria and I also left on Friday so she can stay on top of the flow of information. It seems everywhere she goes, she fits in straightaway. The journos we already have a relationship with like the fact she's "tamed" me and the ones we don't, she doesn't take any shit from. She's tough, efficient, to the point, and they know they can't push her around. It has led to me being as hard as a rock all weekend, much to her amusement.

Saturday goes well. Liam is able to pull off second after touching with another rider, so a top-ten finish next week will secure him the championship. Bria handled the press well yet again and we got a lot more exposure than we ever have before, which is awesome.

The track's four hours away from home, so I took her back to our hotel room and made love to her on every surface, as well as against the door and a couple of walls. It gets me hard just thinking about it. She's currently sleeping as we drive back, and my mind drifts to the ring I've stashed in a box full of my old racing gear. As much as I want to wake her up right now and ask her, I also want it to be special and leave her in no doubt about how much I love and value her. So yeah, it'll keep for now.

Everything went well with Roman too.

Pa helped him move his vehicles and he's safely ensconced at the littles'. Tomorrow, one of Pop's friends, Detective Cameron, will be coming over to take his statement and hopefully that'll be that.

Bria wakes up as we're pulling onto our street.

"Oh, we're almost home, er here," she says.

"Home, angel, we're almost home." I squeeze her thigh. We haven't officially had the "move in" talk but I assumed that as most of her stuff is here and she hasn't slept at her dorm since the night of our first date—except for our "speed bump"—she knows this is her home.

I pull into the garage, turn the car off, and twist to face her.

"You know this is your home, right?"

253

She looks down and plays with her fingers. I lift her chin and cock an eyebrow.

"I didn't want to assume."

"Baby, with us you can assume whatever you want. Whatever is mine is yours, okay?" She nods.

"I'm serious, Bria. I want you with me forever, so that means you've gotta be where I am. Or I'll be where you are, whatever works, but, angel,"—I cup her face—"this is forever."

"Okay." She gives me one of her breathtaking smiles.

I lift her out of the car. She clings to me, wrapping her legs around my waist, her arms around my neck. I get our bag out of the boot and walk us into the house. I love that I'm strong enough to do this. There's nothing I love more than having my girl wrapped around me. I walk into our room and put our bag down before sitting on the bed.

"I love when you carry me," she says, blushing.

"I love carrying you, having you wrapped around me. Nothing better than that."

"I wanted to talk to you about something."

"Okay," I say warily.

"You know I'm on the shot, right?" I nod. "Well, I got it almost two months ago so it'll be effective for just over a month."

"Okay." I'm still not getting where this is going, although I gotta admit, I do like the direction.

"So I was thinking that when that time is up, I wouldn't go get another one." My face splits into a huge grin.

"That puts me right during exams, so I might be too busy

and stressed for anything to come of it, but I don't think I want to wait what will be four months until we start trying for a family."

Happiness swells in my chest. "Me either. If we're not successful the first time, we'll keep on trying. You know I'm all about practice." I thrust my erection against her and she giggles.

"You wouldn't want to be married or at least engaged before we started trying, though?" I ask.

She shrugs. "Not really, just as long as it happens at some point."

"Oh yeah, baby, it'll be happening," I say as I kiss her neck. "You know," I say between kisses, "it's my birthday in six weeks."

"Oh, is it now?"

I nod. "It is, and I think I know what I want."

"And what's that?"

"You, naked, ready, and no birth control to stop my guys from doing their job."

"Your guys, huh?" she asks as I lift her top off.

"Yep, they're gonna get the job of knocking you up done for me."

"So romantic, Mr Ryan," she says, her sarcasm thick.

I make love to her slowly, tenderly, showing her just how romantic I can be.

"You sure?" I ask again.

"Absolutely," she says, her face softening, her hand coming up to cup my face.

"I love you." I begin to move again, my head filled with plans.

CHAPTER THIRTY-SEVEN

BRIA

After this afternoon's romantic interlude, we lie in bed, just holding each other.

"You're gonna be such a great mama," Reed says, his hand running up and down my back.

"And you're going to be one of those overprotective types that think because I'm pregnant, I can't do anything, right?"

"It's not that I'll think you can't do anything, it's that I won't *let* you do anything. Your job is to cook our son so he grows nice and big and strong."

I'm not going to lie, it totally gets me wet to hear Reed talk about our son as if it's a foregone conclusion. I can't wait to see his face if we happen to have daughters instead though.

"What happens if the unthinkable happens and I pop out a daughter?" I ask, giggling.

"Then we'll have to move into a castle or some shit like that so I can lock her up until she's fifty and I'll allow her to date."

"Right, boys it is," I say and snuggle into Reed's chest.

"Have you heard from Roman today?" he asks.

"No. Are you worried?"

"Nah, just thought he might like some company. He's not gonna have a lot to do until we can put Hunter away."

This man….

"You're worried about my friend?"

"Maybe at the end of all this he'll be my friend too."

I smile and lean up to kiss him. "You really are amazing, Reed Ryan."

"I take after my girlfriend," he says, and kisses me. "Come on, let's go over and see how he's doing."

We get dressed and Reed offers me his back. While my leg is still sore, I'm perfectly capable of walking, but it seems Reed likes me being a spider monkey.

"Your chariot, milady," he says, and I hop on, giggling.

Reed walks us over to the littles' and I knock. I don't particularly feel like being dropped today. Rome answers and smiles when he sees us.

"Hey, feel like some company?" I ask.

"Sure." He steps aside to let us in. "Ah, Gray's here too."

It's a good thing Reed's carrying me as I'm pretty sure if I were standing my knees would've buckled.

"Really?" I squeak.

Rome nods and offers a small smile. "We're talking, working things out."

I give him a watery smile in return.

"That's great, man," Reed says.

Rome shrugs and scratches his head. "Yeah, she called me on Friday and we went from there."

"How is she?" I ask, and pat Reed's back for him to let me down, my knees now able to bear my weight again.

"Good. There were a lot of tears, a lot of anger yesterday, but today's better. She's through here." He leads us down the corridor to the living room.

"Hey," Gray says. She's sitting on a couch looking relaxed.

I go over to her and give her a hug. "How are you?" I whisper.

"I'm good."

I pull back to look her in the eyes to make sure she's not bullshitting me.

"Seriously, Bri, it's all good. We spent most of yesterday talking and we each know what happened and what's been happening."

"So what now?"

"Right now we're friends. Will it develop into more? Who knows. But we're in a good place."

"Come on, angel," Reed says, pulling me from Grayson and onto his lap.

"So how'd things go yesterday?" Gray asks me.

"Good. Really good, actually. I managed to handle the press well and I think the coverage reflected that."

"She was amazing," Reed says. "She didn't take any of their shit and they were still well behaved, which makes for a nice change."

Rome nods. "They can be brutal for sure, but then Hunter gives them what they want. Your experience is probably different."

"Usually we have to put out the fires that Hunter starts," Reed says, then winces. "I didn't mean—"

Rome holds up his hand. "It's cool, man. I'll own up to what I did for Hunter. I don't like it but it was me doing it."

Grayson squeezes his hand. I know the development into more won't be long in coming.

"Liam was lucky though, he held on real well," Rome says.

"Stupid fucker," Reed curses. "Who overtakes there anyway? Sometimes I wonder what these guys have in their heads. It sure as shit isn't brains or common sense."

"They think because they have a ride they're hot shit. Someone needs to take them down a peg."

"Or a class or two."

Rome nods in agreement.

"So what are your plans, you know, after?" Reed asks.

"I'm not sure. Just go around town and offer my services, I guess."

"Are we on the list?"

Rome shifts uncomfortably. "I wasn't sure if that was wise after everything. I wasn't sure if you wanted me around, and you've already helped so much."

"So you mean we help a mechanical genius escape his psychotic former employer and we miss out on a chance to snag him ourselves? Not cool, man," Reed jokes.

"You're offering me a job?" Rome asks, bewildered.

"A trial first and we'll see where we go from there. You do all bikes?"

Rome nods. "Racing, street, dirt, freestyle, BMX, mountain, track, and road cycling if you get that business."

"Like Tour de France and Olympics shit?"

"Yeah, man, those bikes are insane."

"Yeah, not so much of that around here, but good to know."

"I mean it's not just for big shit like that. There are triathlons, Ironman comps, that sort of thing too."

"Well, shit."

Rome just shrugs.

"Once we get all this Hunter crap done, we're getting you into the garage ASAP."

"How specialised is a lot of that stuff, Rome?" I ask.

"A bit. I had a lot of downtime over the past five years, so I did a lot of reading, short courses, that sort of thing."

"So not many guys around here would have comparable knowledge?"

"Huh?" he asks.

"Can do what you can."

"Oh, nah."

"And on the flip side, there are not many places people could go for this kind of work either, I'd imagine."

"Nah. Maybe if they went into the city, but that's hours away and pretty pricey too. Those guys tend to be in demand."

"What are you thinking, angel?" Reed asks.

"Just a little promo. You know, a few features in a few magazines, getting Rome and his skills, and the shop he works for a little bit of publicity."

He squeezes me and nuzzles my neck. "You planning world domination too?"

"The two-wheeled world." I give him a chaste kiss.

"Seriously, Bri, you'd do that?" Rome asks.

"Sure, why not? It's great exposure for you, Wheels, and Ryan Racing, and that's my job."

"I thought your job was to cook our sons," Reed whispers jokingly and bites my neck gently. I elbow him in the ribs in reply and roll my eyes at his wording.

We sit and talk for a while, just four friends enjoying each other's company, and I hope this is a preview of many years to come.

CHAPTER THIRTY-EIGHT

REED

The meeting between Rome and Detective Cameron goes well. Rome gives him everything, holding nothing back, even the parts that implicate him.

I told him if he wanted to skirt those, we wouldn't have a problem, but he says he doesn't want to shy away from any of it. He tells Detective Cameron that too and the detective said with his cooperation, it's likely he'll only have to do community service.

The arrest warrant for Hunter was issued today, and hopefully within a few hours, he and his goons will be in custody. I haven't heard from Rome today, so Bria and I are going over there with some food.

We knock on the side door and let ourselves in.

"Hey," I yell, "we brought food. I know the guys live at the diner so there's never much here."

There's no answer and I turn to look at Bria. She shrugs.

"Rome?" she calls. Again, nothing.

We put the food in the kitchen and check the living room; still nothing. We head to the bedrooms and find his door closed.

"Rome," Bria calls softly as she knocks. The door opens slightly against her knock and on pushing it to open wider, we find Rome huddled in the corner, his face a bloody mess.

"Rome!" Bria gasps and runs to him. "What happened?" she asks as she moves his face towards the light, examining his injuries. His lip is split while blood drips from his nose. There's a nasty gash over a swollen almost-closed eye, and his jaw is bruised.

"Hunter?" I ask.

He nods and then winces.

"You need a doctor," Bria says.

"I'm fine," he manages to mumble.

"You're not. Your face is a mess, your hands are torn to shreds, and the way you're sitting and breathing makes me think you have a broken rib or two."

"It's fine, Bria. I'm okay. It's nothing less than I deserve anyway."

"For fuck's sake, Rome," she curses, "you made a mistake. Took one wrong turn. Yes, you did some stupid things but you're trying to fix them now and that doesn't mean getting beaten to a bloody pulp." Geez, my girl has a fiery side! Remind me not to piss her off.

"I'll call Mase," I say. "He's a paramedic. He can come and check you out."

Rome starts to object but Bria shoots him a look.

"Fine," he reluctantly agrees.

Mason tells me he's five minutes out.

"He'll be here soon," I tell them, and Bria and I help Rome get a little more comfortable.

Mase comes in a few minutes later and with Bria glaring at Rome, he lets Mase check him out.

"Just a cracked rib, some bruising, and some cuts," he reports.

"Will he need anyone to stay with him tonight?" Bria asks.

"It's not necessary, although it's going to be kinda difficult for him to move around."

"You don't need to stay, Bri," Rome says from the bed.

"Oh, I wasn't," she says. "Grayson's on her way."

"Oh fuck," Rome curses, and then winces.

"Given his reaction that may not be the best idea," Mase says.

"It's a perfect idea," Bria says cheerily.

"Angel, what are you up to?" I ask. I can see the twinkle in her eye so I know there's something cooking in that head of hers.

"Nothing, honey. I just want to make sure that Rome here has someone to look after him. Or I could stay here tonight with him and you and Mase could go back to our place."

And sleep in our bed without her? I don't fucking think so.

"I think having Grayson come over is a great idea," I say.

"Way to have my back, man," Rome groans.

"Sorry, dude, but I like my girl in our bed, next to me, preferably naked."

"Ah! My ears!" Rome groans and winces when he moves.

"Take it easy, marshmallow," Bria says with not an ounce of sympathy.

"Hey! Injured here!"

"You said you were fine before Mase got here."

"Yeah, if you guys don't need me, Liam and I have plans," Mase says.

"No worries, man." I give him a one-arm hug.

"Thanks, Mase," Bria says and kisses his cheek, blushing. I don't blame her. Mase is a good-looking guy and yes, I'm confident enough in my sexuality to say that.

As he goes to leave, we hear the front door slam and Grayson stomps up the stairs to the bedroom.

"Roman John Thomas, what in all that is holy did you do this time?" she bellows.

Bria when she's pissed off is hot, but Grayson is downright frightening.

"Er, angel, think we might want to get out of here too?" I ask.

"In a bit," she says, taking a seat on the bed and grinning like a loon.

Grayson bursts in and stops short when she sees Mason. "Oh, good, Jamie's here. He'll make it better."

Bria giggles.

"Jamie?" I ask.

"Yeah, Mason is a dead ringer for Jamie Dornan," Bria says.

"The guy from *Fifty Shades*?" I ask.

"*You've* seen *Fifty Shades*?" Bria asks, raising an eyebrow.

"For purely educational purposes," I reply, smirking.

She bites her lip and I can see the possibilities whirring in her mind.

"Well, this has become sufficiently awkward," Mase says, "so I'm gonna go." He's out the door like a shot.

"Yeah, I think we're going too," Bria says breathlessly.

"You don't want to see Rome get chewed up by Grayson?" I tease.

"I think they'll be fine." She takes my hand and drags me to the door.

"Bye, guys. Be nice and try not to kill each other," I say as I'm dragged down the stairs.

Bria doesn't stop until I'm slamming my bedroom door behind me.

"So about this education…."

Early the next morning, after several rounds of very hot, toe-curling, name-screaming sex, my phone rings. Hunter and his goons have been arrested; it's all over.

CHAPTER THIRTY-NINE

BRIA

The next five weeks fly by and before we know it, Reed's birthday is a week away.

Rome has settled into Wheels and Ryan Racing really well, helping Liam to his maiden National Racing Series Championship. We all celebrated long and hard, not only because of Liam's success, but Hunter's downfall.

Reed truly is an adorable drunk, telling me he loves me and he's going to marry me and we're going to have lots of babies.

"Seriously Bria," he slurred, "you don't even know how much I love you. I love you *so* much, baby. We're going to get married and have lots and lots of babies, boys though because I'd lock the girls up, and you don't want that. But if we had girls that'd be okay too, because I know you want girls and I'll give you anything you want. And then while we're doing that we're going to run Ryan Racing and then grow old and grey together." At which point, he promptly passed out. He paid for it the next day but I'll never forget his incredibly sweet words.

The night Rome was beaten up was the catalyst for him and Grayson. They're now back together and better than ever. He's still living with the littles, although he and Grayson have plans to move in together after graduation.

Speaking of graduation, today was my last exam and thank God for that. I feel like I've been studying forever, and I think it's taken its toll. I'm always tired nowadays, but hopefully now that finals are done that'll go away.

I've just stepped into the diner when I bump into Hayley, a ditzy girl in one of my journalism classes. She hates me and the feeling is mutual.

She's clinging to Jax's arm, which isn't surprising. Since I've taken over PR for Ryan Racing, I've raised the team and its riders' profiles quite a bit.

Liam, Mav, and Jax all have several endorsement deals now, and the littles are taking advantage of their higher profiles, as evidenced by Hayley.

"Oh Bria," she coos in her sugary sweet voice. "I didn't expect to see you here. Although, I have noticed you eating more, so I guess it fits." She glances to my midsection, where I *may* have put on a little bit of weight.

"Excuse me?" Jax says as I'm about to offer my own retort.

"Oh, it's nothing, baby," Hayley replies, running her

hand down his chest. "Just a girl around campus. Ignore her, she's nothing."

How she can't see Jax fuming is something I'll never know, but it does make for entertaining viewing.

Jax steps out of her embrace and pushes her hand away. "That girl is my sister and you can get the fuck out."

"But…," she splutters.

"Out!" Jax yells and points towards the door. I step aside to let her pass and Jax slings an arm around my shoulders.

"Hmph." With a flick of her hair, she stomps out of the diner.

"And don't come back," Jax yells at her retreating figure.

"That really wasn't necessary," I say as she drives off, although it was amusing. It always amazes me that during these moments, I feel like I've been teleported back to high school.

"You're welcome." He presses a kiss to my temple and leads me over to the table where Liam, Mase, Grayson, Rome, Chris, and Mav are waiting. The other four Ryans are rushing around the diner.

"Sis, you're positively glowing," Liam says as I reach the table.

"It's all the se—" Grayson begins but then notices Chris. "Sleep she's been getting."

"Aunty Bria sleeps with Uncle Reed," Chris says, to which I blush and everyone else roars with laughter.

"Yes, champ, she certainly does," Grayson says and ruffles Chris's hair.

"To save beds?" he asks.

"Huh?"

"Uncle Reed says dey shower together to save water. Do dey sleep together to save beds?"

In between bouts of laughter, we manage to answer in the affirmative. Reed comes up behind me, resting his chin on my shoulder and pulling my body flush with his.

"Hi," he says, kissing my neck.

"Hey, yourself."

"How'd your exam go?"

"Fine I think, but…."

"You don't want to jinx yourself, I know, but we can celebrate tonight, right?" he asks, a hopeful smile on his face.

"Of course we can."

"An early birthday present?"

"What *do* you want for your birthday?" He hasn't told me and I'm starting to get annoyed. As if men aren't hard enough to shop for in the first place.

"You, angel, just you."

~

As the week leading up to Reed's birthday drags on, I know I can no longer get away with not seeing a doctor. I'm still tired all the time even after a lot of rest and very little stress, and my emotions are all over the place. I'll have to ask whether it's some kind of withdrawal from the shot. I'm also eating like crazy, putting on weight. In the back of my mind, the idea that I may be pregnant constantly drifts in and out. But I keep pushing it aside. One, it excites as much as terrifies me.

Plus it seems too soon for that to even be possible.

It Reed's birthday tomorrow and I have no idea what to get him. When I ask all he says he wants is me. He'll extend that to naked and off contraception, but I don't know how to gift wrap that, plus I'm already off the other. I've bought some new lingerie, so I'm confident he'll enjoy, and an ovulation kit and pregnancy test, but I still feel like I should get him something more.

But it's too late for that as he drives us to a "secret location."

He's been buzzing around all day with excitement. If he were Chris, I'd ban him from ever having sugar again, but as he's twenty-four, almost twenty-five, I suppose that's not entirely feasible.

He drives us up to the lookout. In my four years in Booker, I admit I've never been up here.

Reed shuts off the car, gets out, and opens my door for me.

He grabs a blanket and sets it out before sitting down and pulling me between his legs, his arms wrapping around me tightly.

"It's beautiful up here," I say.

"I used to come up here a lot during all the shit with Hunter, trying to figure out what to do."

"I can see why. It's very calming."

"Mmm." He nuzzles my neck.

We sit in silence for a while before the alarm on Reed's phone goes off.

"It's midnight," he says quietly.

I turn to face him. "Happy birthday." I kiss him.

When we break apart he's beaming, his dimples deep in his cheeks.

"It's time for you to give me my present now."

"But I didn't bring them!" I say, panicked. I hadn't thought that far ahead.

"That's okay. Just stand up for me for a minute, angel."

I do as I'm told, but this is weird.

I look out over Booker and admire the view. It's only when Reed grabs my hand, him on one knee, that I get what's happening. My free hand flies to my mouth as tears start to flow down my cheeks.

"Bria, since the day you first walked through the door of the diner you've been a part of this family, seamlessly fitting into our hearts and our world. You've helped us, laughed with us, and loved us. You are one of us and I can't wait for that to be official. I knew from that first night I wanted to make you mine. I love you so much. I want everything with you: your tears, your happiness, your children. You are my heart, my soul, and I know with you by my side we can do anything."

He swallows and opens the velvet box in his hand. "Bria Marie Adams, will you do me the incredible honour of allowing me to become your husband? Will you marry me, angel?"

I've been nodding since he started his speech and I voice my answer, albeit shakily. "Yes." My heart thunders through my chest. I knew he'd do this some day, but not on his birthday.

He smiles and slides the ring on my finger. It's a plain gold band with a solitaire diamond, I'd say, maybe a carat.

"It was my nan and then my ma's ring."

"It's beautiful," I say as he gets up and takes me in his arms.

"So are you."

I lean up and kiss him, my hands framing his face, his hands digging into my hips.

"I love you," I say.

"I love you, and I can't wait to marry you."

"So how is this your present?" I ask, still confused.

"All I want is you and by saying yes, you've given that to me."

Oh. My. God. I don't say anything. Instead, I let the tears roll down my cheeks. My emotions are spiralling, heat and excitement dancing through me.

"We're gonna get married in your parents' backyard, and soon there's gonna be a little Ryan growing in your belly and we're gonna live happily ever after."

"Reed…."

"Future wife," he says with a smile, and that's all it takes for me to attack him.

I throw all my passion into my kiss, grabbing his shirt. Somehow we manage to disrobe and fall to the blanket.

"The future Mrs Reed Ryan," Reed says as he thrusts inside me.

"Fuck, Reed."

"I love you so much, baby. Thank you for being mine," he manages to get out as he moves in and out of me.

"Mmm." I moan as he goes particularly deep and I arch my back.

273

Reed latches on to a nipple and I moan at the pleasure and slither of pain.

"So good, baby," Reed pants, "you feel so good." I rake my nails down his back.

"I can't wait to marry you," I say and feel my insides tightening. I reach down and grab his arse, pushing him deeper into me, my legs wrapping around his waist. He shifts a little and my clit grinds against his pubic bone, giving me the friction I need.

"That's it, baby, come with me." And a few thrusts later, we're both coming, Reed's hot seed spilling inside me.

He rolls us to our sides, never breaking our connection.

"We're getting married," I say as I run my fingers through his hair. Saying the words aloud sends a shiver of exhilaration through me.

"Best. Birthday. Ever!" he says and we laugh.

"And it's not even mine."

"It's okay, angel. I'll look after you, forever. For the rest of our lives."

"Mmm, that sounds *so* good," I say sleepily as I rest my head on his chest.

"Are you still tired, baby?"

"Mmm." I nuzzle further into his strong chest, his musky, manly scent calming me.

"Baby," Reed says and pulls back so he can look at me, "you need to get checked out. You're going to be a Ryan wife, and bullshit or not that puts you at risk for bad shit happening." His voice breaks. "I can't have anything happen to you. You're my whole life. You know that, right?"

I reach up and cup his face. "It's okay, honey. I managed to get an appointment for today."

"Thank you." He kisses my forehead. "Come on, let's get back to our bed. I want to make love to you all night and I don't think the early morning fitness freaks would appreciate a show. I certainly don't want my fiancée on display like that."

Reed is true to his word and makes love to me all night. The only reason he let me out of bed this morning is because of my appointment. I make the short drive to the doctor's office.

After a few questions, she takes some blood and a urine sample and then we wait for my results.

She comes in after a few minutes.

"So I have your results…."

CHAPTER FORTY

REED

I'm now officially engaged and I can't wipe the smile off my face. I made love to my fiancée all night and would've kept going all day too, if not for this doctor appointment. The thought of Bria being sick scares the shit out of me. I only just got her; surely fate wouldn't be so cruel as to take her away from me already?

My phone rings and I see it's Bria. I swear my heart's beating out of my chest as I answer, praying she's okay.

"Angel?"

She sniffs and my heart breaks. "Can you get down here?" she asks, and I'm already out the door.

"I'm already on my way, baby. Everything's going to be all right. We're gonna get through this together, okay?"

She doesn't reply, just sniffs again.

I talk to her the whole way, the phone at my ear. "It's gonna be okay. I love you and I won't let anything happen to you. Whatever you need you'll get, okay? Whatever we have to do, we'll do it. Between my family and yours, we've got this covered. Don't worry, I'm almost there. I'll be there soon." Thank God, the office is only a short drive away.

"I love you, Reed Ryan."

"I'm just pulling in now. I'll see you soon, okay?"

"Okay."

I park haphazardly, not giving a fuck if I'm blocking anyone, and burst into the office. A moment later, I'm led into an examining room.

Bria is lying on the exam table, her shirt pulled up, the doc squirting some gel on her belly.

"Here he is," Bria says, a smile on her face.

What the fuck? She was crying just a minute ago.

"Angel?" I ask, going over to her side.

The doc starts moving this wand over her belly, and a loud thumping fills the room.

"What—what's going on?" I'm so fucking confused. My head is spinning.

"I thought you'd like to be here for our first sonogram."

"Our whatogram?"

"We're pregnant, Reed. We're having a baby."

"Baby?"

She nods excitedly and holds out a hand. I automatically take it and squeeze it tight.

"But you were crying."

277

"Happy tears."

"Happy tears?"

She nods, her grin never slipping from her face.

"You're about ten weeks along," the doc says. "The heartbeat is strong and everything is measuring on track."

"Heartbeat?" I ask. My head is still trying to process that Bria's okay.

"Yes." The doc hits a button and loud thumping fills the room again.

"That's our baby's heartbeat?" I ask.

"It certainly is."

"And you're not sick?" I ask Bria.

"Nope, just growing a human."

"Our human," I say, and kiss her forehead. *Our human.* The knowledge nearly knocks me on my arse.

"But ten weeks? How did this happen?" I ask, my brain still struggling to catch up. I think I left it at home in the rush to get down here.

"The antibiotics I took for my leg made my birth control ineffective."

"Huh."

"If you'll look at the screen, that's your baby," the doc interrupts.

"Holy shit," I breathe, and tears stream down Bria's cheeks. "That's our baby." I squeeze her hand.

The doc points out some things and then says she'll print us some pictures and a DVD.

"But everything's okay with him, right?" I ask.

"It's a little too early to determine gender, but yes, the baby is fine and healthy and so is mum."

"Technicalities, Doc, that's my son my woman is cooking in there."

She chuckles. "If you say so. So, Bria, start taking those prenatal vitamins, and if you have any issues, give me a call. If not, I'll see you in six weeks."

"Thanks, Dr Lara," Bria says.

"Yeah, thanks, Doc," I say, shaking her hand.

"The nurse will have your pictures and DVD. Congratulations," she says as we walk to the door.

"Holy shit," I say and pull Bria to me. I place my hand on her belly, rubbing gently.

"Happy birthday, although I guess the presents I got you we won't be needing anymore."

"Happy birthday? Fuck, this is so much more than happy birthday. I should go buy a lotto ticket, with the luck I'm having today."

"Do you need millions of dollars?" she asks.

"Baby, I've got everything I'll ever need in one hot, perfect package." She giggles. "Thank you, baby."

"So what now?" she asks, a beautiful smile on her face.

"Call Rome and Grayson. We're starting the party early," I say, the smile on my face is so big it's hurting my cheeks.

CHAPTER FORTY-ONE

BRIA

I hadn't meant to scare the shit out of Reed when I called but when Dr Lara told me I'm pregnant, the tears just flowed and I couldn't speak. Reed's reaction was priceless and his hand has barely left my belly since we left Dr Lara's office.

I call Gray and Rome and tell them to get over to the diner because we're starting the party early.

When we get there, everyone is present and wondering what the hell is going on. Reed has me tucked tight to his side, his hand resting on my belly.

"All right, what is it?" Pop asks.

"We have some announcements," Reed says, shouting over the noise, and things start to die down.

"One, she said yes!" Everyone cheers. Hugs and kisses

flow as I am passed from Ryan to Ryan, Reed never leaving my side. Grayson comes up to me and squeals when I show her the ring.

"It's beautiful, Bri," Rome says, and kisses my cheek.

"You guys next?" They both blush.

"You said *some* announcements," Mav says, "meaning there's more?"

"There is more," Reed says.

"Well?" Grayson asks, clearly impatient.

Reed looks at me and I nod.

"We're pregnant."

This time the roar from the assembled masses rattles the window. The door behind us opens and my parents walk in.

"We heard there's a party going on," my dad says.

I turn to Reed. "You called them?"

"I invited them. I had always planned to propose last night and knew they'd want to be here."

I lean up and kiss him. "I love you."

"And I love you, Mama."

"Mama?" my mum asks.

"You just missed the announcement," I say. "We're pregnant."

"Oh, my God!" she squeals, and pulls me into a tight hug. "How far along are you?"

"Ten weeks," Reed replies and grabs me from behind, both hands resting on my belly.

"Ten weeks."

"Let's go sit," Pop says, and we move to a table. As always, Reed tugs me down on his lap, his hands resting on my belly underneath my shirt. The move is sweet and protective. I don't think I'll ever tire of it.

"So tell us everything," Grayson says.

"Well," Reed begins, "when a man and a woman love each other very much, they have special cuddles—"

"Smart-arse," Grayson says, and flips him the finger, making sure to cover it so Chris doesn't see it.

We all laugh.

"We're ten weeks along. Oh, do you have the DVD?" I ask Reed.

"It's in the car. Jax!" he yells over all the chatter. "There's a white bag in my car with a DVD and some pictures, can you get it for us?"

"Sure thing, Papa." He shoots us a cheeky grin.

"Anyway, yeah, we're ten weeks along. The baby is healthy and measuring on track. We're due for another scan in six weeks."

"But how?" Gray asks.

"The antibiotics I was taking for my leg interfered with my birth control."

"So I owe you a drink or ten," Reed says to Rome, throwing him a wink.

"Call us even," Rome replies.

"Nah, man, you helped give me a family."

I turn and look at Reed. "We're having a family." Tears pool in my eyes as emotion crawls up my throat.

"Yeah, we are."

"Got 'em," Jax says, and pulls down the screen for the projector. He goes to the bar and puts in the DVD. The sonogram comes up on the screen.

"Holy shit," Mav exclaims.

Pop nods. "Yep, that's our baby." I swear my heart almost beats out of my chest.

Four photos were printed, so Reed and I each keep one and we give one to my parents and one to Pop.

"So when's the wedding?" Grayson asks.

I turn to Reed. "Ah…." We laugh.

"We haven't discussed when," I say. "We do know we want it small, just friends and family, at your house." I look at my parents.

"In the garden?" Mum asks.

I nod.

"Lovely."

I nod again and lean back on Reed; he's rubbing my belly gently. I still can't believe I've had another person growing inside me for ten weeks and I didn't know. Yes, the signs were there but I'm amazed I didn't put them all together.

Lunch is a rowdy affair and then rolls into Reed's party.

He parks me in a chair and doesn't let me move all night. He brings me food and drink and anything else I want, never straying far. Grayson and I laugh at his antics.

"He's not going to let you do anything until you pop that kid out," she says with a smile. It's so nice to see her happy again. I'm so glad Rome came to his senses and they were able to work things out.

"I know. He told me it's my job to grow the kid, and he'll do everything else."

"You got yourself a good one, Bri."

I nod. "And it's good to see you and Rome worked everything out."

"Yeah, it is."

A few hours later I'm starting to doze off.

"All right, guys, we're out," Reed says, picking me up. "You ready for bed?" he asks.

I nod, resting my head on his shoulder. We leave to a chorus of "Night, Mama," and I chuckle.

Once home, Reed lays me down on the bed and proceeds to take off all our clothes.

He lies down, his head at my belly.

"Hey there, buddy," he says to my stomach. "I'm your daddy. I just want you to know your mama and I love you very much and we can't wait to meet you. I do want to ask you something though, and that's to look after your mama for me. You've been so good we didn't even know you were there, so good job."

I chuckle. Never in a million years did I expect to ever see this soft side of Reed, but it's what he willingly shares with me every day.

"Anyway, you just chill in there, getting nice and big and strong, and we'll be ready and waiting for you in six and a half months."

He presses a kiss just below my belly button.

"I love you, buddy, sleep tight."

Tears stream down my cheeks. "Jesus, Reed."

"What's wrong?"

"That was so beautiful."

"So are you, even more so now that I know my baby's growing inside you." He moves up the bed and kisses my neck.

He pulls back to look me in the eyes.

"Nothing's going to happen to you, right?" he asks, suddenly getting serious.

"Hey." I cup his face. "I'm going to be fine. The baby and I are fine. You heard the doctor. I've been fine so far and I'm almost through the most fragile part, so, touch wood"—I reach down and grab his erection—"everything will be all right. Okay?" I grin.

He smiles at the gesture, but continues, "It's just—"

"Your family hasn't had the best of luck, I know, but don't you think we've already had our share of bad luck?"

He nods.

"And look how that turned out." I rest my hand over his on my stomach.

Reed smiles.

"See, not so bad, huh?"

"God, I love you. You're so fucking amazing, Bria, and I can't believe you're going to be my wife and the mother of my child."

"Mmm." I move his hand from my stomach to the growing need between my legs. His thumb circles my clit. I moan louder and arch my back.

"Yeah, that's it." He presses down harder.

"More," I pant.

"What's that?" he asks.

"I need more."

"What do you need, baby, tell me."

"You."

"You got me, angel."

"I want you inside me."

"Fingers or cock?"

"Fingers then cock." He shoots me his panty-dropping dimpled smile and slips a finger inside me.

I spread my legs wider and thrust into his hand.

He slides easily in and out of me then adds a second finger. The intrusion is perfect. I rake my nails down his back, my sensitive nipples rubbing against his chest. He curls his fingers, finding my G spot, and I feel a rush of moisture between my legs as I come.

"That's my girl," Reed says as he continues to slide his fingers in and out of me, drawing out my orgasm.

"I love you so much, Reed."

"And I love you and our son, so much, angel." He leans down to kiss me.

I pull him down to me and he slips inside. I hike my leg over his hip. He grabs it and squeezes hard. I'll probably have bruises in the morning but I don't care. I twist my hips and flip us so I'm on top, riding him. His eyes light up as I lean over and my hair falls over us like a curtain. He reaches up, cups my face, and brings it to his.

"You two are the most important people in my life. I don't want anything to happen you, either of you."

I cup his face in return. "Honey, nothing's going to happen. Everything's going to be fine."

CHAPTER FORTY-TWO

REED

I've become addicted to my son's kicks. It's an amazing sensation when you feel the life you helped create kick inside the woman you love. Bria started showing a few weeks ago, and it's so mind-blowing. It's one thing *knowing* our baby is growing inside her, but it's another thing entirely to actually *see* it.

She sleeps on my chest now so her body is aligned mostly with mine. She says it's easier this way. I say, as long as I have my family close to me, I don't give a fuck how she sleeps.

We haven't set a firm date for the wedding yet; we've been so busy. Between Liam's tour as champ, and getting Mav and Jax out there for their invites to the Extreme Games, there hasn't been time. Whenever it is, hopefully our son will make his appearance as a honeymoon gift. God, I can't wait.

But first thing's first, and tonight is the Rocking Racers charity gala.

Bria is wearing a strapless dress that makes her tits look huge. They've grown as our son has, and it's definitely awesome. The dress falls from there, showing a hint of our son growing inside her. She's sitting on the bed putting on her shoes when I notice the height of them.

"What the fuck are they?" I growl.

"Shoes," she replies, not looking up from doing the buckle up.

"Those have to be four-inch heels."

"Yep, boosting me up like a big girl."

"Well that's a shame, because you're not wearing them."

"Excuse me?"

"Those heels are ridiculous! You'll fall and break your neck, or worse, hurt our son."

"I've worn them before, Reed."

"Yes, but you've never been five months pregnant before. What happens if you fall? You could land on your belly."

"You're really worried about this?"

"You two are the most precious things to me," I say, coming to kneel in front of her. "It's my job to make sure you're both safe."

"It'll be fine, Reed. They're just shoes."

"They're *really* fucking high, Mama."

She sighs. "You really don't want me wearing them?"

I shake my head.

"Fine," she huffs. "Go grab my black flats from the closet."

I get up, kiss her forehead, and rub her belly. "Thank you."

With the shoe situation sorted, we head to the car. She sighs as we pass my bike.

"I miss this," she says, running her hand over the seat.

"Mmm, me too. I love having you wrapped around me."

"Guess there's not really room for it in our immediate future, huh?"

"Not with you carrying precious cargo."

"It's a pity. I always had this fantasy…."

"Oh yeah?"

She nods and bites her lip. I go over and hug her to me.

"Tell me, what does this fantasy involve?"

"You and me," she says.

"That much I get." I kiss her nose.

"On that bike." She nods towards it.

"Really?" I arch an eyebrow.

She nods again, still biting her lip.

"I think that can be arranged."

"It can?"

"No rule saying we have to take the bike anywhere, is there?"

"No."

"So as long as we lock the doors, then what's stopping us?" I kiss her neck.

"Nothing, I guess."

"But right now we have a gala to get to, so damp down those hormones and let's go," I say, releasing her and opening the car door.

She pouts as she gets in. "It's not like I'm the only one with a rush of blood," she says, and nods to my cock pressed hard against my zipper.

"Never said you were, but right now we don't have time." I grin, hardly believing it myself that I'm postponing sex.

We arrive with the others, Bria making sure we all do our time with the media on the red carpet. Rome also does his bit. Since Bria had the features done on him, business has massively picked up and Rome's in demand.

I finish with the media and walk over to Bria and Grayson.

"What's with your dress?" Gray asks her. "The hem is drowning you."

"Mr Overprotective over there wouldn't let me wear my heels."

"But it's okay for you to trip over your dress?"

I stand behind Bria and hug her, my hands on our son.

"No, she won't because I'll be right next to her." As I speak, our son starts kicking. Bria grins and grabs Grayson's hand.

"Holy shit," Gray whispers.

"Pretty amazing, right?" I ask.

"It's incredible. You two made that. There's a baby in there!"

"I hope so," Bria says. "I'd hate to think I'm capable of putting on this much weight so quickly."

"You're beautiful," I whisper in her ear.

"All right, kids, that's enough of a show for the media," Jax says. "You're taking the attention away from the real stars."

"I don't see any," Gray says, looking around.

"You know," Jax says, slinging an arm around her shoulders, "it's a good thing you and I didn't work out. I mean, you *clearly* aren't appreciative of my star power."

"If you're such a star, where's your date?"

"No, no girls on the carpet, only forever ones. It sends them the wrong impression. They start thinking it means something and then they never go away. Plus, we don't want any scorned ladies going to the tabloids. It gives a bad impression, right media Mama-boss?"

"You make me sound like a pimp or a madam," Bria huffs.

"Hey, that's not a bad idea," Jax says. "Can you hook me up?"

"You're calling the mother of my child, your nephew, a pimp?" I growl at him.

He holds his hands up. "Course not."

"Didn't think so."

"Go on, we've got the step and repeat and then we can go inside."

We all smile prettily for the cameras then go inside.

Mav and Jax make a beeline for the bar and the women congregating there. They'll have their work cut out for them with this crowd. Rocking Racers brings together rock stars and racing stars, both two and four wheels, to raise funds for a nominated charity. This year it's breast cancer. Every year we make sure at least two of us go but I can see Bria buzzing with the networking opportunities, so I'd say that's going to change and we'll all be attending from now on.

She starts schmoozing right away, impressing some of the hardest men in racing.

I see McKnley Rhodes, spelt without the I apparently. Her sister, Ashton, and Park had a thing going for a while but it was hard with their band, named Places, always on tour.

We sit down for dinner and I'm questioning the waiter on what's being served. There're *so* many things pregnant women shouldn't eat, but I'm pretty sure I know them all.

Tension hits the table.

Hunter and two of his goons saunter over.

"What the fuck?" I ask.

"It's nice to see you, too, Reed. I see life has been good to you." He nods towards Bria.

Hackles rise around our table.

"What the fuck are you doing here?"

"Out on bail before my trial, so I thought I'd come over and say hi, see how you're doing."

"Fuck off, Hunter." He shouldn't even have been able to get into this event.

"Now, now, that's not a very nice thing to say, is it? I was just trying to be friendly. After all, do you really want to test me? You of all people should know how dangerous it is for women to be involved with your family. I still remember poor Emma. Such a beauty. A shame she liked to party, but then I guess it wouldn't have been such an issue if Parker had wrapped his shit up. Having a Ryan baby greatly increases the dangers of childbirth"—he glances at Bria's stomach— "but then just being around you lot is dangerous. Fights at the diner, explosions at garages... not a very safe environment for women or children, is it?"

I don't think, all I know is I have to get to him. I lunge,

fists flying, but am blocked by Rome.

"Leave it," he says to me.

"Nobody threatens my fiancée and baby and gets away with it."

"Let him go, Rome. He's more of a man than you'll ever be," Hunter taunts.

"Shut up, Hunter," Rome says, trying to restrain us both.

"I see you're sitting pretty too. New job, new digs, new girl. A lot to lose right there."

"You leave my girl and home out of this, Hunter."

"Perhaps we could start a curse for your family as well."

"You son of a bitch!" This time it's me restraining Rome as he lunges.

Just then Detective Cameron comes over.

"A problem, gentlemen?"

"No problem," Hunter says.

"You know you're not allowed contact with witnesses."

"I was simply walking past and Roman and Reed here lunged at me."

"You lying piece of shit," Roman curses.

"I've got the whole confrontation recorded," Mav pipes up. He shows it to Detective Cameron.

"Looks like we're going to be adding two counts of witness tampering and harassment to your charges on Monday, Mr David. Turn around."

"This is bullshit," he says.

"Unfortunately for you, Mr Ryan has been filming for a while and captured everything, including you approaching the table. I assume Ms Adams and Ms Dean would like to pursue harassment charges?"

The girls nod.

"I'll have those drawn up. See you Monday morning." He marches Hunter off. His goons have magically disappeared.

I take a breath, running my hands through my hair, and see Cole Matthews approach the table. He and I go all the way back to the juniors; we were each other's main competition.

"Everything okay?" he asks.

"Yeah, Cole, we're good. Just had to throw out the rubbish." I squeeze Bria's shoulder. Cole sees and smiles.

"You must be Bria," he says, and she nods. "Cole Matthews," he introduces himself, extending a hand.

"Oh, you're the guy who won the Supermoto title," she says. My girl's come a long way in six months and now is almost as knowledgeable as all of us in terms of racing.

He nods. "That's me."

"I've heard you're coming over to the NRS next season."

He shrugs. "I need a ride first."

"You looking?" I ask.

"Well yeah. I mean, Supermoto is good, but the level of competition could use some improving."

"Or you could use a change of scenery."

He nods.

"You still got the same management?"

"Yeah, man, family's hard to shake, you know that."

"I do. No promises, but I'll see what we can do."

"Yeah?" he asks, surprised.

I shrug. "We know when we're on a good thing and we're looking to expand."

"Wow, man."

"We'll be in touch."

"Yeah, thanks. It was great to meet you, Bria, guys." He returns to his table, where McKnley Rhodes waits for him, looking anything but impressed.

~

Later that week, Ryan Racing made an offer to Cole. He accepted a day later.

The press loved it. The sponsors loved it more.

The good news was topped off by Hunter's verdict. He was found guilty of attempted murder, arson, assault, two counts of harassment and intimidating a witness. He won't be seeing freedom for a long time.

CHAPTER FORTY-THREE

REED

Today is my wedding day. It's funny, I never thought I'd have one before I met Bria, but since she's been in my life, it was never *not* an option.

The lead-up to today has been pretty chilled. There were no bridezilla moments and everything was done with a minimum of fuss.

It's half an hour before the ceremony is due to start, and I'm going nuts. Grayson insisted on Bria staying at her parents' last night, and as a result, I couldn't sleep. I can count on two hands the nights we've spent apart since we met. I'm not a fan of it happening again anytime soon. I'm pacing and it's driving Park nuts.

"Would you stop that already?"

"I can't. I'm going crazy. I haven't seen them in almost twenty hours. I can't take it."

"Seriously, man?"

"She's carrying my child, Park. I know Emma didn't let you be around while she was pregnant, but fuck, she's got a piece of me growing inside her and I want to be with them all the time. We've hardly ever been apart."

"I always thought Mav would be the next to fall. He's always been so much more serious than the rest of us."

"No rule saying he can't be. Or you," I add as an afterthought.

Park shakes his head. "I just can't see it."

"I couldn't either, and look at me now, twenty-five minutes from being a husband, four months from being a father."

"You've done well, little brother."

"I know, and I'm gonna go check on my family before I wear a path in the Adams's guest room."

The door to Bria's parents' room is closed but I hear giggling come from behind it. I'm able to pick out Bria easily.

"You better not be drinking champagne in there," I say through the closed doors.

"Reed." I can hear her gasp.

"You're not supposed to be anywhere near here," Grayson scolds.

"I'm on the other side of closed doors. What's the harm? I just wanna make sure my soon-to-be wife and son are okay, seeing that I wasn't allowed to spend last night with them. So no champagne, right?"

I can tell Bria's rolling her eyes. "No, I'm not drinking champagne. It's strictly lemonade for me."

"Lemonade? Are you feeling sick? Buddy, remember we talked about being good to your mama."

She laughs. "No, I'm not feeling sick, just felt like lemonade is all."

"Another craving?" I lean up against the door, my hand about level to where Bria's belly would be.

"I guess. It isn't anything bad though."

That's one thing I'm not liking about pregnancy: the daily change of food preferences. One day it's lemonade, another it's apple juice, the next it's iced tea. The only constant is it's never caramel milkshakes anymore. All sorts of things have come and gone from our pantry since we found out we're pregnant.

"That's good. Did you guys sleep okay last night? You weren't uncomfortable, were you?"

Now that she's showing, sleeping is a challenge. It's most comfortable for her to rest on my chest so her belly can rest on my stomach.

"Slept like a baby, thanks for asking," Gray responds. I hear a quiet "Ow," and I know Bria has hit her.

"We slept okay. We missed you though," she answers.

"I missed you too. Are you almost ready? I'm dying from the wait."

"Yes, I'm ready. I've been ready for a little bit now."

"Grayson, are you ready?" I ask, starting to get ticked off.

"Beauty takes time, Reed, and perfection can't be rushed."

"So help me God, Grayson, if you're the reason I can't marry my wife right the fuck now."

"Technically she's not your wife yet."

"Gray," I warn.

"Geez, lighten up," she says.

"Are you ready?"

She starts to say something but is cut off. I imagine Bria has elbowed her. "Yes, I'm ready."

I punch the air. "Good, I'll go down and tell everyone we're ready. I'll see you at the altar, angel."

"I'll be the one in white," she replies.

"I love you two so much."

"Oh, thanks, honey," Grayson butts in, "but I'm taken."

I hear another "Ow," and then Bria says, "And we love you. Now go so we can get married."

I rush down the stairs and swing by the guest room to get Park.

"Come on, she's ready."

"Gotcha, let's go."

Our families, Mike, and the guys from the team—including Cole—are milling around. Chris is running around and Pop is trying to make sure he doesn't get dirty.

They see Park and me and a cheer goes up.

"We're ready if you want to take a seat."

Because there're only about twenty of us here there are no sides, just a group of chairs. We don't have separate families; we're just one now. I shake hands with Minister Hale; he's the one who married Pop and Ma.

Jax must get his cue and starts the music. Grayson comes out of the house and makes her way to us. The music changes, and Bria and Aaron walk out, and I swear my heart stops. She's absolutely breathtaking. Her dress is kind of creamy coloured and her hair is down. Okay, so I suck at details, but in my defence, my brain is being deprived of oxygen because I've stopped breathing.

Personally I don't care what she's wearing. She could walk to me in a hoodie and jeans and she'd still be the most beautiful thing I've ever seen. Aaron shakes my hand and puts Bria's hand in mine. I place my other hand on her belly over our son.

"We are gathered here today to witness the marriage of Bria and Reed and to celebrate the commitment they make to each other," Minister Hale begins.

I can't believe I'm finally marrying Bria, that in a few moments we'll be husband and wife and bound together forever.

"Reed Cooper Ryan, do you take Bria Marie Adams to be your lawfully wedded wife?" Minister Hale asks me.

"Absolutely."

"Bria Marie Adams, do you take Reed Cooper Ryan to be your lawfully wedded husband?"

"I do."

"I believe you have your own vows?"

We nod, and I take a deep breath. "Bria, the moment you walked into the diner and we finally, officially met, I knew you were someone special. From that moment, you've been a part of our family, loving us, laughing with us, crying with us. We are so lucky to have you in our lives and I'm the luckiest guy on the planet because somehow, through everything, you love me. You have changed me so much, Bria. I never gave thought to the possibility of ever having a wife and a baby.

To me, they were a pit of responsibility I never wanted to fall into, but with you, that all changed. Us, being here, was never not going to happen and our child in your belly,"—he starts kicking—"yes, you, buddy. I'm just marrying your mama so if you can behave that would be good." Everyone chuckles. "Our child in your belly was an inevitability. You're the girl of my dreams I never knew I had, the keeper of my heart and the mother of my children. I love you more than I thought was possible to love anyone, and I promise to always love you, protect you, and take care of you until the end of time."

There are tears streaming down her face and I reach up and wipe them away.

"Bria?" Minister Hale asks.

She clears her throat and throws back her shoulders. I smile; that's my girl.

"Reed, from the moment I met you my world changed. It's opened up, and I'm so grateful. You and your family took to me immediately and with no questions asked. You accepted me as one of your own and showed me love and devotion I never knew existed. You have never doubted me or questioned me, you've let me take over your business and together we're going to build it into a powerhouse, just as we're going to grow this." She places her hand over mine on her belly.

"You have loved me more than I thought was possible. You have cared for me, for us, helped my friends and shown me what acceptance and truly belonging mean. You are my best friend, my protector, my lover, and the father of my children. I promise to always be by your side, loving you, looking after you and helping to make your dreams come true until the end of time."

We exchange rings, and then Minister Hale pronounces us husband and wife.

"You may kiss your bride now, Reed," he tells me, even though I need no invitation.

I draw Bria into my arms, one hand resting on her cheek, her eyes shining up at me with nothing but love.

"My wife," I whisper before I take her lips. The kiss is full of passion. I'd keep going, except there are more than a few throats being cleared.

We break apart and I rest my forehead on hers. "I love you, Mrs Ryan."

"We love you, too."

"Come on, I want to show my wife off."

I'm true to my word and drag her round to everyone, asking if they've met my wife. It thrills the shit out of me every time I call her that.

~

The reception is very relaxed, very casual, very us.

We're sitting down having a breather in between dances, my hands, as always, are on Bria's belly. She's twisting my wedding ring.

"You like having me wear your ring?" I ask.

She nods. "I do. It's totally hot. Almost as much as I love wearing your rings."

"So was today everything you dreamed of?"

"Better."

I beam. "Yeah?"

She nods. "Uh–huh." She leans down and kisses me.

"So, you had enough, wife of mine? You've danced with every man here, which I thoroughly enjoyed watching, by the way."

"Is my husband jealous? Does he not remember the vows we said a couple of hours ago? The rings we exchanged?"

I grab her tightly and tickle her. "You just called me your husband."

"Isn't that what you are?"

"Amongst other things, but that's the first time you've referred to me as you husband. I like it, a lot." I push my erection into her backside.

She leans forward so she can whisper in my ear, "Is my husband ready to consummate our marriage?"

"Wife, I've been ready since we said I do."

"So what are we waiting for?" she asks.

In a flash, we're out of the chair and hurrying to the car.

"Going somewhere, newlyweds?" Jax asks.

"Yeah, my wife's tired. The pregnancy, you know," I say. "So we're gonna go."

"Uh-huh, sure," Gray says, but I'm not listening. I'm rushing us away.

"Eager?" Bria asks.

I stop and adjust her in my arms. "To make love to my wife? Always, baby, always."

I get her situated in the car and rush around to the driver side. I turn to her before I start the car and grab her hand. "Thank you."

"For what, honey?"

"For everything."

"I could say the same to you."

"We're married, angel."

"I know, I was there."

"We're a family." I move our hands to her belly.

"We're a family."

"God, baby, is this even real? Did we really do all this?"

"I hope so." Her eyes glisten, reflecting the happiness I feel.

"These months have been the best of my life."

"Mine too, and you know what? It's only the beginning."

"Yeah, it is."

"So what do you say we get started?"

CHAPTER FORTY-FOUR

REED

My wife is miserable and there's nothing I can do to make it better.

She's now officially five days overdue and she's desperate for Avery to come out. We decided to name him Avery Casey after my ma and nan. Ma's maiden name was Avery. Nan's was Casey.

Her back hurts, her feet are swollen, she has to pee every five minutes, and even lying on me at night isn't comfortable for her to sleep. I hate it. I hate that there's very little I can do to help ease her discomfort.

I run baths and massage her feet, but these only make her feel better for a short amount of time.

We've spent the day watching Chris run around with

his friends for his birthday, and it's got us both excited and exhausted. Mostly though, I think Bria just wants Avery to come out.

It's been hectic since the wedding; we had the Extreme Games two months ago, which were crazy. Jax and Mav were in high demand, thanks to the publicity whipped up by my incredible wife, and had a million appearances to make. Of course, I was worried about Bria's workload. She was seven months pregnant after all, but it was only after she snapped at me for suggesting she monitor their media conferences via an earpiece and a live stream that I backed off. Okay, so the two weeks without sex may have been more convincing, but I still think I was right.

In the end, it all worked out. Mav brought home the gold for Moto X speed and style, and Jax gold for BMX halfpipe, unseating the ten-time champion, and silver for BMX big air.

"That'll be us soon," Bria says, referring to Chris's party as I get her ready for bed, which nowadays, much to my delight, involves taking off all her clothes. She can't stand to have anything clinging to her.

"I know. I can't wait." I kiss her belly as I take off her pants.

"How long do you want to wait for the next one?" she asks.

"You haven't even popped out this one and you're already planning the next?" I ask, pulling her body to mine. "I like your thinking."

"It's just something I think we should plan, don't you?"

"I do." I lift off her shirt. "I don't think I'd want too big a gap, but I also don't want you to feel like you're always pregnant. I think my parents timed it pretty well. There's two years between Park and me, then me and Liam, then three years between Liam and Mav but only a year between Mav and Jax. I think anywhere between two and three years is good. What do you think?" I undo her bra and she moans in relief. My dick reacts to the sound.

"I think two to three years is good." She turns around to undress me.

I make passionate love to her, hoping this'll be the last time before Avery comes. I'm just as eager for his arrival as Bria. Obviously, I'm not looking forward to the six weeks I'll have to go without sex, but I think the trade-off, the arrival of our son, will be more than worth the sacrifice.

I swear I've only been asleep for ten minutes when Bria wakes me up.

"Reed, honey, wake up," she says, shaking me.

"What is it?" I ask, jolting awake.

"I went to the bathroom and my water broke. I'm in labour."

"You are?"

She nods.

"Have you had any contractions?"

"One, about ten minutes ago."

"Okay, let's go." I get up.

"Ah!" Bria says, grabbing her stomach.

"Angel?" I rush to her side.

"Contraction," she pants out.

"Okay, let's get our stuff and go to the hospital. Looks like Avery is finally ready to have his birthday." I throw on some clothes, grab a dress for Bria to put on, and get the bags we've had packed for three weeks. I get a glimpse at the clock and see it's two in the morning.

"You okay to walk to the car?" I ask my wife.

She nods and I grab her elbow and escort her to my Mustang. I'm running around to the driver side when I hear her yell out again, another contraction.

"All right, baby, we'll be there soon."

I swear I break every speed limit on the drive to the hospital. Luckily, the town is asleep. Bria calls her parents in between contractions, now eight minutes apart, then rings Park. He's the lightest sleeper and will get everyone else up. I pull into the hospital driveway as another contraction hits, and run inside yelling.

Nurses come running and we get Bria into a wheelchair and up to the maternity ward.

Once she's comfortable in a birthing room, they confirm her contractions have stayed at eight minutes apart and she's three centimetres dilated. They hook her up to all sorts of machines and then we wait and wait.

My family arrive, as well as Rome and Grayson. I'm assuming Park called them. A little while later, her parents turn up.

"Did we miss it?" they ask as they rush in.

"Nope," I reply. "We seem to have stalled at the moment."

"How is she?" Lacey asks.

"Beautiful. She's four centimetres dilated, so almost halfway. They've given her some pain relief so she's fine."

Everyone comes in to say a brief hello, and then at around 7:00 a.m. things happen quickly. Her doctor comes in to check her and tells us she's fully dilated, and on the next contraction she can push. I grab one of her legs and pull it back towards her chest. She pushes and pants and screams and almost breaks my wrist, but after an hour, we hear cries.

"You did it, angel," I say and kiss her sweaty forehead.

"Congratulations, it's a girl," the doc says.

"A girl? We have a daughter?" I ask, tears in my eyes.

"You certainly do," the doc says. "Do you want to come and cut the cord, Dad?"

I'm stunned and still can't believe I have a daughter, that Avery is here.

"Go get our girl, Daddy," Bria says, a loving smile on her face. I bend to kiss her quickly and make my way to the end of the bed. I grab the scissors from a nurse and cut where they tell me, and get my first glimpse of my daughter.

She's perfect.

The nurse takes her away to check her and clean her up. I go back to Bria and kiss her forehead again.

"We have a daughter, angel," I say.

She nods and wipes her tears away.

"Yep, a very healthy baby girl, three kilos exactly," the doc says, and places her in Bria's arms.

She has blue eyes and a mop of brown hair. She has Bria's cute button nose and my lips, the perfect mix.

"She's perfect," I say and give her my finger, which she grasps tightly.

I unwrap her a bit and count her fingers and toes several times. Ten of each, for the record.

"Thank you so much," I say, pulling them towards me, my girls.

"She's the perfect mix of both of us," Bria says, tears streaming down her face.

"She's perfect, our little Avery Casey Ryan." I kiss her forehead, inhaling her sweet baby scent.

"Good thing we picked a unisex name."

"You knew, didn't you?" I ask, my eyes not leaving my daughter.

"I may have done," Bria says slyly.

"I don't even care. We have a daughter."

"Do you want to hold her?"

"Absolutely." Bria gingerly scoots over and I join them on the bed.

She transfers Avery to me and my heart explodes. This little girl I've watched grow in her mama's belly and is only twenty minutes old totally has my heart. Anyone does anything to her, and I swear I'll kill them. No one hurts my daughter.

"Hey, princess, I'm your daddy. You are the most precious thing I've ever seen, and I promise I'm going to look after you and protect you forever."

Bria sniffs and I finally look away from Avery.

"You two…," she says, tears streaming down her face.

"She's amazing. I thought I couldn't love anyone as much as you, but now…."

"I know."

"It's amazing. I can't believe we made her." I lean down

and kiss her forehead again.

"I'm so glad to meet you, beautiful girl. I know we've already talked lots, but I'm so glad you're here. You mean the world to your mama and me, Avery, and we love you so much." The moment is surprisingly calm as she falls asleep in my arms, and Bria takes a few quiet moments. I breathe it all in. Not wanting to forget this feeling.

Lacey and Pa poke their heads in. "Can we come in?"

"Sure. Meet your granddaughter and great-granddaughter, Avery Casey Ryan," Bria says.

Pa puts a pink teddy on the table beside the bed.

"You knew?" I ask.

"I guessed. Bria kept saying 'them' or 'the baby,' not 'our son' so I figured…."

"You said him with me," I say to her.

She shrugs. "It was habit."

"Can I hold her?" Lacey asks. As much as I want to say no and never let anyone hold her but us, I know that's not feasible. I nod and hand her over reluctantly.

"She's beautiful," she says, and Pa nods.

"Your pop and I appreciate the sentiment too, so thank you," Pa says.

"Sentiment?" Lacey asks.

"Avery was my mother's maiden name, and Casey was my nan's," I say.

"Lovely."

Avery stretches in Lacey's arms and I jump at the movement. Everyone laughs at me.

"She's okay, Reed. She's just stretching," Lacey says.

"It's just she's so little and new."

"And your baby. Don't worry, Reed, I've done this before."

"I know, but she's ours and so damn precious."

So. Damn. Precious.

Over the next few hours, everyone comes to visit.

The standouts are Chris, with his eyes as wide as saucers, and Rome, who upon holding Avery for the first time, asks Gray if he can't put in an order. She tells him she'll consider it.

We're able to take Avery home the next day. I never leave their sides at the hospital.

I got up with her every time last night, telling Bria she did the hard work, now it's my turn. I've barely left her side, but then again, neither has Bria.

So far, she's been a good baby, not fussing too much, and took to Bria's breast easily. My shorts got very tight the first time I saw her feed her. It's too bad we have to wait six weeks.

Bria's just finished feeding her and we're standing watching her sleep when she asks, "You're not disappointed we didn't have a boy?"

I sling an arm around her waist, pulling her tight to me and kissing her temple. "Nothing you could've given birth to would've disappointed me."

"She's perfect."

"I know. I don't ever want to leave her, even for a second. I know it's not practical, but I guess I just don't want to be without her. It feels like I'm missing something, like how I feel when I'm not with you."

"Oh, honey." She pats my stomach.

"We're a family. We have a daughter."

"I know, I was there," she jokes.

"Nine and a half months ago I was looking for my next lay, and then you walked into the diner and my whole world changed in an instant. Now I'm a husband and a father and I couldn't be happier."

"I always thought I'd get married and have kids, but when I was at least twenty-seven. I wanted to graduate and work a few years to build my career before I did all this. Then I walked into the diner and all that rolled into one. It's been a whirlwind but I wouldn't change anything. I have a loving husband and a beautiful daughter. I don't need anything else."

"We are going to give that little girl the world. Anything she wants is hers."

CHAPTER FORTY-FIVE

REED

Avery is four months old and perfect. Not long after she was born, her eyes changed from baby blue to a hazel, green and brown.

We've been pretty lucky. She's a great baby and doesn't fuss too much.

We've both been able to spend time with her at home and if Ryan Racing requires our attention, we can usually do it separately, like today.

The NRS starts up next week, and Liam and Cole had media stuff to do. The hype with Liam as reigning champ and Cole coming on board is insane.

When Bria comes in she looks exhausted, but the moment she sees Avery resting on my chest, that exhaustion disappears.

"Hey, beautiful girl," she says, coming over to us as we chill on the couch. My girl and I are watching *Mulan*. She likes Mushu.

"Hey, we missed you today."

Bria kisses me then picks up Avery, smothering her face in kisses. She laughs her baby laugh and I smile at the sound. There is no doubting this girl, well, both of them, have my heart.

"I missed you. Were you a good girl for Daddy?" Bria sits on the couch and I pull her tight to me. I love having my girls close.

"She was. She's a daddy's girl, so of course she was good. How about you? How'd it go today?"

She blows out a breath. "Hectic. I know Cole and Knley are great together but her family is *crazy*. They hate Cole and aren't being shy about hiding it. The media's having a field day. Add to that the fact they don't get to spend a lot of time together, and poor Cole's a bit lost. At least he's got the series to focus on and take his mind off things, but I have a feeling it's going to come to a head soon."

"Shit, does he know?"

"I think he's smart enough to realise it's got to, soon, but I'll have a chat with him and Knley about it. She's coming in for the race but it's not going to be pleasant. I mean, it's her family, after all."

"Mmm. I don't like the fact you're being put in the middle of all this."

She shrugs and bounces Avery in her lap. "It's part of my job. Cole is a Ryan Racing rider and unfortunately his private life is part of his public image."

"I don't miss that."

"Just the nature of the beast. To a certain extent he's used to it, but add in Knley, her star power and family, and it's a little bit of a freak show."

"Where's her PR in all of this?"

"Her mum, or mumager, as she calls herself, like she's some kind of Kardashian wannabe, does it."

"Oh."

"Yeah, she's loving all the extra attention. Even if Knley and Cole aren't doing anything, it's insane. It's not like I can do anything though. Knley and Places have their own agenda, their own stuff they want to achieve. I'm just the PR manager for Cole's team."

"Oh, you're a lot more than that." I lean over and kiss her cheek before moving down to her neck, nipping, licking, and sucking lightly.

"Mmm," she moans and my dick stirs to life. With Avery being so settled, our sex life hasn't taken that much of a hit, a fact my dick and I are eternally grateful for.

In Bria's lap, Avery squawks as the movie ends.

"You ready for dinner, baby girl?" my wife asks our daughter after clearing her throat a few times.

"We'll finish that later," I whisper in Bria's ear as we get up and go to the kitchen.

Bria gets Avery settled in her high chair while I heat up the veggies I mashed for her today.

"So what's on the menu?" Bria asks.

"For mademoiselle, mashed pumpkin, sweet potato, and apple."

"Mmm, yummy," Bria says, and makes a face. She hates pumpkin.

"And for sir and madam, a slow-cooked beef massaman curry with coconut jasmine rice."

"You really are too good to be true."

"No, just nothing short of what you deserve."

"I love you." She leans over to kiss me.

"And I love you. Now, let's get our little princess fed and bathed, then we can put her to bed and the fun stuff can begin." I wiggle my eyebrows at her.

Avery laughs at the movement.

"Is that funny, baby girl?" I ask, directing the gesture to my daughter and she laughs again. I lean over and kiss her chubby cheek.

The two of us get Avery fed and into her bath. She splashes around in the water, soaking both of us, but we don't mind.

After dressing her in her Saints onesie, it's then the best part of the evening. Bria sits in the rocking chair that's been used for three generations of Ryans and breastfeeds our daughter.

I sit on the daybed we have in here and watch them until Avery's little eyelids start drooping and eventually close. We both kiss her forehead before Bria places her in her cot and closes the door.

I pull Bria into my arms. "So how are you doing?"

"I'm better now I'm here with my husband and perfect daughter." She leans up and kisses me.

What started as a quick kiss quickly turns passionate.

"Dinner will keep for a bit, right?" she asks breathlessly as we break apart.

"Yeah." I nod. "It's good."

"Good." Bria turns and starts walking to our bedroom, shedding clothes along the way. I waste no time in following her and ridding myself of my clothes as well.

When I get into our bedroom, Bria is naked and waiting for me. I step through the door, closing it behind me, and Bria attacks. She pushes me against the wall and kisses a path down my body to my rock-hard cock. Without hesitation, she sucks me deep and I hit the back of her throat.

"Oh fuck!" I exclaim and my head rolls back.

"Mmm." She moans and the vibration goes straight to my balls.

She alternates between sucking me deep and licking the crown and my slit. She reaches for my balls but I stop her, grabbing her under her arms.

"Uh-uh, I'm not coming in your mouth tonight." I pick her up and toss her on the bed, her hair flying everywhere. She giggles and leans on one arm, one of her knees bent.

"You're a vision," I breathe.

"You're not too bad yourself."

I slowly stalk over to her. I get to the edge of the bed and crawl up between her legs, kissing as I go. Her flavour bursts over my tongue and I moan.

"So good."

"Reed." My name is a moan on her lips as she runs her fingers through my hair.

I circle her clit with my tongue before moving down to slide in and out of her, sucking up her juices. I replace my tongue with my fingers, one at first, before adding a second. I nibble and suck on her clit before she comes, tightly squeezing my fingers.

I lick my fingers clean before crawling up my wife's body and sliding into her wet heat.

Leisurely, I slide in and out of her, her hips rising to meet me, my mouth attached to hers, my tongue mimicking our movements. I pull back to look her in the eyes, smoothing her hair back from her face.

"I love you so much, Bria."

"I love you so much, Reed."

I thrust into her a few more times before we're both coming hard. Bria bites down on my shoulder to stop her screams from waking Avery, and I swear I come again.

"Jesus," I say as I roll us to our sides, my semi-hard cock still buried in my wife.

"Did you come twice?" she asks.

"I think I did," I reply, running a hand through my hair.

"Impressive," Bria says as she tries to catch her breath.

"What can I say?" I kiss her neck. "My wife does it for me."

She giggles and I reluctantly pull out of her and go get a washcloth from the bathroom to clean her up. I come back into our room and find Bria throwing the old Ryan Racing shirt she sleeps in over her head.

"Open for me, Mama." I hate to wipe away the evidence of our lovemaking but it's messy and no one wants to sleep in the wet patch on the bed.

I throw the washcloth back in the bathroom and pull on a pair of boxers. Even though my family are pretty good at giving us space now Avery's here, they still walk in unannounced and it's not good for sibling relations for my brothers to see just how blessed I am. Plus, my pop and pa don't need to see me naked.

The phone rings, so Bria grabs it and I go get our dinner. By the time I make it back, Bria's wrapping up the call.

"Yes, Mum, I'm sure we'll be able to handle Avery at the track." She pauses. "Yes, we've got baby ear muffs and no, she won't be exposed to any heavy fumes."

"Tell her if she wants," I say, "we can get her, Aaron, Colt, and Anne passes and they can sit in the box. I don't think anyone's using it."

"Did you hear that?" Bria asks. "We were going to try and send Pa up there and if you guys are there, he might stay. It would mean Chris would be there as well though," Bria says. I don't think that'll matter to the Adamses, they love Chris as if he were their own grandson. They spoil him rotten, saying that since his maternal grandparents don't give a shit about him, they will.

"Yes, I'll leave Avery with you. I was happy to have her with me, and then Reed would take her after the race, but yes, you can have babysitting duty." She rolls her eyes.

I smile and motion to the bowls of curry and rice I'm holding.

"Look, Mum, your passes will be waiting for you at the gate on Saturday along with directions to the box, and I'll see you when you get there. Just text me. Right now I've got to go. Reed made dinner and it's getting cold."

A pause.

"Okay, I will."

Another pause.

"Yep, I will." Bria rolls her eyes and nods. "Yep, I got it. Mum, I really have to go. Okay, I love you both, bye."

"Bye, Lacey," I yell before Bria hangs up.

"I swear she'd be here 24/7 if she could."

"She wants to be near her granddaughter. I can understand that."

"Yes, but she needs to realise we're Avery's parents and we know what we're doing, sort of."

"Hey, I'm never going to fault anyone for falling in love with our little girl. She has a way about her so you just can't help wanting to be near her, just like her mama."

"Smooth, Ryan, real smooth," she says and leans against my chest. I hand her a bowl and she thanks me with a kiss.

We sit, eating and chatting about general things before making love a few more times.

Around eleven, Avery wakes for a feed. She'll wake again at three. Quietly and as gently as I can, I slip out of bed and go heat my daughter a bottle. I walk into the nursery and pick her up.

"Hey, baby girl, are you hungry?"

I sit in the rocking chair while she hungrily sucks down her bottle.

"You, my princess, are one of the most precious things in my life. I love you so much, Avery."

I kiss her forehead, inhaling her sweet baby smell that's even better than her mama's, burp her, change her, and tuck her back in.

I stand and watch her sleep for a while and kiss my thumb and index finger and point to the sky. As I do, I think about all the women in my life, both here and those no longer with us, and I realise just how damn lucky I am. My nan, who, despite only having eighteen months with Pa, blessed him with Pop. My ma, who had five sons before succumbing to ovarian cancer, and my own wife, who overcame Hunter and his goons plus our own insecurities before blessing me with the princess sleeping in front of me. All three women are strong in their own ways, each taking on a Ryan male and winning his heart. I look at Avery and know that despite whatever may happen in the future, this little girl is lucky because she has Bria as a mother, just as I am to have had Elizabeth Avery as mine.

I go back to Bria and pull her over my chest, her breath soft against my neck.

I still worry that something is going to happen to her, that around the next corner lies a tragedy waiting to befall her, but if the little girl in the next room proves anything, it's that together she and her mother are beating the odds and breaking the cycle.

EPILOGUE

BRIA

Twenty-five years later

Life with the Ryans is never boring, and with Avery, the first Ryan granddaughter, was no exception. She's taken the racing world by storm. As an eleven-year-old, she started on the junior circuit before turning pro at just seventeen. I'm sure I went prematurely grey when that happened but Reed assured me she was a natural. Our little girl was racing bikes before she could even legally drive, naturally.

Now at twenty-five, she's starting the upcoming NRS season as the previous season's runner-up, second only to Chris. Together they're continuing Ryan Racing's reputation as a powerhouse in action and motor sports.

Our second child, Chase, is burning up the motocross circuit, and our youngest daughters, Peyton and Kennedy, are taking the cycling world by storm: Peyton as a mountain bike and downhill BMX rider, and Kennedy in road cycling. Kennedy is hoping to compete in grand tours soon, and both have the Olympics in their sights.

At every race, the whole family is in the Ryan Racing garage Avery and Chris share. The team's chief engineer is the kid's "Uncle" Rome, with his adopted son, Xander, assisting. Ryan Racing's freestyle rider is planning on putting a ring on her finger very soon, or so Grayson tells me. This is despite Reed still insisting she and her sisters aren't allowed to date until they're fifty.

Even though traditionally Ryans only have boys, Reed always did give me what I wanted, so a house full of girls and the boy I asked for is what I got.

We've been married twenty-five and a half years and are still in love as ever, and still as healthy as ever. I know Reed worried, and still worries, that something might happen to me, as had happened to his pa and pop's wives, but if being with me taught him anything, it's that the women in his life are always up for breaking the cycle.

ACKNOWLEDGMENTS

I never thought this book would ever make it to print. Yes, I wrote it and sent it to a publisher in the hopes it would be picked up, but I didn't actually think it would happen.

I'd like to thank Becky, Liv, and everyone at Hot Tree Publishing. Thank you for all your hard work and for believing in me and seeing the potential of the manuscript I sent you. It was the most stressful thing I've ever done but I'm so proud of the finished product. I'm still not sure whether I can believe this is happening but it truly is the biggest honour of my life.

To my parents, Dave and Trish Lowe, thank you. From the young girl who used to make issues of the Woodvale News on the family PC to the university graduate who decided she didn't want to pursue a career actually using the degree she just spent three years studying for, I want to thank you for loving and supporting me through all of it. I love you both so much. There have been some rough patches but hopefully, this is a sign of better things to come.

To Anne Stewart, who always encouraged me, thank you. I'm so sorry Jen never got to see her name in print, so Jennifer Stewart, this is for you.

To Jaelene Hilcke, you are an amazing woman who constantly inspires me and puts me to shame. You are a living example of great strength of character and determination. Better times are coming for you.

To my friends, workmates, and managers, thank you for putting up with my addled mind while Bria, Reed, and the Ryans filled my head.

To Sadé Norris and John Steele, thank you for not laughing at my idle scribblings, also known as my first pathetic attempts at writing. It took a lot for me to open myself up like that so thank you for your kind words and encouragement.

To Tijan, L.P. Maxa, Kaylee Ryan, Ahren Sanders, and Cambria Hebert, thank you for your books, providing me with endless hours of entertainment and inspiration.

To the millions of women out there who believe they're not worth as much as their male counterparts, who are fighting their own personal battles and those who have not yet found their way, keep going. One day better things are coming, we just have to have faith and believe in us; after all, if we don't, who will?

And finally, to you who is reading this, thank you so much. It's such a thrill to know you are reading the words I've spent hours upon hours slaving over. I hope you enjoyed *Breaking the Cycle* and fell in love with Bria and Reed just like I did. If so, please leave a review, blog, tweet or post about *Breaking the Cycle* and recommend it to all your friends!

ABOUT THE AUTHOR

Megan Lowe is a lost journalism graduate who after many painful years searching for a job in that field, decided if she couldn't write news stories, she would start listening to the characters whispering stories to her and decided to write them down. She writes primarily new adult and contemporary romance stories with sport and music themes.

Based on the Gold Coast, Megan's heart belongs to New York City. When she's not writing, she's either curled up with a good book, travelling, or screaming at the TV, willing her sporting teams to pull out the win.

Megan would love to hear from readers.

Facebook: FACEBOOK.COM/MEGANLOWEAUTHOR
Twitter: MEGANLOWE87

ABOUT THE PUBLISHER

Hot Tree Publishing opened its doors in 2015 with an aspiration to bring quality fiction to the world of readers. With the initial focus on romance and a wide spread of romance sub-genres, we envision opening up to alternative genres in the near future.

Firmly seated in the industry as a leading editing provider to independent authors and small publishing houses, Hot Tree Publishing is the sister company to Hot Tree Editing, founded in 2012. Having established in-house editing and promotions, plus having a well-respected market presence, Hot Tree Publishing endeavours to be a leader in bringing quality stories to the world of readers.

Interested in discover more amazing reads brought to you by Hot Tree Publishing or perhaps you're interesting in submitting a manuscript and joining the HTPubs family? Either way, head over to the website for information:

WWW.HOTTREEPUBLISHING.COM

CPSIA information can be obtained at www.ICGtesting.com
Printed in the USA
LVOW08s1632211016

509750LV00001B/61/P